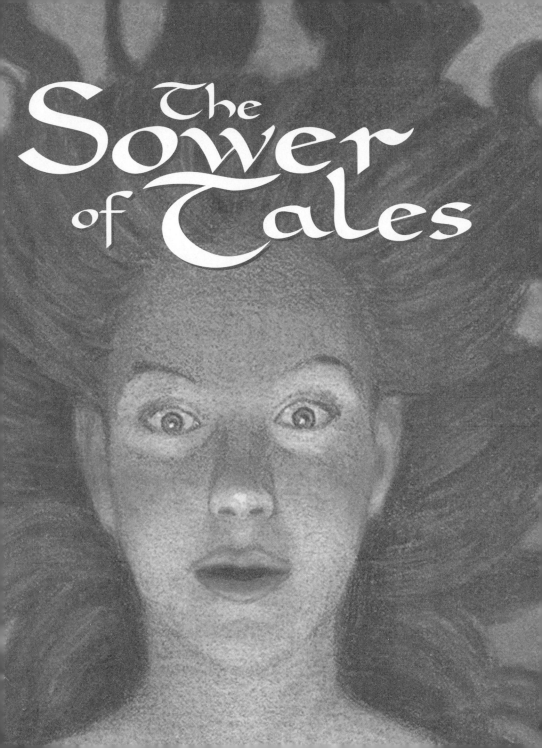

The Sower of Tales

Published in Canada by Fitzhenry & Whiteside,
195 Allstate Parkway, Markham, Ontario L3R 4T8

Published in the United States by Fitzhenry & Whiteside,
121 Harvard Avenue, Suite 2, Allston, Massachusetts 02134

www.fitzhenry.ca godwit@fitzhenry.ca

10 9 8 7 6 5 4 3 2 1

Library and Archives Canada Cataloguing in Publication
Gilmore, Rachna, 1953-
The sower of tales / Rachna Gilmore.
ISBN 1-55041-945-5
I. Title.
PS8563.I57S68 2005   jC813'.54   C2005-903642-7

U.S. Publisher Cataloging-in-Publication Data
(Library of Congress Standards)

Gilmore, Rachna, 1953-
The sower of tales / Rachna Gilmore
[385] p. ; cm.
Summary: When the story pods stop growing in the Plains, a stubborn young
girl undertakes a dangerous journey to seek the help of the legendary Sower of
Tales; but she is plunged into a desperate struggle against a sorcerer who plans
to use the story pods to destroy the world.
ISBN 1-55041-945-5
1. Fantasy. I. Title.
[Fic] 813/.54 dc22   PR9199.3.G55So 2005

Fitzhenry & Whiteside acknowledges with thanks the Canada Council for the
Arts, the Government of Canada through the Book Publishing Industry
Development Program (BPIDP), and the Ontario Arts Council for their sup-
port of our publishing program.

Cover illustration by James Bentley
Illustrations by Tara Anderson

Design by Wycliffe Smith

Printed in Canada

The Sower of Tales

RACHNA GILMORE

To Mary Lou & Chris' Class,

May the Tales always

delight you!

Rachna Gilmore

May 4 2006

FITZHENRY & WHITESIDE

To all Sowers of Tales
who nourish, delight and inspire us
with the joy and power of their tales.

—R.G.

Acknowledgments

My thanks to the following people:

Karleen Bradford, for going through umpteen drafts of the manuscript and for her encouragement and insightful comments; Melanie Colbert, Jan Andrews and Alice Bartels, who all gave useful feedback at various stages of the novel; Louise Young, for her feedback and enthusiasm for this novel; my agent Marie Campbell, for her encouragement and support; Laura Peetoom, editor, for her part in helping to focus this manuscript; Tom Tomlinson, for the wonderful term "roffe" and for helping me to sustain the energy to write with clarity; my husband Ian, for his unfailing and generous love and support; and to all the Sowers of Tales who continue to delight and inspire me with the power of their words.

The Sower of Tales

About the Story...

Calantha twirled and jumped. She'd picked the the story pod for Talemeet. She had!
Then her smile faded. That twisting again. Something wasn't right.

King's men on horseback, riding the Plains. Rumors and fear.
Fingers flicked to ward off evil, whenever the Sorcerer Odhran
is mentioned. Something is definitely not right, and Calantha is
not the only one to feel it. The Seers, the Gatherers all agree:
the Essences have become twisted, hard to read. But why? No
one seems to know.

Then the unthinkable happens. There are story pods in
the fields, as always, but there is no new growth. Where are the
seeds? What will become of the Plains people, with no Tales to
bring them together? Has the Sower of Tales abandoned them?

In this riveting tale, a stubborn dreamer sets off on a har-
rowing journey to seek out the Sower of Tales, only to be burdened with a terrifying task. Others will help her, if Calantha
can trust them. Her dearest dreams—and her worst nightmares—
will guide her, if Calantha can face them.

And she must. For the fate of the Plainspeople, the fate
of the Sower of Tales herself, rests in Calantha's hands. And her
one passion, the Tales, will make her more vulnerable—and
more powerful—than anyone could have known.

PART ONE

THE STORY PODS

Robbers with swords are easier to fend off
than the thief who creeps silently in.

Traditional Plains saying

"S narking bograts! I hate this!" Calantha flung the sharo thorn and sucked her pierced finger.

Oh, pustering toadstools. Her mother had heard. With a swish of skirts, Luvena erupted from the cooking chamber onto the back porch. Her nostrils pinched as she took in the one piece of crooked thatch among the mess of ruined sharo leaves.

"Is that all you've managed?"

Calantha rolled her eyes. Why should she learn sharo thatch? She was not going to apprentice with Saeward the thatcher—never mind that Saeward himself would have ten fits at the thought.

She shoved the spray of tattered blue-gray leaves

off her lap. "I can't do this."

Luvena's face tightened. She tried to speak coaxingly, but her voice soon rose—sharper, faster. "Calantha, for pity's sake, all you do is stack five leaves together and roll the edges toward the center so the top is wider and the bottom narrow to direct the rain downward. Then pierce the edges with thorns to hold. It's an easy enough task, if you will only apply yourself."

Calantha's jaw clenched. She deliberately turned her head and fixed her eyes on the path that led from the back of their yard to Kasmira's hut.

Her mother's face blotched with anger. "Don't give me that mule face, Calantha. I know what you're thinking, and you will put it out of your mind. Look, story pods are all very well, and I'm the last to say they don't matter. But for goodness sake, child, think on a Gatherer's life. You must have a trade that will allow you to barter for at least some comforts beyond the basics of life."

Calantha stared stonily ahead. Five more moons. That was all. In five moons she'd be fourteen, and then, by the Sower of Tales, she *would* apprentice with Kasmira, no matter how her mother pleaded or ranted. It was the only thing she'd ever wanted—to be a Gatherer of Pods—even if it didn't meet Luvena's notions of a fitting occupation for her daughter.

Luvena's voice softened now, plying the old familiar arguments. With the ease of long practice, Calantha slipped by her mother's words into one of the tales from the story pods. The sideways rolling of the leaves reminded her of the one about the snake who saved the angry dog.

"Did you even hear me, Calantha? Move!"

Calantha blinked.

Luvena thumped her hand against her dark hair. "For patience's sake! Go! Get some more sharo leaves—and from the copse beyond the Cheesery, not from the Mid Plains road. You are not going anywhere near your precious Field of Gathering. And while you're about it, Calantha, reflect on why Greeley the potter is so pleased with your sister Freya. Because she applies herself!"

Her face flaming, Calantha sprang to her feet,

scattering the heart-shaped sharo leaves. She ran full tilt into the blazing heat of the afternoon sun.

Snake's venom! If she heard once more how pleased Greeley the potter was with her sister, Calantha would throw something. As if Freya didn't give herself enough airs already; Freya, who was capable and beautiful, like their mother, with her silky, dark hair and round, smooth face. Calantha just seemed to offend every one of Luvena's standards and hopes—dusty, bumbling, and plain besides, with a long, bony face, a curved nose, and coarse, brown hair that never stayed in place.

As Calantha passed Freya's pottery shack at the rear of the yard, she saw the neat row of pots her sister had made earlier that day. All plain and alike. Dull and smug, just like Freya.

She strode by her mother's Cheesery onto the path that led to Kasmira's. It wound through a mass of trees, scrub, and grass, past a tangle of purplish harwenberry bushes, then alongside some sharo trees—the wide, blue-gray leaves casting deep shadows on the path ahead.

Calantha let her breath out in a huff. Sharo

thatch! Her mother's latest scheme was insane. But she'd been desperate since she'd realized that not even her good friend Benigna, First Herbroffe, would take Calantha as apprentice. Benigna had nobly picked Calantha for service a few times, but now she pointedly avoided her.

Calantha groaned. She detested offering service in the Green, which all unapprenticed youngsters did when they could be spared from home—she was almost always the last to be picked, and how Julissa gloated. But any service was better than the flikketting sharo thatch, or, for that matter, helping her mother in her precious Cheesery. At least when she'd been gathering herbs with Benigna, she'd been able to wander away to look for story pods.

She scratched her fingers. The wretched sharo sap made her itch, but what did her mother care? Well, she could send her for all the sharo leaves in Grenlea, but her mother would tire of teaching her long before Calantha would tire of not learning.

Something among the purplish harwenberry bushes caught her eye. A story pod! A beautiful yellow story pod, with traces of pink, nodding above the bushes. Calantha's heart leaped. It was ripe! She could tell from the size, and the humming she sensed, even from here.

She glanced back. The Cheesery and Freya's shack blocked all view of the house. Oh, she must touch the pod. Just see what kind of tale it held.

Hands tingling, she pushed her way along the faint track through the shrubs, her skirt catching on the sharp branches. Gently, she cupped the story pod in both hands. Delight prickled through her at the familiar humming. It was ripe, all right! And there was a thrum to it that made her quiver. The tale would be mysterious and full of adventure.

She looked back again. She'd never harvest a ripe pod from the Field of Gathering; they were always to be saved for the Gatherer's choosing for Talemeet. But here...

She must hear this tale, she must. She'd take the pod to the woods beyond the sharo copse and open it there. Tell her mother she'd taken extra time to find sharo leaves of the same size. So what if Luvena didn't believe her and was angry—her mother was angry anyway.

Calantha closed her eyes and let her heart sink into the pod. She must wait for the right moment or the pod would tear and the precious seeds fly upward, back to the Sower of Tales, leaving behind only murmurs of the lost tale.

She waited, waited. Her whole body eased and settled. Any moment now—

"For pity's sakes, are you never done getting into trouble?"

Calantha gasped and swung around. Freya. She carried a bucket of clay at each end of the pole balanced across her shoulders.

The pod. Oh, the pod! Broken. Tantalizing words whispered and danced as the milky blue-white seeds flew upward.

A bitter taste flooded Calantha's mouth. Her eyes pricked. "You dolt! Look what you made me do!"

Freya's jaw dropped. "What I made you do? You—you stupid little... Can't you do anything without stopping for your flikketting story pods?"

Calantha gasped. She bent down, grabbed a handful of wet clay from Freya's bucket, and flung it at her face.

The clay spattered right across Freya's open mouth. Freya screamed, then sprang at her, hands like claws. The buckets clanged backward, and Freya fell.

Choking with laughter, Calantha scrambled through the harwenberry bushes on to the wider path.

Freya screeched, "Wait 'til I tell Mother!"

Lifting her skirt high, Calantha tore past the sharo copse toward Kasmira's hut.

No! It was the first place they'd look.

She spun around in a cloud of red dust and pushed through the scrubby plum bushes and wild grasses to her left. When she reached the Shernthrip road, she bounded across it to a small track in the middle of a lorsha field. Luckily they hadn't harvested yet, and the grain was high enough to hide her. She ran through the field, turned left on the path at the edge of the woods, then reached the North Plains road. The big chernow tree. She'd hide there. The feathery red branches made a perfect curtain.

She stopped, gasping. No, she mustn't. King Ulric's men had been around lately, and they'd likely pass this way. Her father had forbidden her to come here alone. Then where could she hide?

The woods near Xenyss' hut—they wouldn't think to look there! She'd keep away until her mother cooled down, maybe even cut some sharo leaves from the grove nearby. Calantha tore down the road, back toward the Green. Story pods at various stages of growth winked at her along the ditches, but she didn't dare stop.

If only her mother wouldn't look out the window.

Calantha flew across the Green, and as she swung onto the Blackthorn road, which led westward from the village, she darted a look backward.

Crash! Down she fell, the breath punched out of her.

Xenyss.

"Oh, my b-blessed stars!" Xenyss was sprawled in the dust, his blue eyes blinking, his Seer's cap twisted partway off his bald head.

"Oh, Xenyss. I'm sorry, so sorry," Calantha babbled.

She pulled and tugged at him, but he was heavy, his crooked leg slow to find ground.

At last he was up, puffing, arms flailing. Calantha thrust his stick into his hand and straightened his cap. "I didn't mean...let me dust you..." She flapped at his pale blue Seer's robe, leaving behind reddish smears of clay.

"S-s-slowly, Calantha," wheezed Xenyss. "What are you up to n-n-now?" He put his hand awkwardly on her back and peered at her in his mud-turtle way—head tilted and half sunk into his shoulders.

Calantha groaned inwardly. If he were a better Seer, she wouldn't feel guilty running off like the boys usually did; but she couldn't just shake his soft kindly hand off her shoulder.

"Xenyss, I have to go. I'll tell you later—"

"Calantha! Wait!" Luvena's voice cut like an icy wind through the heat and dust.

"Oh d-dear," whispered Xenyss.

"It doesn't matter, Xenyss," said Calantha. "She'd have found me anyway."

Her mother advanced across the Green like a dark cloud, her skirt rustling, her eyes like lightning. She grasped Calantha's arm and shook it, paying no mind to Xenyss. But then, no one paid mind to Xenyss.

"Calantha, this is beyond belief, even for you."

"But, Mother, Freya—"

"The trouble, Calantha, is that you did not listen to me. Yet again."

Xenyss said feebly, "Now, Luvena, p-p-perhaps she—"

Calantha closed her eyes in despair.

"With respect, Xenyss, this is between me and my daughter." Luvena couldn't keep the sharpness out of her voice.

She marched Calantha back to their house, scolding in a low roll, like water on the boil. Why couldn't Calantha manage the simplest task without fumbling and bumbling? If she would apply even half the effort she wasted on her wretched story pods to something useful—

Calantha felt hot and scratchy. She said nothing— she'd learned that much at least—yet when her mother steamed on about how Calantha could do better, for she was not stupid, Calantha's chest constricted.

Not stupid.

Somehow, those words always had the power to

wound. Calantha turned her head away—and saw Julissa gaping at them from the window of her small white-washed home on the southern side of the Green. She held a brush against her golden hair, and a smirk spread like grease across her face.

"Mother!" whispered Calantha urgently.

Thanks be to the story pods, her mother saw Julissa and stopped. She even turned the full power of her terrible smile on Julissa, whose smirk withered. Ha!

As soon as they were out of sight, her mother resumed her tirade, then stopped abruptly as the thud of hooves rang across the Green.

A group of horsemen galloped around the curve of the Mid Plains road, raising a swirl of dust. Luvena's eyes narrowed as the horses slowed on the Green. They were fine beasts—one roan, two gray, and one white. The riders were helmeted and wore scarlet and gray. King Ulric's livery.

Calantha's eyes jagged over them. A wizened man, stringy as an old hen; a couple of beefy young lads, raw and red; and a sleek, plump man with a wide mouth who looked sharply around.

The pit of her stomach tilted. Years ago, when she'd

been playing with Neola, she'd tried to tell her how she sensed things about others, how it was like smell but not smell. But Neola had looked strangely at her and told the other children, who'd laughed at her and called her a witch. Calantha had since learned to keep quiet about her feelings, but something about the horsemen—and it wasn't just their livery, or the way her mother gripped her arm—made her insides churn.

A couple of the men doffed their helmets. Calantha turned away, glimpsing on one of the men a pair of plump earlobes, tilted upward like succulent new dignes leaves.

"Good day, Mistress," one of them called out.

Luvena barely nodded. Pulling Calantha by the arm, she hurried across the Green and down the road to their large, red-washed home. Calantha felt the men's eyes boring into their backs.

As they entered the house, Freya's face gladdened with spite.

Luvena said breathlessly, "Anwyll, they're here again. King Ulric's men. It's the fifth or sixth time these past two moons."

Calantha's father strode to the window facing the Green. He stood still, but the muscles along his cheeks tightened. Beagan ran up beside him and stood on his toes to look out, his mouth half-open. Calantha could just see the men on the Green, turning their horses in a circle, eyeing the houses. The roiling inside her grew.

At last they trotted toward the North Plains road and disappeared from sight. Thanks be to the Sower of Tales, she hadn't hidden there!

"Well." Anwyll slowly rubbed the side of his strong hooked nose. "They're going north, probably back to Jaerlfin. It's nothing, Luvena; they're just passing through."

Luvena's forehead creased. "But why do they keep passing through? And asking questions? Eythun says they were counting cows last time. I don't like it, Anwyll. What if King Ulric's after the plains, like his grand-father? People say with Sorcerer Odhran—" Luvena's breath caught. She flicked the fingers of her right hand to ward off evil, as did Calantha, Beagan, and Freya.

Anwyll said firmly, "Ulric won't be that foolish. We'll never be part of his kingdom again. He knows it. We've been freemen for over six hundred years, and we're well prepared to repel any attack. As for Odhran, half those tales are made up just to frighten children."

Beagan cried shrilly, "But doesn't the Sorcerer send bad dreams? Didn't he send Calantha's witch dreams?"

Calantha flushed as Freya snorted. She should never have told Freya.

Her father said, "No, Beagan, he did not."

Beagan's face crinkled. "What does he do, then? Can he tell weather? Better than Xenyss?"

Freya's eyes narrowed. "Mother! What about Calantha? Aren't you—?"

Luvena frowned abstractedly. "Not now, Freya."

Despite the uneasiness still coursing through her, Calantha couldn't stop her smirk.

"And you, Calantha, go wash yourself and grind the lorsha. We're behind enough already, thanks to your idleness and mischief." The distracted look left her mother's eyes. "You will continue to learn sharo thatch. And don't for one instant think you can go running off to Kasmira's without doing your chores after dinner."

Calantha glanced at her father, who fleetingly put

his finger to his lips. She bit back the hot words and swished past the curtain into the cooking chamber. Her mother didn't try to prevent her anymore from accompanying Kasmira to the Field of Gathering. Luvena had stopped that long ago, when she and Anwyll had realized that the screaming tantrums Calantha threw—if not able to go—caused her real harm. But she still resented it, and she took every opportunity to delay Calantha.

Calantha's mouth tightened. As fast as she could, she flung handfuls of the coarse grain onto the stone mortar and turned the heavy pestle round and round, scooping the crushed grain into the nearby pot. By the time the pot was full, her hands and arms were numb and her shoulders and neck throbbed right up to her ears. But all the lorsha was ground, and finely enough for her mother's exacting standards.

She stretched to ease her back. Her stomach felt slightly queasy, as though it held traces of undigested porridge. She couldn't think why.

Then she remembered the horsemen.

CHAPTER TWO

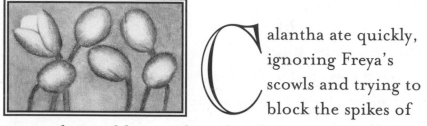

Calantha ate quickly, ignoring Freya's scowls and trying to block the spikes of worry she could sense from her father and mother. She only half-heard Beagan, who rattled on, between mouthfuls of lorshcake and rabbit-and-arrac stew, about the striped snakes he'd found by the river. She'd have to scurry through her chores to reach Kasmira's on time. What kind of story would they pick today? If only she'd been able to catch the tale in the broken pod. Her mind slid into yesterday's story of the fierce mountain lion.

When the meal was over and she'd scrubbed the stew pot, helped put away the dishes, and swept the chamber to Luvena's satisfaction, Calantha rushed to the back door. No time to tidy herself.

Beagan cried, "Tell Kasmira a funny tale! Like the one of the toad." He flicked his tongue.

Anwyll, who was oiling the harness, said, "My greetings to the Gatherer of Pods."

"Aye, mine too," said Luvena, reaching out to caress Calantha.

Calantha dodged her mother's hand and dashed outside. The only reason her mother sent any greeting was because she prided herself on observing the proper conventions—and because Kasmira was a distant cousin.

Raking her fingers through her hair, Calantha rushed along the narrow path, past the tangled mass of shrubs, trees, and grass, past the harwenberry bushes and the sharo copse, and on to Kasmira's faded whitewashed hut. Breathless, she dashed through the crooked door, blinking to adjust to the gloom of the interior.

The one-chambered hut was scrupulously clean as always, with the bed curtained off against one of the whitewashed walls, and a small table with two chairs near the fireplace. Kasmira, who was putting away her plate and cup in the narrow corner cupboard, turned around.

She looked at Calantha and rasped, "What have I said about tidiness when gathering story pods?"

Calantha's lips pinched. "I didn't have time; Mother's been at me and at me." She stopped, her voice shaking.

Kasmira's brown eyes gazed steadily at her. Then she nodded slightly and picked up the comb from the shelf. "What happened this time?"

Her matter-of-fact tone eased the knots inside Calantha. As Kasmira began to unsnarl her tangled hair, Calantha launched into the events of the afternoon—the wretched sharo leaves, the story pod she'd found, her anguish at losing the tale.

"Then horsemen came. Four of them, Kasmira, King Ulric's men, heading north. There was something wrong." Calantha twisted around to look at Kasmira. "Some...some awful sense of purpose about them. But I couldn't make out what. What do they want of us?"

Calantha sensed Kasmira stiffen, although she only said, "Maybe nothing. But when the Kings of Jaerlfin turn their eyes onto the Plains, it's not usually for our good." Pulling at a stubborn knot, she murmured, "I must tell Xenyss."

"Xenyss!" said Calantha.

"Xenyss has more skill than anyone realizes," said Kasmira sharply.

"Oh, Kasmira, Xenyss is kindly—and none more so—but he can't even divine the weather anymore." Guilt washed over her. She rushed on, trying to justify her words. "Even Father's losing patience, but Mother says, 'What can you expect from a Seer who never apprenticed at the Place of Knotting?'"

Calantha stopped, appalled. Was she actually quoting her mother?

Kasmira twitched her hair. "You know better than that! Xenyss says there's some kind of shift in the Essences. They're becoming harder to garner, let alone read properly, so of course the weather is difficult to tell."

It was on the tip of Calantha's tongue to say that was just Xenyss' excuse, but she stopped herself and shrugged. "What does it have to do with the horsemen?"

Kasmira answered severely, "Maybe nothing, but

maybe something. How many times do I have to tell you? Everything is connected. Part of the larger web. It isn't always easy to see how, but it is connected." She tugged Calantha's freshly braided hair. "There. Turn around, Wild One!"

Calantha grinned. "Don't forget 'mule.'"

Kasmira's face creased like fine old leather. "I'll leave that to your mother. Now, come. We're late." She gave Calantha's cheek two swift pats.

Calantha rushed to get the Gatherer's red-green cloak from the back of the door. She placed it reverently around Kasmira's shoulders, brushing aside her own lingering uneasiness. Nothing must mar the harvesting of a story pod for Talemeet.

They hurried down the winding road toward the Green. Kasmira's hut was well past the other houses, and although it would have been quicker to take the back paths to the Field of Gathering, Kasmira insisted on going formally through the Green when picking a story pod for the nightly Talemeet.

Farther down the road, near the houses, people were already sauntering about in the cool evening air. The houses were all thatched with blue-gray sharo, and washed yellow, white, or red like Calantha's—although, of course, none were as fine as theirs, as Luvena was so fond of noting.

Saeward the thatcher bowed exaggeratedly as they passed his plain yellow home. "Ah, the Gatherer and her little shadow."

Calantha scowled at him. He was a squat, balding man, with dark, sarcastic eyes under peaked brows. He never bothered with Talemeet.

A snort of laughter escaped her. He really had no idea why Luvena had begun plying him with her cheeses! Imagine his horror if he knew of Luvena's scheme to have her, the clumsiest child in the village, apprentice with him.

"Behave," said Kasmira.

It took Calantha a moment to wipe the grin off her face.

Clusters of people stood about the Green. Old Berwin, his face as red as a ripe harwenberry, flashed a gummy smile. "Greetings, Gatherer of Pods. Oh, pick a tale of true love!"

Kasmira twinkled. "It's always the fickle who ask for those."

Neola, shadowing her father Tabbert, waved her good arm. Neola always came to Talemeet, like most of the children. Tabbert and a few others called out, "Greetings, Gatherer of Pods."

Calantha glared at Anyon and Selwyn—Earthroffes like her father. It was bad enough that they never stayed for Talemeet, but couldn't they at least greet the Gatherer?

Kasmira shook her arm. "Stop it! How many times do I have to tell you? Dignity!"

Julissa's voice shrilled from across the Green. She, along with Cybella and some boys, had joined hands in a circle, and they were shrieking, "Break-the-circle-at-your-peril! Break-the-circle-at-your-peril!" They were too old for the game, of course, but it was a chance to flirt. Eadric, in the center, swung around and around, judging where he should charge through, looking hopefully at Julissa.

The scar on Calantha's knee, from when Julissa had knocked her down years ago, twitched. How she hated that game! When they'd been little, Julissa had only let her play in order to target and pummel her, usually when the other children paid too much attention to Calantha's tales. She'd quickly learned to save the stories for her doll; at least then she'd only had to endure her mother's scoldings about wasted time.

Near the north end of the Green, First Elder Argenta, her silver hair gleaming, stood by the fire, talking to Xenyss. Calantha caught a strand of something not quite right coming from them, like twisted ribbon, but lost it as she followed Kasmira down the Mid Plains road.

As usual, no one else joined Calantha and Kasmira. Calantha was glad to have Kasmira to herself, glad no one else wanted to apprentice with her—and yet resentful. Kasmira had told stories of how, in the olden days, long before her time, Gatherers always had many to accompany them. And many who'd wanted to apprentice. After the story pod at Talemeet, Kasmira had said, villagers would even sit around and tell tales to one another.

The sounds of the village faded as they passed the last houses along the road. The fields beyond were empty of workers, their red furrows scattered with stooked bundles of gray-green lorsha, harvested just that day. Wide sharo leaves rustled as they passed the grove on the right. Calantha made a face. The very sight of sharo made her itch.

She gazed at the story pods trembling among the grasses in the ditches and trailed her fingers across the fuzzy curves of a nearly ripe, pinkish pod.

At last, beyond the pasture fields, they reached the Field of Gathering. It was the one field never harvested but left for the Gatherer, and it was here that the story pods grew thickest. The red story pod stalks gleamed at various heights throughout the tall, rippling grass, with small buds swelling at the tips of the eight-day-old pods, and the rounder, fully ripened fourteen-day-old pods swaying above.

Calantha's body eased as she followed Kasmira into the field. Such a chorus of colors—misty greens, furry dusty blues, pinks, reds, and every other color imaginable. It was only here among the humming pods that she moved softly, at harmony and peace with her body, as though she fit right.

Her eyes lilted across the muted rainbow shades of the ripe pods. Which one would Kasmira pick today? What tale would it hold?

As Kasmira began to move about the field, Calantha stopped to stare at the tallest peak of the distant Eastern Mountains, the one sloped like Eythun's broken nose. Every time she looked at it, her heart lifted and filled.

That was where the Sower of Tales lived. It was from there that she nightly scattered the seeds, which grew in just half a moon to fully ripened story pods. Kasmira had told her long ago, when she'd been puzzled by the Plainsfolk's differing ideas on where the Sower lived. Kasmira had charged her not to speak of it, and Calantha hadn't. Except that one time.

She hadn't been able to help it. She was only nine, and when she'd heard Hardwin, the village blacksmith, boasting about how he'd climbed to the very top of that mountain, she'd blurted eagerly, "Did you see the Sower of Tales?" Hardwin had just laughed and laughed, but afterward Kasmira had scolded her, reminding her that she must never speak of it. When Calantha had continued to fret about why Hardwin hadn't seen the Sower, Kasmira had retorted, "Of course he didn't find her. He doesn't have the key." She'd refused to say anything more.

Calantha sighed. She couldn't believe that she'd actually ransacked Kasmira's hut for the key all those years ago. When Kasmira had found out…Calantha drew in a deep breath. It was the only time Kasmira had threatened not to take her to the Field of Gathering. But in five more moons she'd be fully apprenticed. Then, and only then, Kasmira had said, she would give Calantha the key.

Calantha had never really understood why there was need of a key. Did the Sower of Tales live inside the mountain, behind a locked door? But no matter; once she had the key, she'd go there someday. She'd meet the Sower of Tales!

Calantha tore her eyes from the mountain and watched Kasmira cup the ripe pods in the field, one by one.

At last, Kasmira beckoned. "All right, Calantha. Which pod?"

Calantha brushed eagerly through the tall grass. She touched a large, dusty blue pod; she couldn't glean any words yet, but she knew by the deep hum-

ming and the tingle along her palms that it was fully
ripe, and with a lively tale. Another, a silvery one,
was ripe too, but somehow she knew it held no
laughter. She almost passed the small, grayish pod—
it was so plain, except for the hint of scarlet at the
base. But something made her stop. And when
she cupped it, oh, how it sang through her veins;
there was a tickle and liveliness to it that suggested
laughter.

"This one," said Calantha, breathlessly. Beagan
had asked for a funny one.

Kasmira beamed. "Good! It's the one I'd choose.
Always go by the feel, Calantha, not the look."
Casually she said, "Go on, then. You pick it."

Calantha gaped. "Me?"

Kasmira twinkled, but said dryly, "Well, there are
others if this one tears."

Calantha's heart fluttered. She'd picked many a
pod—and even managed to open some of them with
greater success lately—but she'd never yet picked a
pod for Talemeet.

She moistened her lips, then cupped the story
pod in both hands. From the depths of her being,

she breathed, "Thanks be to the Sower of Tales, she who scatters the seeds."

She could sense a strand from Kasmira guiding her, almost as though the Gatherer's hands were also on the pod. Calantha let herself sink into the humming of the pod until her palms were one with it.

Hardly breathing, she allowed her wrists to suggest the merest thought of release. And the pod was loose—and whole—in her hands.

"Nicely done, Calantha," said Kasmira lightly.

Calantha's face almost split with smiling as she handed the pod to Kasmira. Oh, this almost made up for the tale she'd lost earlier.

As they left the field, she looked longingly at the ripe story pods nodding above the grass. They'd open at night of their own accord, of course, and their seeds would return to the Sower of Tales, but...who would hear those lost tales? Would the night sky catch whispers? Would the stars? If only she could hear them all.

The sun had set, with pink and red laughter, by the time they returned to the village. Calantha twirled and jumped, running ahead and back. She'd picked the story pod for Talemeet. *She* had!

Kasmira cracked out laughing. "You remind me of the tale of the cat that tried to fly."

Calantha was still laughing as they crossed the Green toward the fire, where folks had gathered. It was a large group—larger than usual, even for the informal exchange of the day's events before Talemeet. She didn't at first notice a strange something flickering at the edge of her elation.

Then her smile faded. That twisting again. Something wasn't right. She knew it, even before she heard the voices, before she recognized the burly figure that stood before the fire to speak.

CHAPTER THREE

ardwin's deep voice rumbled, "...and I say we send a strong party to Jaerlfin, to demand that he explain these incursions. We must act, I tell you, before King Ulric grows bolder." He smashed a giant fist into his equally giant palm.

Calantha shrank inward, trying hold onto the humming of the pods. They were talking about the horsemen. She might have known— it explained the size of the gathering. Why did Hardwin always stir trouble? Why now, before Talemeet?

The seven Elders of Council sat together on the stone benches by the fire; Argenta, First Elder; Xenyss, his head tilted; Kerwin, the First Defenseroffe, gray, grizzled, and taciturn, with whom everyone past the age of sixteen had to train for at least three moons; and the other four Council members, Calantha's own father, Frensha, Eythun, and Benigna.

Argenta tapped her stick on the ground. "Friends, it is not Councilmeet, and the Gatherer approaches, so we will spare but a few moments to this matter. Speak, then, who will."

Calantha and Kasmira paused at the edge of the gathering, as Eythun, First Herdroffe, stood up. He was short and stringy, but his muscles were like whipcord. There wasn't a bull in the herd he couldn't wrest to the ground.

His clipped voice rang out, "I went to Wrenford last week, trading cattle. They'd been there too, King Ulric's men. Asking questions. About distances to nearby villages, market days, livestock. They made no threatening gestures, but it's clear enough, isn't it?" His bright eyes darted around. "They're taking stock."

As voices rose in agitation, Kasmira made her way toward the fire. Calantha wove among the villagers to her family, who sat near the front, facing the Elders. She slipped down beside Freya, who was frowning, with quivers of worry coming from her. Impulsively, while still expanded by the story pods, Calantha hugged her and whispered, "I'm sorry, Freya."

Freya hugged her back and Calantha settled against her, glad of her familiar earthy smell and the warmth of her arm, muscular from kneading clay. Luvena rubbed Calantha's back approvingly. Beagan's wide eyes were fixed on the central fire where Argenta was asking Xenyss to speak.

Xenyss stood, leaning heavily on his stick.

"Mud-turtle," snickered Freya.

Calantha bit her lip but said nothing. She didn't want to quarrel with Freya again.

Xenyss stuttered, "Th-there is s-s-something s-s-strange afoot. Th-the Essences h-have b-been h-h-hard to read and there is unrest in the air. B-b-but it is d-difficult to s-see the c-c-cause of it. We m-must n-not be hasty and p-provoke a conflict."

Muffled snorts broke out among Eadric and the boys. Calantha wanted to throttle them but also to shake Xenyss. Why couldn't he find a spell to speak clearly? From a Sorcerer at least, if he couldn't manage it himself.

The snickers died as Anwyll, her father, stood to speak. As First Earthroffe, in charge of all the fields, he commanded respect, but he was also personally valued for his measured, cautious nature.

"Friends," he said, "we must pay heed to our wise Seer."

Calantha's heart lifted with gratitude.

Anwyll continued, "Before we act rashly, we must consider the nature of this King. He has been in power for four years since his father died, and there is no more indication of his gathering arms than with any of the previous Kings of Jaerlfin. It is possible that he sends his men to assess the riches of the Plains in order to see what he might gain by trading with us."

A relieved murmur arose. Many voices shouted out in agreement.

Calantha twitched. She loved her father, but why did he have to be so...so pedantic? When were they going to get to the tale—the one that *she'd* picked?

Anwyll held up his hand. "But he is also reputed to be a hard taskmaster, and greedy. And we all know that the Kings of Jaerlfin are not above resorting to trickery. Friends, we must remain vigilant. And we must, we *must* remain freemen. We must never lose what we gained in the Great Liberation."

A burst of agitated voices rang out. Freya nudged Calantha.

Everyone had heard of the Great Liberation, but Freya, who had finished her apprenticeship with First Defenseroffe Kerwin not so long ago, had told Calantha more about it. Long ago, before the Great Liberation, the Plains had been part of the kingdom of Jaerlfin. The Plainsfolk had lived in poverty and misery, but none of the independent rebellions and revolts had succeeded, until some six hundred or more years ago, when the Plainsfolk had risen up together. They'd driven King Theron back to JaerlzGate, up in the northern mountains, and at last won their freedom.

Kerwin had also explained that the reason all Plainsfolk must train in defense was that ever since the Great Liberation, the kings of Jaerlfin had periodically tried to retake the Plains. The last time had been years ago, before Luvena was born, but one of the kings, hundreds of years before that, had even had his Sorcerer conjure up the illusion of a fierce army to trick the Plainsfolk into surrender. But he hadn't counted on the pluck and vigilance of the Plainsfolk, and when they engaged in battle, the deception was discovered.

Calantha flinched from the edginess spiking through the Gathering. Why did her father have to bring this up now? It only gave credence to Hardwin's agitations and Xenyss' vague mumbles. Snake's venom, it was *Talemeet*, not Councilmeet; everyone should be eager for the tale, not fretting and scattering like this.

Hardwin leaped to his feet, but—thanks be to the Sower of Tales—Argenta forestalled him. She tapped her stick and said clearly in her soft voice, "Friends, enough for now. Alarm is premature, and it is unwise to stir worry without cause. The Council of Elders will meet tomorrow, before Talemeet. Any who wish to speak further may come. Kerwin." She turned to the First Defenseroffe. "We will hear your thoughts then, and decide whether we should send word of our concerns to the Grand Council in Maernlea."

Kerwin grunted. He rarely spoke at Talemeet. But Freya had said he missed little.

At last, the tale.

Argenta asked, "Are there any other accounts of this day? Eythun, First Herdroffe?"

Calantha groaned softly.

Eythun stood and said quickly, "The cows all give

milk. We are content."

Laughter broke the tension as Argenta tapped her stick once more. "Then it is time for the tale."

Kasmira came forward, and there was a rustle of movement as the usual group of older folk slipped away. They were mostly men, Hardwin and Eythun of the Council among them. Calantha glowered after them. Bad enough that they never stayed to honor the tales, but did they have to set the whole gathering in snarls first? Argenta was too mild and complacent; she should say something, especially to Eythun. Elders, at least, should always stay for Talemeet.

Kasmira stood at last, beside the fire.

Calantha breathed deeply, to untangle herself. Beagan squirmed against her, and sighs of anticipation arose as people moved closer together, filling the spots vacated by the others. The feeling at Talemeet was shifting, thank goodness; the turbulence was subsiding and they were coming together into the familiar eagerness for the tale.

Kasmira bowed to all and held up the story pod. Her voice rustled through the clear night air. "Today's story pod was chosen by Calantha. Moreover, it is she who harvested it."

Calantha flushed. She sensed her mother's twitching displeasure, but Freya nudged her and Beagan looked at her with open-mouthed admiration. Others smiled and nodded at her too, but in the distance, she saw Julissa toss her fair hair.

She began to quake inside. What if she hadn't chosen well? What if the tale wasn't quite ripe?

No. She'd felt it; it had thrummed with life.

Kasmira gave thanks to the Sower of Tales, and most of the villagers echoed it by rote. Kasmira brought the pod down to her heart. The silence of the gathering was broken only by the crackle of the fire and the sputter of the lorsha torches.

Kasmira murmured the words of opening:

"Story Pod
Yield the treasure
Of your words
Now
Swirl and spin your tale
Now,
Let it circle, wind,

And wing
Hearten us and
Sing,
Charge and fill our hearts
Now
Now!"

The last *now* was barely whispered but it was as direct and deep as an arrow finding its mark. The words were so simple, but Calantha knew that there was more to it than just the saying of them; you had to sink your heart into the pod to make it open.

Slowly, the pod glowed from within, gray shifting to blue, then green, while the scarlet at the base blazed, blazed. At last, the five petals curled back and the silky, blue-white seeds rose to circle the gathering.

The familiar words—*Once, so begins this tale*—rang inside Calantha's head, and then she was caught in the flow.

Such a funny tale! About a princess who, bored with her finery, ran away; and of the lost herd of pigs she found and restored to the farmer, who gave her the runt of the litter; and how she persuaded her father to let her keep the piglet at court, even having a small crown made for it....

Beagan shrieked when the princess was dragged
through the mud, and Xenyss' abrupt snorts mingled
with the general laughter.

When the tale was done, Calantha sat motionless,
savoring the delight. The spent blue-white seeds rose
higher, still circling the gathering. Slowly, they took on
muted shades, as though drinking color from the air.

Calantha sighed happily at the faces around her.
Berwin looked less prune-like and Xenyss' head was less
tilted. Even Laerissa, Julissa's mother, no longer wore
her habitual frown. It was only at this time that Calantha
felt at one with the villagers, instead of always on the
outside. This harmony after the tale was so *right*, so seamless and easy, with everyone joined by the tale.

Someone murmured, "Well chosen, child." It was
Frensha, a weaver and a good friend of her mother. Her
bright eyes twinkled and she flashed her quick, warm
smile.

Luvena grunted slightly, but others said, "Fine tale!
Well picked!"

Calantha flushed.

"I liked the part when the princess fell into the

mud," chortled Beagan.

Other children called out their favorite parts. Eadric, who apprenticed with Herdroffe Delmer, croaked, his voice partway between boy and man, "I know I'll dream of pigs swarming out of the sty tonight."

Laughter erupted as Delmer twitched his wide moustache and boomed, "Never mind dreaming, boy. Just wake early and mind the pigs. There be no princesses in these parts to tend them."

Frewen, who was short and freckled, always mocking, nudged Eadric and looked pointedly at Julissa. Everyone in the village knew of Eadric's feelings. A burst of teasing broke out. Then people began to stretch and move, chattering of the day, making plans for the next.

Glancing upward, Calantha saw the spent seeds of the story pod slowly beginning to rise, to return to the Sower of Tales.

A strange sensation built inside her, like something waiting to burst. It was wrong, all wrong, that they tossed the tale aside so soon. Hadn't Kasmira said often and often that long ago they'd mulled the tales, treasured the stillness? Why couldn't they keep that togetherness longer, just for once?

She found herself blurting, "Do you think the princess kept her promise not to stray if the king let her keep the piglet?"

Faces turned to her, some amused, some even interested and surprised, but some disapproving. Calantha's own face flamed. They thought she was puffed up because she'd picked the tale!

"Calantha, hush," whispered Luvena severely. Her irritation burned Calantha like a rash.

Benigna smiled kindly and said, "Who knows, child. The tale ends there."

Calantha sprang to her feet and moved away beyond the light of the fire and the lorsha torches, to wait for Kasmira. Hardwin and a group of men appeared from the darkness and went over to speak to Kerwin. Folk rattled on, some low, some loud, some laughing, all scattered into their separate concerns.

Calantha stared at the mist of spent seeds, barely visible now, rising upward. Once, when she'd been very small, she'd caught some of the spent seeds and planted them to grow her own story pods. How heartbroken she'd been at the stubbly twisted stalks that grew! Kasmira had gently consoled her. "Child, only the fresh seeds scattered each night by the Sower of Tales can bloom into pods bearing tales." Of course, Freya had laughed hysterically—imagine not knowing that!

Calantha watched until the seeds disappeared into the night sky to return to the Sower, then pulled herself inward to stay with the tale, going over it again and again.

Kasmira joined her at last. Her dry voice crackled, "Never mind, pigeon. They're all too busy with doing, nowadays, to ponder the tales. But you picked a fine one."

The tightness inside Calantha eased. She grinned widely.

Kasmira shook her by the back of her neck. "Now what have I said? There's no room for pride in the picking, none whatsoever. You'll pay a price for that."

But Calantha couldn't help the elation bubbling inside her as they crossed the Green in the dark. Back at home, she lit a candle from the embers of the fire, and as she prepared for bed, sank again into the delight of the tale, savoring its smooth curves and flow, imagining what might come next.

Her mother, father and Beagan soon came in, chat-

tering good-humoredly. Luckily Luvena was too busy
setting blue plums to soak for tomorrow's cake to scold
Calantha for her outburst. Freya straggled in later, having lingered with her friends.

When the candle was blown out, Calantha rustled
contentedly into the straw mattress next to Freya. It had
been such a wonderful tale! So rounded, full of heart.
Satisfying. And she had chosen it, *and* harvested it!
Kasmira could say as much as she wanted about not having pride, but she'd been sixteen when she'd first harvested for Talemeet, and Calantha was not yet fourteen.
In five more moons she'd be properly apprenticed, and
then she'd live with Kasmira, no matter what her mother
said, and she and Kasmira would listen to all the story
pods they wanted, and she'd never have to fiddle with
any more sharo thatch, *and* she'd pick all the pods, and
the villagers would love and honor the tales, and she'd be
famed as their Gatherer, maybe even praised by her
mother and Julissa....

CHAPTER FOUR

 Screams. Piercing, terrifying screams, screams.

Someone was shaking her.

"For pity's sake, Calantha, wake."

Calantha sat up, heart thundering, eyes wide with terror. Slowly, in the faint moonlight, her surroundings fell into place—familiar walls, bed, the curtain billowing lightly at the door. She was in her bedchamber. Drenched in sweat. Freya was beside her, patting her back, her face concerned.

It was *she*, Calantha, who had screamed; her throat was raw and ragged.

Her mother, holding a candle, peered in at the doorway. The frills of her nightcap cast strange shadows on her face and on the curtain behind her.

"Calantha, what now? Did you get into those unsoaked plums last night?"

Calantha's heart still punched against her throat. She shook her head, shivering.

"Then what?"

"Another dream," grunted Freya. "Probably *two* witches this time."

Calantha gripped her hands around her knees.

It wasn't the same as the dreams she'd had over a moon ago, of a dark-faced woman, with wild hair and a pointed chin, who stared and stared with her misty, gray eyes as though trying to pull at her. Those dreams had made her start and wake, but they'd never made her scream. The eyes in this dream, even though she hadn't seen them, had been...different. And the dream itself...

"It's nothing," said Calantha, her teeth clenched. "Nothing. I'm sorry."

She sank down into the mattress, trying to ignore Freya's mutterings, the deep rumble of her father's voice, her mother's chittering replies.

She pushed herself into the first tale that sprang to mind, the one of the cat who braved the water. It came in jerks and staggers at first, but as she plowed on, it became smoother, and at last she was caught in the flow. She told herself tale after tale. Her body ached from lying clenched so as not to disturb Freya. But she didn't sleep any more that night.

At last, there was a lessening of the dark. She watched the sky through the window, dark eased by a hint of pearl light on the horizon. The first hesitant twitter of birds sprayed the air like cool, clear water.

It was a dream. Only a dream. Wasn't it?

Her stomach twisted again with fear. She had to go and see.

Slowly, she started to climb out of bed. Freya turned, murmuring. Calantha froze, one leg half out of bed. Freya would try to stop her if she woke.

She remained motionless until Freya settled, then carefully stood up and unhooked her green shawl from the wall. Picking up her shoes, she slipped past the curtain to the main chamber. Father and Mother would be up soon. She must be fast. She tiptoed to the front door and lifted the latch. It rose without a squeak. Thank goodness her father greased it regularly.

She shut the door silently behind her, and drank

in the crisp morning air. The road was still and silent, the sky clear. Xenyss had said it would be overcast.

Hands trembling, she put on her shoes. For a moment she hesitated. Should she take the quicker back path? No, it would be wet and muddy. She flung her shawl around her shoulders and began to run down the road toward the Green, her jaw tight, partly from fear, partly from cold. She raced through the dew-wet Green, her braid coming undone, her breath in puffs, then swerved onto the Mid Plains road, past the last few houses, only one with a stir of smoke; past the empty lorsha field with mist ghosting along the furrows; past the rustling sharo grove on her right, the pasture fields on the left, and at last, to the Field of Gathering. Chest heaving, she hurtled into the field. The sun hadn't risen, but there was enough gray light to see.

They were still here! The story pods were here!

Her knees buckled and she bent over, almost sick with relief. Gasping, she straightened up, flicking back the strands of hair across her face. She stumbled deeper into the field and touched the pods.

They hummed with tales; oh, thanks be to the Sower of Tales, they were here, and humming.

"A dream, just a dream," she whispered. Her voice sounded harsh and hoarse in the stillness of the morning. Slowly, her heartbeat steadied. Could the children be right about the Sorcerer Odhran sending nightmares? She shivered and flicked her fingers.

It had been so vivid. She could feel it still. She'd stood in the field, alone. And there hadn't been a single pod in the field. Not one. Despair had filled her. Gray, numbing desolation had weighed and pressed her down, crushing her. And then the eyes. She couldn't see them, but she'd sensed them, searching, searching, as though through a mist. She had stood frozen. She knew the eyes were searching for her but she couldn't move. The sense of malice was overwhelming, intent. So cold. The eyes were turning, turning, toward her. Terror clawed at her throat, and she screamed....

Calantha shuddered. She reached for another story pod, then started at the lilting whistle coming down the road. She ducked down, and peering through the grass, recognized Eythun's quick springy walk. Of course, he checked the herd in the far pasture first thing. And here she was in her nightdress!

Bent double, Calantha scurried to the end of the field. She clambered down to the grassy ditch next to the lorsha field, jerking back her hair. The grass was soaking wet, the ground sticky with mud. She wasn't halfway past the field before her new shoes were caked and her nightdress drenched, clinging and twisting around her legs like a fretful child.

"Flikketting lizards! Pustering toadstools! Snarking, *snarking* bograts!" Muttering every foul word she'd ever heard Hardwin say—and Hardwin knew many—Calantha struggled to the end of the ditch, then followed the track behind the clusters of pale green brinlow trees scattered along the rear of the houses on the Mid Plains road and the eastern side of the Green. She reached the back of her own house just as the sun rose, dazzling her eyes. The pungent sweet smoke of burning lorsha stalks filled the air.

She caught her breath. Her shoes were smothered in red mud, her nightdress spattered almost to the waist, and her new green shawl puckered where she'd caught it on a branch. If her mother saw her…Calantha shivered.

She turned toward the path to Kasmira's, then froze. In a sickening flash, she understood.

How many times had Kasmira said there must be no pride in the gathering, that there was a price to it? Last night, she'd been full of pride. The dream— was it her punishment?

Calantha's chest constricted. If Kasmira knew, it would be a long, long time before she'd let Calantha pick a pod for Talemeet again.

No. She'd rather face her mother.

Calantha crept onto the back porch and peered inside. Thanks be to the Sower of Tales, the cooking chamber was empty.

She slipped inside, shoes in hand, heard the clip and trot of her mother's voice, punctuated by the measured rumble of her father's from their bed- chamber. She scurried to her bedchamber.

Freya, braiding her long, dark hair, swung around. Her mouth dropped open. "Now what have you been up to?" she gasped.

"Never you mind," said Calantha, struggling out of her wet nightdress. The bottom slapped against her face, reeking of musty water.

Freya steamed in low fury as her fingers flew, tying the blue ribbon to the end of her braid. "Were you listening to story pods at this hour? Were you? Wait 'til Mother sees that nightdress."

Calantha's fingers itched to slap Freya but the last thing she needed was her mother coming in. She couldn't tell Freya about the nightmare, either. She'd made that mistake when she'd told her of the witch dream, and Freya'd been sympathetic only until their next fight. Then she'd mocked and laughed, and spread it around to half the village.

Whipping around, Calantha hissed, "You be quiet, you preening little toad! If you say one word to Mother, I'll tell her and everyone how you've been ogling Frewen."

Freya gasped. "I haven't...I never!"

Calantha's eyes glittered. "Ah, but will they believe you?"

Freya turned an unbecoming shade of purple. "You...you...stupid *mule*!" In silence she doubled up her braid, tied it in place, then flounced past the curtain to the main chamber.

Calantha scrunched up her nightdress and tossed it under the bed. She'd scrub it herself later. She washed quickly and dressed, ran a comb through her hair and quickly braided it, tangles and all, then scraped her shoes as best she could at the window.

"Calantha, for the Creator's sake," her mother's exasperated voice rang out. "It's high time you were ready. Be quick, now."

It was almost a relief to hear her mother's sharp tones. It made everything seem familiar and ordinary. Normal.

And yet, nothing seemed quite normal. Everything was soupy and blurred. When she slopped breakfast dishwater on the floor for the third time, her mother, with an air of frazzled weariness, packed Calantha off to the Green to offer service.

Calantha dragged her feet toward the Green, her head hazy. She hated offering service, but at least she'd be away from her mother's eagle eye and the dreaded sharo thatch. If only Benigna would take her, just once more. Benigna never told on

Calantha when she wandered away to pick story pods—although it was probably why Benigna rarely chose her.

Youngsters had already clustered in the Green; Breanna with her red hair, Listha, Fenwick, Cybella blinking palely, as well as others. And, of course, Julissa in the center, her fair hair glistening. Calantha groaned softly. Julissa was always there. Probably because Laerissa, her mother, couldn't endure Julissa's sharp tongue either.

The weaver Frensha, with her quick, darting movements, was already eyeing the helpers, along with Farnell, an Earthroffe, Tubbunte the round-shouldered cobbler, and others. Calantha brightened at the sight of Benigna's tall spare figure. She moistened her lips and smiled ingratiatingly, but Benigna avoided her eye and picked Cybella.

Calantha's breath escaped in a hiss. Cybella was small, quick, and sickeningly obedient. Also exhaustingly, grindingly, eye-gougeingly dull—she'd never been the least interested in Calantha's stories when they'd been little.

Julissa lifted a disdainful eyebrow at Calantha and

muttered audibly to Breanna, "Thinks she's so clever just because she picked a story pod. Too bad she can't do anything else...." She stopped as Frensha called her name.

As usual, Calantha was the last to be picked—by Frensha, who took her with weary resignation, and probably out of friendship to her mother. Calantha lagged behind the others as they headed to the weavery. Her head felt as though it was stuffed with uncarded wool. Despite Julissa's glee, Calantha was relieved to be assigned the task of stirring the vat of orange dye outside Frensha's weavery. Anything was better than having to fiddle with those looms like Julissa, who was surprisingly adept with her hands. Calantha had only to look at the looms for the threads to snarl.

As she stirred the hot, heavy cloth, Calantha let herself drift with the tales of the pods. The sun's reflection in the orange dye dazzled her eyes and made her head spin. As she stopped to ease her back, her mind skittered sideways at the dream, cautiously licking it, as at a wound. Something twisted sharply inside her. She whipped her mind away and began to stir again, faster; it was just a nightmare, a silly nightmare for her pride. It was only the lack of sleep that made everything seem so strange. It must be.

Chapter Five

And yet that strange, snarled feeling remained all week. It was as though her insides were full of knots. At times the knots tightened, at times they loosened, but they were always there.

For a few nights she was terrified to sleep, but thank goodness, she had no more nightmares. Not even of the witch. She still liquefied with fear when she remembered the dream and she found herself running to the Field of Gathering again and again, just to see; relief flooded her every time she touched a pod and felt the familiar humming.

But in spite of that, everything continued to feel strange. *Askew*. That was the word that kept coming to her mind. But why? No more horsemen were seen in the village or nearby. Of course, Hardwin was still agitating the Council to send a party to Jaerlfin, which her father steadily opposed because of the heavy harvest work. Luckily, her father said, Kerwin had too good a head on his shoulders to let Hardwin do anything rash. Kerwin insisted that this was too big a matter for just one village to act on; it was best left to the Grand Council of the Plains.

Calantha sensed something strained from Xenyss too, a kind of cramped, twisting worry. He seemed to stumble through the village more and more, and once, when she saw him talking to Argenta, she caught a strand of something badly wrenched.

Even Kasmira seemed preoccupied somehow, and quieter when they met for the daily harvesting for Talemeet. Calantha wasn't sure why, but part of her was glad of it; the less she talked to Kasmira, the less likely she was to blurt out everything. Part of her did wonder guiltily if Kasmira already knew, and was waiting for her to confess, but she thrust that thought aside. There was no need to say anything. She'd learned her lesson, hadn't she?

More than ever, to escape the strangeness,

Calantha let herself drift with the tales in her head. It only made her more forgetful and awkward and she got into dire trouble when her mother found out that she'd stolen away to pick story pods when she should have been harvesting the gray balmberries under the kerlnut trees with Benigna—who had actually picked her for service one day, along with Cybella. Benigna hadn't told, but Cybella conscientiously reported it to her sister, who told Freya, who told their mother because Calantha had lost the hair clip that Freya had never even wanted until it was gone. Luvena became more determined than ever to teach Calantha sharo thatching, and Calantha grew equally determined not to learn.

It was unseasonably warm a few days later, when Calantha accompanied Kasmira to the Field of Gathering. Kasmira walked faster than usual, and in abstracted silence. Calantha scratched her fingers and held her tongue resentfully. Kasmira didn't seem to care any more than Luvena did that the sap from the sharo leaves made her fingers itch and itch.

When they reached the Field of Gathering, Calantha breathed deeply, to unsnarl herself. A

Gatherer must have harmony around her to pick a pod. She gazed at the Eastern Mountains, at the highest peak, but it was covered in mist. Calantha sighed and turned to watch Kasmira, who was wandering about the far end of the Field of Gathering.

Calantha frowned. Kasmira wasn't touching the ripe pods. She wasn't even looking at them. Calantha's back prickled with uneasiness.

Why was Kasmira staring downward?

Kasmira turned and beckoned. Calantha rushed through the tall grass. The tightness of Kasmira's mouth reminded Calantha of her mother.

"Calantha, do you see any new ones coming up?"

The knots inside Calantha wrenched. She stared numbly at Kasmira. Then she shoved aside the grass, searching for the telltale red shoots poking through the soil. Why hadn't she thought of this, oh, why hadn't she thought of *this*?

There were plenty of ripe story pods nodding above the grass, and at every height, from her knee upward to her chest. But none below that. Two days to germinate and poke through the soil, another four to grow knee high....

Somehow she found her voice. "How long...?" she asked.

Kasmira's mouth was grim. "Six days, I think. I sensed something wasn't right, but I just couldn't see what."

Six days.

Calantha moistened her lips. "Kasmira. Six nights ago, I had a dream."

"The witch again?" Kasmira frowned. "I thought that had stopped."

"Not the witch dream. This was...different."

Kasmira turned sharply. "Then what?"

Somehow, Calantha forced the words out. "I dreamed there were no more story pods."

Kasmira's eyes blazed. "What exactly did you dream?"

What was the matter with her tongue? It felt like an old rag. "I...I stood at the edge of the field. There were no story pods. None. Eyes..." Calantha's throat went dry. "Eyes were looking for me. I woke up screaming."

Kasmira's face turned gray. "Why, by the grace of the pods, didn't you tell me?"

"I went to the field that morning. The pods were there." Calantha looked desperately at Kasmira. "I was afraid it was because of my pride, after the gathering. I was afraid you wouldn't let me pick a pod again."

A hard stillness came into Kasmira's face.

Calantha choked, "It isn't because of that, is it? I never meant—"

Kasmira shook her head impatiently. "No, of course not. Pride makes it difficult to harvest a pod, but not—"

Relief flooded Calantha, followed by a swoop of fear. "Then why? What's happening? Has the Sower of Tales abandoned us?"

Kasmira didn't seem to hear. "I must tell Xenyss."

"Xenyss?"

Kasmira's face was drawn. "This must be tied to the change in the Essences he's been sensing." She looked around as though in a daze, then began to move. "A pod. I must pick a pod for Talemeet."

Calantha cried, "But we can't just—"

"Calantha, what good will it do to deny everyone

a tale this night?" Kasmira's voice was harsh.

Calantha stared at her.

Kasmira said shortly, "Come to me tomorrow morning. We'll see Xenyss together, then we'll tell the Council. But for now, you are not to breathe a word of it to anyone, d'you hear?"

Calantha managed to nod. As she watched Kasmira move through the field, cupping ripe story pods, her thoughts screamed and bit like swarming clonthip flies. How could Kasmira be so calm? So unhurried?

But Kasmira tore the first two pods she tried to harvest. Calantha couldn't remember when that had ever happened before.

In stupefied silence, she walked back to the Green with Kasmira, and listened to the tale with frantic, distracted attention, barely able to sit still.

That night she maddened Freya by rustling and turning in bed as she swung between disbelief, guilt, and terror. She clung to every story she could remember, and lacerated herself for not telling Kasmira sooner. If only, if only...she fell into an exhausted sleep.

But when she awoke, it washed over her, like a burst of cool water, just exactly what she must do.

She could barely choke down her lorsha porridge at breakfast and her mother felt her forehead to see if she was ill. As soon as the pot was scrubbed, she blurted, "Mother, I have to go to Kasmira. She asked me for service today."

Luvena huffed, "But she should go to the Green, then. What if I need your help in the Cheesery? And are you well enough? You look so pale." She touched her forehead again.

Calantha jerked her head away. "I'm fine, Mother. I must go." Ignoring Luvena's protests, she tore down the dusty path to Kasmira's hut.

She could tell from her face that Kasmira hadn't slept much either. "Kasmira," she began, "I know what to do."

"Just wait 'til we've spoken to Xenyss," said Kasmira.

Calantha sighed but held her tongue as they set out down the road and across the Green. It seemed strange to see youngsters there waiting to offer service. How could the world go on as though nothing had happened? Julissa turned to stare at her, but for once, Calantha didn't care.

They continued silently along the westbound Blackthorn road; it narrowed beyond the last of the houses, pressed in by brinlow trees, wide-trunked kerlnuts with their deep green leaves, and chernows with their low, swaying, feathery red branches. Xenyss lived a long way out of the village, as did all Seers, and Calantha was hot and sticky by the time they reached his large, sagging, whitewashed hut.

She rarely came here, except when sent by Luvena with some food or gift for Xenyss. The first time had been when she'd been small and Julissa had pushed her down, saying she was too ugly to play with. Calantha had split her knee and she'd been crying when Xenyss had found her. He'd taken her to his hut and tended to her, ignoring the blood she'd gushed all over his pale blue robe. She'd been afraid of him before that, for he was a Seer, and she'd been too young to understand the mockery of the older children. But she'd never been afraid afterward, and she'd never forgotten his shy kindness.

They climbed the worn, crooked steps to the

porch. Kasmira knocked, and Xenyss' voice bid them enter.

Calantha blinked to adjust to the gloom inside.

A small fire glowed in the fireplace along the far wall; a bench stood in front of it, as well as a table, two chairs, and a footstool. Xenyss' plain, low bed with its worn gray blankets was tucked in the corner. A few old pots as well as an assortment of herbs hung on the whitewashed walls, filling the hut with layers of green smells.

In the middle, taking up most of the space, was the traditional divining square; a large, low, wooden frame, filled with sand. Xenyss stood motionless in the center of the square, his back to the door.

Kasmira put a warning finger to her lips. Xenyss was in the middle of a divination.

The four corners of the square each held a plain earthenware bowl, the kind that Freya had first learned to make. One was empty, another held a lump of clay, a third gleamed with water, and red embers smoldered in the fourth. Earth, air, water, fire; Xenyss in the center. Lines were marked on the sand, some straight, some curving, some joining one corner to another, others joining a corner to the center.

Calantha stared; she'd never seen a divination at work. Suddenly, she sensed a change, as though the air had shifted. Her eyes widened as new lines appeared in the sand, from the air corner to the earth corner and some to the fire, but yet more toward Xenyss.

Xenyss' head turned, tilting and sinking as each new line appeared. He gazed longest at the deep lines from the air corner to the earth—and at the harsh jagged line scouring toward him in the center.

Calantha stood motionless, mesmerized by that jagged line. Something about it made her shudder and she had to drag her eyes away.

At last, Xenyss turned around.

"Kasmira." He nodded. As they focused on Calantha, his eyes cleared and sharpened.

He motioned them to sit. Calantha sat on the bench, hands gripping the edge, as Xenyss, grunting, lowered himself into a chair.

"What c-c-can I d-do for you?"

Calantha opened her mouth, but Kasmira was

quicker. She rasped, "There are no new story pods growing, Xenyss. We saw yesterday evening."

"There haven't been any for seven days," cried Calantha. Why were they wasting time? There was only one thing to do.

Xenyss' head straightened in alarm. "Th-the Essences. This m-m-must b-be tied to the change...they are b-becoming m-more and m-m-more askew."

Calantha started. *Askew* was the word that had sprung repeatedly to her mind a few days ago.

"There's more," Kasmira said crisply. "Calantha, tell him about the dream."

Calantha took a deep breath and somehow forced the words out. As she finished, she sensed the alarm in Xenyss. It was almost like a sharpness in the air.

Xenyss asked urgently, "What d-did you f-f-feel in the d-d-dream, when you saw there were n-no s-story pods? What d-d-did you sense?"

Calantha drew in a shuddering breath. "Despair," she said. "The air...everything, felt drained. Half alive."

Xenyss leaned forward, the loose skin along his

jaw shaking. "Th-the eyes. Were they the s-s-same as in your witch d-dream?" He too, then, must have heard, like half the village.

Calantha swallowed, trying to stop the roiling inside. Somehow, Xenyss had gone to the heart of the matter. "I...I didn't see the eyes. But they weren't the same. I just know it." She wrapped her arms around herself.

Xenyss put his hand on her shoulder and warmth slowly flooded her. He sat back heavily, his eyes darting to the divining square. "D-d-does anyone else know of the d-dream?"

"No. Well, Mother, Freya...I woke screaming. Only they thought it was the witch dream again, and I didn't say..."

Kasmira turned to Xenyss, her face drawn. "What's the meaning of all this? What is happening?"

Xenyss shook his head. "I n-n-need t-time to unravel—"

Calantha sprang to her feet. "We don't have time. There haven't been any new story pods for seven days now. In seven more they'll be gone." Her breath caught in her throat. "I've been thinking and thinking—there's only one thing to do."

"Calantha, settle down—" began Kasmira.

But Calantha plunged on. "The Sower of Tales. I have to go to her. She scatters the seeds. If she has stopped, we must find out why." Calantha gripped her hands together. "Kasmira, give me the key. I know I'm not yet apprenticed, but give me the key and let me find her."

"N-no!" Xenyss voice was surprisingly forceful. "The d-d-divination reveals s-s-strong s-signs of d-d-danger. And your d-dream shows you m-m-must be t-t-tied to it."

Calantha's eyes flicked to the jagged line on the sand. She said, too loudly, "Then I should be the one to go, shouldn't I?"

"No!" Xenyss almost shouted. "It is real d-d-danger. This is n-not a game for children to m-m-meddle in."

Calantha's stomach jolted, but she flashed, "I'm not a child, I'm nearly of age to apprentice and—"

"You're not going anywhere," said Kasmira harshly.

Calantha turned to her. "But we can't just wait for Xenyss to...to...." She bit her lip.

Xenyss looked pale, exhausted. "Calantha, it t-takes t-t-time to unravel causes, b-because everything is intert-t-wined. The Essence of the wind is harnessed s-s-strangely. B-but I c-cannot yet m-m-make out how. Or b-by whom." He put his hand on her arm. "Other Seers and Sorcerers in the P-P-Plains have m-marked it as well. Sorcerer Theora in Shernthrip is also t-trying to unravel it."

Calantha stared stonily past him.

Xenyss gripped her arm. "C-Calantha, listen! You have a g-gift that not all have, but it is untried and r-raw. W-wait until I know b-b-better how you are t-tied in this, so I c-can g-guide you if—"

Kasmira interrupted, "She's not going anywhere."

Calantha's jaw tightened. "I have to—"

"Don't be a mule," snapped Kasmira.

Calantha flinched. Kasmira never used that word—her mother's—except in jest.

Xenyss nodded urgently. "You m-m-must keep low. And tell no one of the d-dream."

"The Council of Elders?" asked Kasmira.

"N-not of her p-part," said Xenyss. "I t-tell you, the d-danger is—"

Rage filled Calantha. She wasn't a child, incapable of making her own decisions. "I'm going. You can't tell me what to—"

"You are not going," said Kasmira. "I won't give you the key. If anyone has to go, it will not be you." Her eyes were hard and merciless.

For the first time Calantha glimpsed the true power of the Gatherer. But what shook her to the core were the spikes of fear she sensed from Kasmira. Fear for her.

"Promise me, Calantha," said Kasmira. "Or you will never apprentice with me."

Calantha's eyes widened in shock.

Kasmira said coldly, "You will promise me. On my life."

CHAPTER SIX

he next two days seemed like a nightmare. Calantha went about in a daze as the news spread and the village flamed with speculation and talk. But the only thing the villagers did was talk, even the Council of Elders—just talk and talk and more talk.

Calantha scratched her fingers until they bled. Why wasn't anybody *doing* anything? She should be on her way; she should be on her way to the Eastern Mountains. And she'd have gone, too, promise or no promise, except that Kasmira had made her promise on her life. Kasmira had been viciously clever to insist on that.

Never had Calantha been so ashamed of her father and his plodding caution. At first, he and

Eythun were alarmed only about the crops. Once they discovered that the crops and vegetables still grew, they actually seemed relieved. When the Council considered sending out others to search for the story pods, it was Anwyll, her own father, who objected because he couldn't spare hands from the heavy harvest work.

Calantha thought she'd explode as Laerissa, Julissa's mother, kept insisting that maybe for once the story pods were taking longer to sprout. Hardwin, big and important, strutted beyond the western woods, and a couple of other folk went to the nearest villages. A few searchers from nearby villages even came to Grenlea, on the same quest, but still the Council did nothing, and still Xenyss mumbled about being in touch with the other Seers and Sorcerers in the Plains and needing more time.

Time! Snake's venom, they didn't have time! Kasmira, of all people, should know that. Even if she'd sent someone else to the Sower of Tales, Calantha wouldn't feel so helpless. So terrified.

At least her mother didn't try to make her roll thatch or offer service. When Luvena heard the news, she looked long at Calantha, with an awful pity in her face. It scared Calantha, but also infuriated her. Her mother also noticed, at last, how sore Calantha's hands were from the sharo sap. Now she kept at her and at her to rub them with Benigna's linth balm.

The only thing that stopped Calantha from drowning in fury and despair was roaming the laneways and opening any ripe pod she could find outside the Field of Gathering. She tore more than she could bear and yet she couldn't stop trying. And she went over all the stories she could remember, every single one, melding parts of different stories to make new ones, trying to hold them, hold them.

At last, two torturous days after they'd first heard the news, the Elders cautiously decided to call a Councilmeet—mostly because of the arrival of a couple of strangers, who had come by horse and cart from a distant northern village, asking about the story pods. When they reported seeing no new ones along the way, the Council finally began to believe.

Calantha seethed with rage. Councilmeet! Flikketting lizards, what good was that? It was just

more talk; hadn't they wasted enough time already?
It was nine days now, since the dream, since the
story pods stopped growing! In five more days,
there'd be none. They'd harvest the last pods, keep
them for a day or two at most, before they burst
open, and then…Calantha felt drained, exhausted at
the thought. The desolation she'd felt in her nightmare was coming true. And those eyes…she shuddered. She didn't want to think of them.

As she passed the Green in the early afternoon,
Calantha saw a large group of villagers around the
newcomers, Flenart and Shraelyn. They too seemed
to have nothing better to do than talk—to each and
every villager they met, and about the most trivial
matters. They didn't care about the story pods
either, for all they'd been sent by their village to
look for them.

Lurking at the edge of the group, she overheard
Flenart making friendly enquiries about the
Gatherer and her apprentices. Cybella, who stood
beside him, murmured something and pointed to
Calantha. As Flenart tucked in the edge of his turban
and turned toward her, Calantha left abruptly, her

stomach suddenly uneasy. She didn't like Flenart, despite his broad, smiling face; and she didn't much like Shraelyn either, who was thin and fidgety, with pale, darting eyes. But then, everything made her stomach twist right now. She hated everyone.

Especially Kasmira. Calantha could hardly bear to look at her with that boulder of a promise lying between them.

And yet, when Kasmira went to the Field of Gathering later on, Calantha accompanied her as always. She couldn't stay away. Argenta had decreed that they'd meet early that evening so they could make time for two tales before Councilmeet. Several villagers came with them to the Field of Gathering now—a gaggle of curious boys; Neola and a few others who were concerned; and some stragglers who tagged along just because others did.

The sun was low in the sky as the villagers gathered on the Green. Such a large gathering, more than twice as usually came to Talemeet. Calantha sat still as the tales unfolded, soaking in the words as though parched. A funny tale of a farmer's child who befriended a snake, and another of hardship and danger, of a warrior searching for a curing stone from the depths of the sea for his wife. Kasmira had picked both the pods. Calantha hadn't even asked to pick one.

She blinked as the last tale ended, and watched the seeds change color and rise to a sky streaked crimson and magenta with the setting sun. If only she could shut out the spikes of worry around her, the sharp intent from Hardwin and some of the men. Her mother emitted a low, grinding concern; Calantha knew that much of it was for her, but she didn't care. Freya was worried too, but she wasn't talking to Calantha—they'd fought like fire lizards the past two days. Most of the faces were more somber than usual after a tale; Berwin's face prune-like, Frensha's smile forced, Delmer's moustaches drooping, Julissa's face more spiteful and fretful. Even Benigna's smooth forehead had twitched into faint lines.

Calantha sensed someone nearby looking at her. Flenart. He smiled at her, his blue eyes twinkling. Calantha scowled and turned away, trying to brush aside her discomfort. She stared at the Council; the

various First Roffes, including her father, and
Argenta and Xenyss, who sat on the stone benches by
the fire. Kasmira sat with them for once, her brown
face wrinkled and pinched. Calantha's chest constricted. They'd never been this distant. Not even
when she'd ransacked Kasmira's hut for the key. If
only she'd found it....

Argenta stood and banged her stick on the
ground. "Friends, as First Elder of Council, I greet
you. You have all heard by now that there are no new
story pods growing. In a few more days, there will be
none."

Fear prickled across Calantha's back. It made it
real, to hear it said aloud at Councilmeet.

"We meet, then, to consider what action to take.
We have visitors from the village of Braeshin to the
north." She nodded at Flenart and Shraelyn. "They
are here because of the story pods too, and they have
seen no new ones along the way." Argenta banged
her stick again. "Speak, then, who will."

Of course, it was Hardwin who first leaped to his
feet.

"I say we send a strong armed party to JaerlzGate,

to talk to King Ulric."

Calantha's jaw clenched. She might have known Hardwin would try to twist this to his cause.

Frensha rose exasperatedly. "By the Creator's Grace, Hardwin! What does King Ulric have to do with the story pods? No, I say we seek the assistance of the Sorcerers at the Place of Knotting."

Many voices cried out in agreement, but Hardwin shouted over them, "It's a long journey across the seas to the Place of Knotting. We don't have time. King Ulric's behind this—why else have his men been meddling here of late?"

Some folk shouted in agreement, while others scoffed.

Calantha closed her eyes in despair. Oh, why were they wasting time? There was only one thing to do.

Tubbunte's high-pitched voice rang out, "For goodness' sake, man, do you think King Ulric sent his men to pull up the story pods one by one? Why? To plague the children?"

Titters broke out.

Hardwin rubbed at his ears and glowered. "All I say is, who most wishes us harm?"

The titters died.

"Aye," rumbled Hardwin. "Him and his Sorcerer Odhran."

Fingers flicked at the mention of the name.

Calantha's nails dug into the palms of her hands. Hardwin was just eager to fight, to make swords in his smithy—he'd already started. He didn't care about the story pods any more than most of the villagers.

Eythun stood up and barked, "If King Ulric wanted to harm us, there's much worse he could do. The crops still grow, my cows give milk." His strong nose jutted the air. "Perhaps we are too overwrought. The story pods may grow again. And if not..." He shrugged. "They'll be missed, mostly by the children, but..."

Rage tore through Calantha. She leaped to her feet but her mother pulled her down.

"Quiet," hissed Luvena. "You will not make an exhibition of yourself."

Calantha's face flamed.

Flenart looked at her sympathetically. "I hear you are much attached to the tales, Calantha, and skilled at the gathering."

Her mother glowered.

Flenart smiled and scratched a fat earlobe under his turban. Some unsettling memory flickered in Calantha's head, then skittered away, lost.

Xenyss was speaking. Despite her anger, Calantha ached to see him leaning on his stick, looking so worn.

"...t-t-tied together," he was saying, stammering worse than ever, his face red and earnest. "You *c-c-cannot* affect one Essence without ch-ch-changing every other. I t-t-tell you, there is g-grave d-danger t-to our way of l-life. T-t-to the very f-f-fabric of our b-being. You m-must listen. No one c-can be c-certain how it will impact on us, b-b-but be assured, it w-will. *D-d-drastically*."

There was an uneasy silence. Even though Xenyss' words chilled her, Calantha felt a spark of hope. Maybe now they'd do something.

Argenta's voice carried clearly in the gathering dark. "Friends, there is no question that this is a matter of concern, even as Xenyss says, because it is a change in the very fabric of our beings."

Calantha felt, rather than heard, the scoff from her mother. Someone began to light the central fire and others the lorsha torches, now that the sun had set.

Argenta continued, "There are many who wish to speak, but I ask that we now hear from the one most closely concerned with this matter. Our Gatherer."

From across the crowd, Calantha sensed someone's eyes on her. It was Julissa, staring, her expression a mixture of spite and gloating. Calantha turned away. Julissa didn't matter now.

Kasmira's red-green cloak swirled as she stood. Her voice rasped, "Friends, much has been said, but there is one thing that *must* be done. We must seek the Sower of Tales."

Calantha leaned forward. At last! Oh, would Kasmira relent now and let her go? In the turmoil around her, she sensed a thrusting skewer of interest.

Hardwin leaped to his feet. "No one knows for certain where she dwells. We don't have time—"

Frensha interrupted, "The Gatherer is right—we should seek the Sower of Tales."

Benigna stood up and said mildly, "Maybe the Sorcerers at the Place of Knotting can direct us. The

Gatherer of Banthrip says the Sower of Tales lives on an isle past the Place of Knotting."

Hardwin shouted, "She could be in the Northern mountains, and if we go to King—"

Kasmira held up her hand. "I am Gatherer and I know where she lives."

Calantha winced. Sharp, sharp interest, it was knife-like, painful. She tried to trace its source, but in the turbulence around her it was like trying to trace one thread in a fistful of snarls.

Kasmira continued, "The Sower of Tales dwells on the highest Eastern mountain. Aelthea, who was Gatherer before me, told me, and she—"

Hardwin cried out, "No, she does not. I've been there, I tell you, and Cyneric too, all over the Eastern Mountains. There's nothing but rock and rubble. The Gatherer at Wrenford says the Sower of Tales lives past the Northern mountains. If you Gatherers have no common direction, I say we go to King Ulric. Even if he isn't behind it, his Sorcerer might know how to find the Sower of Tales."

Kasmira started to say something but Xenyss shouted, actually shouted, "We m-must not waste t-t-time there if H-Hardwin f-found n-n-nothing."

Kasmira called out, "But Aelthea went to the Sower of Tales and—"

Xenyss shouted louder, "Aelthea d-d-disappeared. We all know her m-m-mind wandered!"

Calantha's head began to throb sickeningly. How could Xenyss discredit Kasmira so openly?

Kasmira tried to speak again, but was drowned by Hardwin, Saeward, and others.

Calantha rocked back and forth. Nobody cared about the story pods. Nobody. A spear of clear understanding lanced through the pain in her head—without the story pods to join them, the disagreements would only widen and grow. And she could do nothing about it because Xenyss thought he saw danger. Xenyss, who couldn't even divine the weather, let alone untie the knots of his own tongue.

She sensed a flash of blue tugging her. Xenyss was looking at her, eyes urgent as though trying to tell her something. She wrenched her own eyes away. She wanted nothing to do with him. Not after what he'd just done.

Julissa's voice cut through the babble. "I know

why they've stopped growing." Julissa stood, triumphantly. Laerissa, her mother, also stood, mouth
pursed, nodding self-righteously.

Voices subsided into an edgy silence. Someone
tittered nervously.

Julissa looked around and shrilled, "Think on it.
When did the story pods stop?"

Calantha's heart began to thud.

"It was when Kasmira let *her* gather a pod." Julissa
jabbed a spiteful finger at Calantha. "She must have
something to do with it. She has offended the Sower
of Tales."

In flashes, Calantha saw faces turn toward her;
Frensha's concerned; Freya's frightened; Beagan's
eyes wide; her father's grim, as he sprang to his feet.

But Kasmira was first. "Nonsense! There have
always been others who pick, apprentices and—"

Julissa cried, "But she isn't apprenticed!"

Kasmira snapped, "That has no bearing..."

Between the peaks of pain in her head, Calantha
spied an unexpected passage of hope. She leaped to
her feet. "Yes," she cried out. "It may be true."

There was a shocked silence.

Then Kasmira began to speak, and her mother, but Calantha shouted, "Maybe I was too proud. Maybe I offended the Sower of Tales. If so, I must make amends."

Above the general agitation, Calantha sensed her mother's alarm, Kasmira's stab of fear, and something roaring from Xenyss. But she rushed on, her voice hoarse. "I'm willing to go and find the Sower of Tales. The Gatherer has a key, and if she gives it to me...." She stopped as a sharp pain jagged through her head.

Her mother yanked her down while she herself stood, keeping Calantha pinned under her strong hand. Freya gripped her with one hand, tears gathering at the corners of her eyes, while her other hand made panicked circles on Calantha's back.

Luvena's voice cut through the babble like a knife. "Enough."

There was absolute silence. Calantha struggled to stand but couldn't.

Luvena's eyes flashed. "There is nothing but spite and envy behind Julissa's remark."

Laerissa sputtered, but withered into silence at a glance from Luvena.

"I know my daughter can be difficult," said Luvena.

"She is stubborn, unruly, and wilful; those of you who have had her for service know that."

Calantha tried to swallow the familiar waves of bitterness rising inside her.

Luvena's voice rang, "But she also has a good heart. And I defy anyone to say different."

Calantha's jaw dropped open.

Luvena forged on. "You all know that I do not want my daughter to apprentice with the Gatherer. Yet even I cannot deny that she has a skill that others do not have."

Calantha felt dizzy. Had her mother really said that?

Luvena continued, "It is a gift, I tell you, a gift! How can her harvesting a story pod possibly offend the Sower of Tales?" She looked around the silent gathering, and her voice lowered. "Friends, I warn you! If there is any further talk of this nature, you will have to deal with me."

Neola's robust voice cried out, "Well said!" Many chorused in agreement. Others still looked dubious.

Calantha's throat went tight as her mother sat down behind her and put a strong, steadying hand on her back. Like a blessing. Calantha blinked and blinked, and leaned against the comfort of her mother's arm. She had a sense of more shouting, people looking at her, before the discussion turned again.

By the time Councilmeet ended late that night, Calantha felt like a wrung-out rag. Her head ached, worse than ever. Kasmira hasn't even tried to mention the Eastern Mountains again, or the key, and nothing of worth had been decided that Calantha could see. The Council had agreed only to send small search parties farther afield—but just a few because, again, Anwyll insisted that folk couldn't be spared from the harvest. The parties would search for news of the story pods, and also try to discover more about the whereabouts of the Sower of Tales. A journey to the Place of Knotting was considered too long and dangerous to undertake without the help and agreement of the Grand Council in Maernlea. But at Hardwin's insistence, the Council agreed to send him with Kerwin to Maernlea to report their findings and to request that the Grand Council send a group north to JaerlzGate, to see King Ulric.

Calantha stood up shakily as the villagers began to stir and chatter in groups. Her headache threatened to pound her into the ground.

Her mother briefly touched her cheek. "All right, Calantha?"

Calantha nodded, managing a shaky smile.

She drifted away from the crowd. She wouldn't wait for Kasmira today. She couldn't. In the darkest pit of her being, Calantha knew that her nightmare was coming true. The desolation she'd felt in the dream swamped over her.

She caught sight of Xenyss stumbling in her direction from the far end of the Gathering, and even through her headache sensed a frantic tug of urgency from him. He was coming to talk to her.

Well, she didn't want to talk to him. Luckily Argenta stopped him to say something and Calantha seized the chance to move out of sight. Flenart and Shraelyn stood at the edge of the crowd and as she passed by, they called out to her. Calantha pretended not to hear.

Alone in the dark of the Green, Calantha stopped to collect herself, pressing a hand against her head. Her headache was subsiding a little, now that she was away from the worst of the confusion. She blinked and looked up at the sky. Heavy lowering clouds. And Xenyss had said it would be clear. A sobbing laugh sprang to her lips.

She stumbled onward through the Green to the dark road on which she lived, stopping to draw in gulps of air. She'd never before had a headache this bad. Maybe she should bathe her forehead with balmberry water, even crush part of one into her drinking water. But not too much. Two of those tiny gray berries could knock out a grown man, as Benigna had repeatedly warned her—she'd managed to pick up that much at least before running off to the Field of Gathering the day that she'd offered service. How long ago it seemed. Another life.

What was that? She jerked around.

Something twisted toward her, like sly fingers trickling across the back of her neck.

Was she being watched? Her eyes strained against the dark, but she could see nothing apart from the dim outlines of some of the houses and shrubs. In the distance, the fire at the Gathering flickered, surrounded by the fainter glows of lorsha torches moving about as folk carried them home.

Maybe she should have brought a torch. Should she go back and get one?

She shook herself, rubbing the back of her neck. She'd never needed a torch before. It was just her headache.

On she went in the dark, but just as she reached her gate, she felt that prickling again.

Before she could swing around, there was a thud of footsteps and a hand clamped across her mouth, while another banded like iron around her arms and waist.

Calantha struggled, tried to bite and scream, scratch and kick.

An angry voice muttered, "Wildcat!"

Then something hit her on the head, and darkness swallowed her.

PART TWO

THE JOURNEY

Thunderous clouds may shroud the peaks,
yet lightning shows the way.

Traditional Plains saying

CHAPTER SEVEN

Clopping. The clopping of hooves. Her whole body jolted with the clops. A hard surface under her. Where was she? Why did her head hurt so?

Calantha struggled to open her eyes. The effort made her moan. From a soupy distance she heard a woman's voice. "She's coming around."

A man's voice rumbled something.

Calantha tried to sit up—if only that jolting would stop. A cart. She was in a cart.

The man said, "Keep her quiet. Here comes someone."

A woman's face, all blurred, bent over her. She hissed, "Not a word, d'you hear, or I'll hit you." She sat down on Calantha, knocking her breath out, and covered her mouth.

Calantha heard more hooves and tried to move, scream, but couldn't.

The man said, "Goodeve, Mistress." Where had she heard that voice before?

Then the other clopping receded and the woman moved off her, although she still kept her hand over Calantha's mouth.

Calantha twisted. She'd placed that voice now. Flenart. She struggled again, but the more she struggled the harder she was held.

She went limp.

"That's better," said the woman. "You be still and you won't get hurt."

Calantha's head swam as she tried to focus her eyes. As though through water she saw Shraelyn's face. "Be quiet, all right?"

Calantha nodded, her heart hammering. Slowly, Shraelyn removed her hand.

Calantha gasped for air. She closed her eyes, to stop the swirling in her head.

"That's right," said Shraelyn. "Best go to sleep like a good child."

Calantha lay still as the cart clopped on. Then with a sudden burst, she sprang upward and tried to jump off the cart.

She hadn't even made it to her feet when she was downed. Shraelyn swore and cuffed her ears. The cart stopped. Flenart loomed over her. Scowling.

"You give us any more trouble, I'll knock you out for good."

Shraelyn whispered, "Careful! He said he wants to question them, remember?"

"Shh!"

"What do you want?" cried Calantha shrilly. "Where are you taking me?"

"You'll find out soon enough," said Flenart. He turned to Shraelyn and growled, "Tie her hands and feet. And gag her. The sooner she's off our hands the better."

Calantha fought them, but they were too strong for her. She was bound. A dirty rag was pulled across her mouth and tied behind her head; it smelled foul and tasted worse, but she couldn't shift it.

"Be still," said Shraelyn warningly as the cart started again. "It'll go easier with you."

Calantha struggled and struggled. She should have waited 'til she was stronger instead of trying to escape while dizzy. Her mother was right; she was stupid. The gag was choking her; she couldn't breathe.

Kasmira's matter-of-fact tones rang in her head—*That's enough Calantha, calm down.*

Yes, calm down, breathe, breathe. She made herself go limp, trying to breathe deeply through her nose. A tale sprang to mind—the one of the crow who used patience and cunning to get the butter from the Earthroffe. Patience and cunning. That's what she needed. As the cart clopped on into the dark night, she traced the story to steady her heart and settle her mind. Exhausted, she fell asleep.

When Calantha awoke, the sky was dark gray. Just before dawn. Her arms were numb, the rope around her wrists and ankles burned and chafed, and her tongue was dead and dry against the gag.

Shraelyn lay beside her, asleep, close enough for Calantha to see the wisps of hair escaping her scarf, the soft fuzz between her eyebrows and her mottled cheeks. Her breath, whistling through the gap between her front teeth, smelled foul.

Calantha blinked to try and clear her head. It throbbed dully but at least it wasn't as bad as before. She must escape. But how?

The cart slowed and Flenart called out, "Wake up, woman."

"Hnnnh?" Shraelyn murmured.

Calantha snapped her eyes shut. She'd learn more if they thought she was asleep.

The cart turned, and Calantha heard Shraelyn yawn and stretch.

"Best stop for the day," said Flenart.

"But we should make haste, get rid of this child. What if someone comes looking for her?"

Calantha's heart leaped. Of course. They'd think she'd run away to find the Sower of Tales. Her father would resent the waste of time during harvest, but they'd go eastward to look for her. Only she had no idea where Flenart and Shraelyn were taking her; if they were anywhere but east...

Flenart growled, "That's why we hide for the day and go on at night."

Calantha's hope sank like a rock.

The cart jounced over rougher terrain, and branches scraped and rustled against the sides of the cart. At last, the cart stopped. The back tilted down and bumped up as Shraelyn got off. Calantha peered through her eyelashes. Kerlnut trees and feathery red chernows with drooping branches surrounded them like a curtain. No one would see them here. She fought against the panic threatening to drown her.

"This will do," said Flenart, yawning.

"What about her?" Shraelyn asked.

"Leave her in the cart," huffed Flenart. "More trouble than she's worth. Just hope she's what he's looking for...don't know what he's after."

Shraelyn said nervously, "Well, he said, didn't he, anyone young, with an affinity to the story pods? And anyone with strange dreams, or a keen interest in the Sower of Tales. That pale one, with the blinking eyes, she pointed straight to this one."

"Dreams and schemes," muttered Flenart. "I don't like all this skulking. Why the King gives Odhran so much rein—"

Odhran! Terror speared through Calantha's heart.

"Stop it!" cried Shraelyn. "It's not for us to question. What if he hears?"

Flenart said uneasily, "Come now. He doesn't have ears here, does he?"

Shraelyn's voice was breathless, raw with fear. "Just shush! Who knows what he—"

"Shh! Keep your voice down," growled Flenart. "Go check on her."

Footsteps rustled around to the back of the cart. Calantha felt Shraelyn's eyes crawling on her skin. She lay still for a moment, then fluttered her lids open.

Shraelyn looked at her unsmilingly. "Awake, are you?"

Calantha raised her head, moaned, then flopped down again, closing her eyes.

"Flenart, she doesn't look too good."

Calantha lay still as Flenart tramped nearer.

Shraelyn said nervously, "You shouldn't have hit her. She'd have come with us if we'd been clever, but no, you had to—"

"Be quiet, woman," said Flenart. "They'd never have let her go. Not with that fury for a mother."

Unexpected anger twitched through Calantha. How dare they talk about her mother like that? *Calm down*, she told herself, *be calm*. Slowly, she opened her eyes again, rolling them weakly.

Shraelyn climbed onto the cart and removed the gag from Calantha's mouth. Calantha gasped for air and tried to move her tongue.

"Be quiet, or I'll put it back on," said Shraelyn.

Flenart snorted. "She can shout as much as she wants. Who'll hear her?"

"Water," croaked Calantha.

Shraelyn muttered, then lifted a full skin of water.

"My hands, can you untie...?" Calantha made her voice weak and frightened.

Flenart and Shraelyn whispered together. Calantha caught snatches—"...can't trust her...where can she go?"—before Shraelyn turned to her and grimly untied her hands.

Calantha gasped at the pain as she tried to move her arms from behind her back.

Shraelyn said severely, "The slightest bother from you and you'll be tied up again. Understand?"

Calantha nodded and rubbed her arms, wrists and hands.

Shraelyn helped her to sit up and, unstoppering the skin, handed it to her. Calantha drank deeply. The cold water helped to clear her head. The crow. Patience and cunning.

Flenart grunted and stretched out under a tree with a blanket. "You watch her now. I've got to sleep."

Shraelyn nodded and settled down in the cart, cushioned by blankets.

Calantha quavered, "Where are you taking me?" Best if they thought she was afraid. Not that she had to pretend much there.

Shraelyn looked away. "Never you mind," she said gruffly. "You be quiet and you won't get hurt."

Calantha fixed her eyes pleadingly on Shraelyn, trying to draw the answer out. "Just tell me, where are you taking me?" She made her lips tremble.

To her surprise, Shraelyn said shortly, "North. Now be quiet."

Calantha sank down again, her thoughts scattering like a broken pot. They must be taking her to

Jaerlfin. To Odhran. But why? What did he have to do with the story pods? Could Hardwin actually be right? She must escape. But how? And where were they? They could have taken any of the roads from Grenlea and still turned north.

She heard Shraelyn fidgeting, then the sound of chewing.

After a while, Calantha stirred again and moaned.

Shraelyn was eating cold lorshcakes, her pale, watery eyes fixed on Calantha.

"More water," murmured Calantha.

Shraelyn made a face but handed her the skin. Calantha drank slowly, an idea forming in her head. Eyeing the lorshcake, she said timidly, "I'm hungry."

Shraelyn clicked her tongue, but untied a cloth and gave Calantha the smallest lorshcake.

It was coarse and dry, but Calantha ate it, stopping every few bites to droop against the side of the cart. When she finished, she groaned, her hand pressed against her stomach.

"Now what?" Shraelyn scowled.

Calantha whispered, "I have to...to relieve myself."

Shraelyn's eyes narrowed.

"I don't want to soil..." said Calantha, trying to sound embarrassed.

Shraelyn glanced at Flenart, then huffed, "All right, all right." She glared at Calantha as she unbound her feet.

Calantha rubbed her ankles and wobbled as she stood. She didn't need to feign; her legs were stiff and weak.

As Shraelyn got down, the cart made a banging sound. Flenart was up in a flash. "What are you up to?" he growled.

Calantha smiled waveringly.

Shraelyn muttered, "She has to...you know. It's all right; I'm going with her."

Flenart sat up and scratched his head. His turban had fallen off. Calantha saw his earlobes—as fat as new dignes leaves. Snake's venom! He was one of the horsemen who'd come through the village the day she'd thrown the clay at Freya! She'd had a glimpse of recognition at Councilmeet but she'd been too distracted to follow it.

She limped on through the trees, with Shraelyn

gripping her arm. "Behind there," said Shraelyn, pointing to a wide kerlnut trunk. "Don't try anything or you'll regret it. I'm watching."

Calantha squatted behind the trunk, her eyes darting frantically for a way to escape. They swept across the base of the tree, over a small gray vine, then swivelled back. Balmberry vines! Heart thudding, she followed the twists of the creeping vine. Were there any berries? They were so hard to find. There! A cluster of the small, almost invisible, gray balmberries. She snatched up all that she could see, about six or seven. Thank goodness Benigna had persevered in showing her how to spot them. If she ever offered service to Benigna again, she'd never complain.

"Aren't you done yet?" growled Shraelyn.

"Coming." Clutching the berries in the palm of her hand, she emerged shakily from behind the tree, her hand limp against the folds of her skirt. No, she mustn't run now. She'd never get away.

Back at the cart, Flenart was eating.

Shraelyn said sourly, "You watch her while I go behind the bushes."

Flenart jerked his head at Calantha. "Get back in the cart." He tied Calantha's ankles again and tethered the rope to the side of the cart, but he didn't meet her eyes. There was a strange wobbly feeling coming from him, gray and blurry. Guilt! He was embarrassed to look at her.

Oh, thanks be to the Sower of Tales, she was starting to sense again, now that she wasn't drowning in her own fear. Calantha sagged against the side of the cart as though her head ached. Her hands began to sweat.

Softly, she said, "Water, please."

Flenart looked at her suspiciously. "Drinking a lot, aren't you?"

"My head still hurts," said Calantha weakly.

Flenart handed her the skin, his eyes suspicious. Just then, Shraelyn came back, mumbling something, and Flenart turned his head.

Quickly, Calantha crushed the berries as hard as she could, and, pressing her palm against the open mouth of the water skin as though wiping it, scraped the berries inside.

Hands shaking, she tilted the skin to her mouth,

making a ring with the fingers of her clean hand so the skin didn't touch her lips. Once, twice, she dropped the skin and lifted it, sloshing the water so the berries would mix.

"Here, you've had enough," growled Flenart. "Leave some for us."

Calantha jerkily handed the skin back to Flenart.

He took a long, deep drink. "Water's turning brackish," he muttered. "We'll need more soon." He glared at Calantha.

Calantha's heart thumped. Traces of the berries were stuck to the sweat in her palm. She wiped her hand against the folds of her skirt. She mustn't let the smallest bit come near her mouth.

Now if only Shraelyn...

Shraelyn climbed back onto the cart, looking suspiciously at Calantha. Calantha lay down and closed her eyes. Had Flenart drunk enough? Benigna had said two berries would knock out a grown man, and she'd put in six or seven, but there was a lot of water in the skin.

Every fiber of her body screamed to be up and running, but she kept her eyes tightly closed. She must wait.

As she continued to lie still, Flenart and Shraelyn relaxed and began to quietly plan the journey. "Take two nights at most to get to Jaerlfin," said Flenart. "Stopping for the days." He sighed. "It's longer this way, but at least it's quieter and there are more places to hide."

So they couldn't be on the North Plains road. That wouldn't take any more than a day by horse and cart. Then where were they?

Flenart muttered, "Can't see how anyone like her can be danger to his plans, no matter what his divining told him."

Shraelyn hissed, "Stop it! He'll be angrier still if we don't bring anyone." She paused, then said uncertainly, "Let's hope he'll be pleased with what we heard of the whereabouts of the Sower...."

Flenart yawned noisily. "Well, there's others looking, too. Maybe Farlwen or Tabbard will find someone more fit."

"Aye," said Shraelyn. "It's not all up to us."

Calantha's chest squeezed. More of King Ulric's men? Disguised as Flenart and Shraelyn? The jagged line in Xenyss' divining square flashed across her mind. She must get away.

Calantha heard Flenart yawn again. If only Shraelyn would drink!

Unexpectedly, she had a fleeting sense of Xenyss' calm, blue presence. His words flashed into her head—*C-Calantha, you have a g-gift that not all have.* Then the blue presence was gone, but a clear thought remained behind—if she could sense others, maybe she could also influence them.

Heart racing, Calantha gathered herself as best she could and with all her force sent out just one thought to Shraelyn—*thirsty, thirsty, thirsty*! Her own mouth became dry, begging for moisture. Desperately, she directed the feeling to Shraelyn, along with *drink water, drink water.*

Suddenly, Shraelyn said, "Pass that skin, I'm parched."

Calantha tensed as Shraelyn took a deep swig.

Flenart climbed down from the cart, making it bump. "Must sleep. I'm so tired I can barely walk straight. You watch her. I'll let you have a spell later."

Calantha lay still, but directed toward Shraelyn, *sleep, sleep, sleep*. She bit the insides of her cheeks until the salty taste of blood filled her mouth; she herself must not fall asleep.

It felt like hours, but at last, when Calantha peered through her eyelashes, she saw Shraelyn's head droop down over her chest.

Now. She wanted to run, but she made herself repeat the story of the crow.

Slowly she opened her eyes wide.

Silence.

Shraelyn was slumped over, a trail of drool coming out of the side of her mouth.

Calantha sat up cautiously.

Six or seven berries. Oh, flikketting lizards, had she killed them? What had Benigna said about too many berries? Cybella would know— dull, conscientious Cybella. Calantha peered over the side of the cart. Flenart was fast asleep on his back, his hand across his face. He was snoring, his chest rising and falling. Still alive.

Slowly, Calantha began to untie the rope holding her ankles. It was tight, the knots difficult to loosen.

She tore at them, glancing nervously at Shraelyn. At last she was free. She edged toward the back of the cart, eased one leg out, and slipped off. Her heart sprang to her mouth as the cart tilted, then thumped, but Shraelyn slept on.

The horse was tied to a low branch, munching on the scrub underneath. The harness and reins were tossed over a branch.

Calantha hesitated, then quickly untied the horse. No time for the harness—she didn't know how to put it on anyway. She led the horse out from under the trees, wincing at the deafening rustle of branches. As she cleared the trees, she darted a quick look behind, then, grabbing the horse's mane, somehow managed to scramble onto the broad back. Gripping the coarse brown mane, she dug her heels hard into the side of the horse.

Chapter Eight

S he couldn't see clearly; she was being tossed up and down on the horse like a sack of potatoes. A field. Grass cropped close. A pasture field? There was no one in sight.

Her stomach rushed to her mouth as the horse picked up speed and cantered across the field, making for the tall grass in a ditch along a road. Calantha bent low and clutched the mane with both fists; she'd never ridden a horse before, just Eythun's mule a few times. She nearly toppled as the horse stopped abruptly at the ditch and lowered its head to pull up a mouthful of grass.

Gasping, Calantha caught her balance and looked around. Story pods nodded in the grass. There was a nearly ripe bluish one nearby. She leaned over and touched it. Oh, the humming! No...there wasn't time. She mustn't get caught.

Where was she? Calantha looked around and around. The Eastern Mountains, with their familiar crooked slope, were off in the distance to her right.

They might have gone east, then! This could be the Shernthrip road and someone might come looking for her! She'd be safe.

Then a cold wave washed through her.

No. Whoever came looking for her would insist on taking her back.

Calantha's fingers tightened in the horse's mane. She was not going back. She couldn't. Flenart and Shraelyn had started her on her journey and now she must go on. Somehow, she must find the Sower of Tales. Even without the key.

She drew in a deep breath and peered up and down the road. No one in sight. She tugged at the horse's mane, but it just rolled a placid brown eye at her and kept eating. Darting a look at the distant smudge of trees behind her, Calantha kicked her heels hard into the sides of the horse.

Startled, the horse lifted its head and began to

plod. Calantha dug her left heel into the horse's side and made it turn eastward along the road toward the mountain. Her teeth rattled, her bones shook, but at least she was moving.

She tried to scan the landscape for anything familiar. Trees fringed the road, offering glimpses of the odd field beyond; they could be anywhere. The few times she'd taken the Shernthrip road with her mother to barter her cheeses, they'd gone through Jontherp to Wrenford. Could this be past Wrenford? It was a half-day by cart from Grenlea. Flenart and Shraelyn had traveled all night, hadn't they? Snarking bograts! How could she think with that pustering horse jolting and jostling her?

She dug her heels hard into the sides of the horse and the dreadful trotting changed to a canter. Calantha's breath caught in her throat; she clung to the horse's mane as the road narrowed and turned into a wooded area. Trees on either side jumped up and down dizzyingly.

Then a low branch rushed toward her head. She screamed and ducked. She was falling. She thudded to the ground, rolling over and over.

Stunned, she lay still. The horse galloped on, around the curve of the road, and disappeared.

Calantha sat up, head spinning, her whole body shaking. Her left knee was skinned and the heels of her hands scraped and bruised, spotted with blood. The horse was gone, gone.

She leaned against a young brinlow tree and began to cry. "Pustering pustules. Flikketting lizards. Snarking, snarking bograts!"

At last, wiping her face with the back of her hands, she got to her feet. Through blurred eyes, she spotted a dignes plant. She broke a few of the plump leaves and eased the clear, cooling jelly onto her knee and hands. The stinging subsided.

Calantha sniffed, rubbed her arm across her nose, and began to walk. She was better off without that stupid horse, anyway. Yes, she was. A girl on a horse would attract more attention than a girl on foot. And it would be harder to hide. She clenched her jaw. Sooner or later, she'd come to a village. If they had gone east and she was past Wrenford, then Shernthrip should be next. She'd never been there, but her father said it was one of the bigger villages in

the Plains, with a thriving market; they even had
their own Sorcerer, not just a Seer. She didn't know
how far it was but if she got there by evening, maybe
she could join Talemeet. The darkness inside her
lifted at the thought of the healing silence of
Talemeet, the Gatherer opening the pod.

The Gatherer! Of course! Hadn't Kasmira said
that Gatherers had the key? The Gatherer at the next
village would have one, too—there must be more
than one.

Calantha began to walk faster, staying close to
the trees in case anyone came by. Her thoughts
turned to what she'd overheard from Flenart and
Shraelyn. They'd obviously come looking for her—
or someone like her, with a keen love of the story
pods. It must have been their skewering interest
she'd sensed at Councilmeet, and Xenyss had tried
to warn her. That's why he'd stopped Kasmira from
saying anything more about the Sower of Tales.
Calantha pressed her hand against her mouth.
Oh, but what had she said? Apparently, enough for
Flenart and Shraelyn to take to Odhran. Her
insides roiled. But what could Odhran possibly

have to do with the story pods?

Calantha flicked her fingers and tried to think of a tale to still the churning. The first one that came to mind was the one of the princess and the pig—the tale from the first pod she'd picked for Talemeet. How long ago that seemed.

The woods seemed to go on forever. Even in the deep shade, the day grew hotter, and soon clouds of small green clonthip flies began to hover, buzzing, kissing, biting. She swatted at them, her tongue swollen with thirst, and immersed herself in the tales of cool places where water froze into ice during the winter.

Twice someone came by and she hid. Once, a young man with a Herbroffe's green-gray clothing went by in the opposite direction. She didn't sense any danger from him, and when she saw his full skin of water she nearly came out. But something made her stop and she remained crouched behind the tree, her mouth aching with thirst. The second time, it was two men on horseback. They wore the brown breeches and tunics of Earthroffes, but there was a pointed air of searching about them. Were they looking for her? Or were they just Plainsfolk looking for story pods?

After they'd gone, she walked on, scratching at her bitten neck, face, and arms, her head strangely light. Hunger gnawed at her belly. How far was Shernthrip? When would she get there? She should have taken the lorshcakes from the cart; even dry ones were better than none. She darted a glance backward. Would Flenart and Shraelyn be awake now? She tried to walk faster.

To her relief, she soon came upon the damp traces of a stream alongside the road. Snapping past the undergrowth, she followed it eagerly into the woods, where it gushed strong and clear. She drank and drank, then washed her grimy face and arms, before continuing on.

It was hours later when she at last reached the end of the woods. One moment she was in the deep shade of the trees, and the next moment she was out

in bright sunshine, squinting against the hot afternoon sun.

Story pods nodded in the ditch beside the lane.
She rushed toward a yellowish pod and cupped it. It
wasn't quite ripe but the familiar humming was like
balm. Her eyes raked the ground for signs of new
story pods. No new ones. None.

She looked around through the shimmering heat.
She was on the crest of a hill. Below, in the distance,
was the largest cluster of blue-gray thatch she'd ever
seen, with a river gracing the far side. It *must* be
Shernthrip. There were cultivated fields on either
side of the road sloping down to the village, some
harvested, with stooked lorsha bundles. In a distant
field, a group of men were harvesting the last of the
grain, and cows ambled about in another. Near as
she could make out, the distant grassy field between
the pasture and the lorsha grain might be for story
pods, but she couldn't be sure.

A full red story pod dancing in the afternoon sun
caught her eye. Calantha scrambled partway down
the ditch to reach it. Delight flooded her as she
cupped it. It was ripe, and pulsing with a lively tale.

Her whole body eased and settled. She took a deep breath and willed the pod to release, but she was too hasty and it tore and split. She stared longingly at the seeds drifting upward, traces of words murmuring disconnectedly. She began to reach for another ripe pod, a greenish-gray one, when she heard the clop of hooves.

Someone was coming from the village! Calantha scrambled to the bottom of the ditch and lay flat amid the grass, her heart thudding with the hooves as they neared, then passed by.

Slowly, she got up and dusted herself off. Her mother's voice rang in her ears, "Apply yourself, Calantha, instead of forever fumbling and bumbling." Suddenly, she longed for her mother. Luvena might be hard and demanding, but she'd never be caught face down in a ditch!

Calantha shoved the hair off her face. Flikketting lizards, she was not going to start wishing for her mother; Luvena would march her straight back to Grenlea and make her learn sharo thatch!

She climbed out of the ditch and began to walk toward the town below, then stopped abruptly. What if there were searchers from her village down there? Or the others that Flenart and Shraelyn had talked about?

She couldn't go down there. She mustn't. She'd attract too much attention with her dress all torn and muddy, and her wrists red with rope marks.

Oh, she couldn't join Talemeet.

Eyes pricking, she crouched behind the grass and scanned the town. Where was the Gatherer's hut?

A small whitewashed hut, well beyond the other houses, seemed to leap out at her. There was another hut by itself near the river, but she was drawn to the first one, pulled to it. It must be the Gatherer's. Quickly, she traced a path to the hut, through several fields and woods, trying to fix the way in her mind. She'd wait until after dark to approach the Gatherer and then…somehow, she'd get the key.

Straightening up, she continued on. Her body ached even more for having stopped that short while, but she stumbled along the ditches between fields until she reached the woods. Shaking with fatigue and hunger, she pushed on through the cluster of pale green brinlow trees. There was no path and the undergrowth snapped and whipped against her. Part of her longed to lie down and rest, but she knew she must find the Gatherer's hut while it was still light.

When she came out of the woods, she stopped, trying to remember which way she was supposed to go. Why was her head so stupid and dazed? A few story pods grew at the edges of the trees, near ripe, and she stopped to touch one, letting the humming work through her, then dragged on, skirting the woods leftward, until at last she came to a lane.

No houses in sight and no one about. She crossed the lane and stumbled along toward the right. *Oh, Sower of Tales, let this be the right direction!* Her knees shook with relief when at last she saw the small whitewashed hut. The Gatherer's hut!

Ducking low, she scuttled along the trees beside the hut, and around to the back. Cautiously, she peered through the one window.

Still blinded by the early-evening sun, she couldn't see clearly at first. Then her eyes adjusted to the gloom.

Herbs on the wall. A small bed. A divining square.

She slid down, her head flopping onto her knees.

Not the Gatherer's hut, then! She'd been so sure this was the right one, so certain. Bitterness flooded her mouth.

A hand dropped on her shoulder. Calantha gasped and scrambled to her feet.

A small birdlike woman, hardly bigger than Calantha, stood in front of her with a big stick in her hand. She wore the white robes of a Sorcerer. Her dark, bright eyes probed Calantha as she lowered her stick partway.

"Calantha, yes?" whispered the woman.

Calantha nodded. How did the woman know? She was too tired to run.

The woman bobbed her head up and down fiercely. She looked swiftly behind her at the scrubby woods in a way that made Calantha's skin crawl.

"Inside, quick!" whispered the woman. "You mustn't be seen."

Pulling Calantha by the arm, the woman led her to the door, then inside. Quick as a fire lizard, she locked the door and closed the shutters over the window.

As Calantha's eyes adjusted to the gloom of the

firelit chamber, she saw the Sorcerer's hands sweep and pluck across the walls and the edges of the door and window, as though pulling and knotting something together, while she murmured softly.

At last she stopped and turned to Calantha.

"There," she said.

Calantha jumped. The sound of her voice was so loud after the silence.

The woman's small bright eyes crinkled. "I've sealed the hut, so no one can hear. Yes. I put on a drawing spell, hoping to bring you, but there's always a risk of pulling others, too."

Calantha's head felt swollen, stupid. "Bring me?" she croaked.

The woman nodded. "Yes. I've been expecting you. Xenyss sent word to look for you."

Chapter Nine

Xenyss! Calantha's heart leaped, then plummeted like a rock. This woman would send her back.

She whirled to the door, but the woman was faster, blocking the way.

"Easy, child. I'm not going to send you back. I am Theora. Sorcerer of Shernthrip." The woman's head bobbed again, birdlike. "Xenyss knows you must make this journey. He asked me to help you."

Calantha stared at her. She sensed the truth radiating from the Sorcerer and her head spun with relief.

"Yes," said Theora. "If the Essences are willing you can speak with Xenyss later."

Calantha glanced at the tangle of lines in the

divining square. Her breath caught as she recognized the jagged line she'd seen in Xenyss' hut.

Theora turned her away from the square and made her sit. "Come, drink something. Eat."

Calantha started to speak, but Theora shushed her, bringing her a cup of water, into which she crumbled a reddish herb. Calantha gulped it down. The slightly bitter taste made her mouth pucker.

"Loosethorn," said Theora. "It'll clear your head. Yes. Ease your aches."

Calantha ate the arrac-and-bean stew Theora ladled for her from the pot over the fire, mopping it with lorshcake. Her mother would have scoffed at the coarseness of the grain, but Calantha ate it eagerly, washing it down with some hot loosethorn tea.

By the time she finished, her head had cleared and her body felt less stiff. She looked at Theora and said bluntly, "I must see the Gatherer. Get the key to the Sower of Tales."

Theora's head bobbed. "Yes. I'll bring him after Talemeet."

"After? But—"

"You must not attract attention," said Theora.

Calantha sighed. Talemeet. Without her. Wearily, she asked, "Xenyss let you know I'd be by?"

Theora nodded. "He divined you coming this way. With others. Yes. That you were in trouble. Now tell me, child, what has happened."

Calantha drew in a ragged breath. "Flenart and Shraelyn came to our village; they said they were from Braeshin, to the north, but they kidnapped me. I heard them talk. They were to look for young folk with an affinity to the pods, and...and an interest in the Sower of Tales. They mentioned King Ulric and..." Calantha's voice shook, "Odhran."

Theora's face seemed to turn gray. "Go on, child."

Stumblingly, repeating things as Theora questioned her, Calantha told her everything that had happened. Theora's face grew more and more somber, but when Calantha described how she'd escaped, a strange gleam came into Theora's eyes.

"Xenyss was right. Yes. You do have a strong gift." Her head bobbed up and down.

Calantha blinked in surprise. She hadn't felt

particularly strong or gifted. Just scared. She leaned forward and asked, "Sorcerer Theora, do you know what's happening to the story pods?"

Theora shook her head, her small face troubled. "There are layers and layers of concealment. Xenyss warned me the Essences were twisting. Yes. And I sensed it too. But I didn't see that the story pods had stopped. Nor our Gatherer. And I didn't trace Odhran's hand in this until after you were taken. I never thought him capable of—"

"You know him?" whispered Calantha.

Theora nodded abruptly. "We apprenticed together at the Place of Knotting. He was older than I. Yes. Small and weedy. Not the most skilled, but he was persistent. And hungry."

Calantha asked nervously, "But...what does he have to do with the story pods?"

Theora shook her head. "I don't know. I don't know yet. But, child, the Essence of the story pods is tied to the very fabric of our beings. Can you even imagine a time without them?"

Calantha's eyes pricked. She shook her head.

"But they were not always here."

Calantha's head jerked. A time with no story pods? It was like saying there was once no sky, no air to breathe.

Theora's head bobbed up and down. "Yes. Only the Sorcerers at the Place of Knotting remember. Long ago, there were no story pods. The time they say the story pods began is some six hundred and eighty years ago. Now mark this well—the Great Liberation was six hundred and seventy years ago."

Calantha stared at her. The liberation had been ten years after the story pods?

"What...what will happen if they...disappear?"

Theora sucked the air in through her teeth. "The Sorcerers at the Place of Knotting will not speak of it. They do not teach how the story pods are woven into the wider web. But I have never seen the Essences without the story pods. Never. The tales are knit deep into the heart of all Essences. The very heart. Without them..."

"Everything will change," Calantha whispered, remembering her dream. Icy fingers brushed over her. "Xenyss said that, too."

Theora nodded, her eyes bright and hard.

"Xenyss saw the change in the Essences early. He is a skilled Seer. Yes, for all he did not apprentice at the Place of Knotting."

Calantha flushed. Did Theora know what the villagers said of Xenyss? Quickly she asked, "You said I could speak to him?"

Theora nodded. "Come. I'll prepare the water."

Erasing all the lines in the divining square, Theora placed a large stone basin of water in the center and motioned Calantha to kneel in front of it. She drew fresh lines linking each of the corners—earth, air, water, fire—to one another and to the center, then added a fine series of circles around Calantha and the basin. Last of all, she wiped her own footprints and knelt over the basin of water, beside Calantha, within the circles.

"It must be quick," she said. "It's best not to use the Essences too long. I've added extra protection but even so.... We don't want to be noticed."

Calantha sensed sharp concern behind her words.

Theora closed her eyes and Calantha felt the air tighten and shift.

"Look at the water," breathed Theora. "Below the surface. Think what you have to say, don't speak."

Calantha stared. Water. Just water.

Then a twist in the air, and Xenyss' face appeared in the water. It wavered as she fought to see him clearly, but as she let her eyes sink below the surface, she saw him again.

Calantha's eyes stung. If only she could reach out and hug him.

Xenyss smiled. Words reached her, although Xenyss' lips did not move.

"Calantha, forgive me."

Calantha began to speak and the face in the water blurred.

"Think it," breathed Theora.

Quickly, Calantha thought in reply, "No, I should have waited to hear what you had to say."

Xenyss' words came clearly in her head, "I was coming to tell you to leave. I should have seen that there was more danger in you staying—I should never have stopped you or let Kasmira extract that promise."

"Tell her I didn't break it," thought Calantha.

Xenyss nodded. "She knows. She releases you. You go with her blessing, and mine."

Calantha blinked hard. "Tell her—"

Xenyss' voice sounded urgently in her head, "Calantha, we don't have much time. There is more at stake than anyone realizes. We have just uncovered that the Sorcerer Odhran is tied to this; he hopes to gain power in some way, but we don't know the how or why. Only one person will know."

"The Sower of Tales!" thought Calantha.

Xenyss' words came fast, "Yes. She knows how the Essence of the story pods is knotted into the heart of our existence; she will know what Odhran is after. Get the key from the Gatherer and go to the Eastern Mountains. Find the Sower of Tales. Make haste, Calantha, but be careful. Odhran must be trying to stop anyone from finding her."

Calantha's insides began to twist with panic.

"Be calm, child. I will keep a thread of mind tied to you, and try to send help along the way. You must find the Sower of Tales—she too may be in danger."

"The Sower of Tales, in danger?" Calantha felt numb. "But—"

Suddenly, the water wrenched and all the breath was sucked out of her. She barely glimpsed a pair of deep-set, icy cold eyes before Theora smashed the water with both fists.

Calantha gasped and gasped, trying to suck in air. At last, she managed a painful, strangled breath. She fell back, chilled to the core, shaking.

Theora held Calantha close. "He didn't see you, he didn't see you. I stopped the water in time."

But Calantha smelled her fear and uncertainty.

Theora let her go and with quick, birdlike movements, wiped the square clean of lines. But not before Calantha saw the deep jagged line sawing harshly toward her—right through the protective circles.

She stumbled as Theora helped her to the low bed by the fire. She was cold, so cold.

"I should have been more careful," said Theora. "There is always danger of others tapping into the water."

"Was it...?"

Theora sucked in her breath. "Yes. I'd know those eyes anywhere."

Calantha rocked back and forth as Theora piled blankets around her. A thought came to her. She unclenched her jaw and forced the words out, "The Sorcerers at the Place of Knotting." She jerked her head toward the divining square. "Can't you reach them? Get help somehow..."

Theora shook her head. "The Sorcerers live apart; they don't engage with our world. We can't reach them through divining. The Place of Knotting is outside our time; it is a space where other worlds knot together. But to go there..." She drew in her breath with a hiss. "There isn't time."

Calantha stared at her dazedly. Her head felt bruised. Theora pushed her down gently, whispering healing words under her breath. Slowly, slowly, Calantha began to warm up.

"Take heart, child," said Theora. "You are not alone. Xenyss and I work with you."

Exhausted, Calantha murmured, "Xenyss didn't stutter over his words."

Theora smiled. "You don't think he stutters in his head, do you? It's only the body that betrays him. Sleep now. Yes. It will be a while before the

Gatherer comes."

As Calantha's head sank into the pillow, a warm blue presence seemed to wrap around her. Xenyss. She slept deeply.

CHAPTER TEN

M ist. A blurred
face. Dark hair,
sharp chin. Gray
eyes pulling,
pulling at her.

Calantha sat up in bed, gasping—and remembered where she was. The hut was dark except for the
flickering glow of the fire and the orange light of the
two lorsha torches on the wall.

Theora hurried over. "What did you dream?" she
asked sharply.

"The witch," blurted Calantha. "Only not as
clear as before." Her voice caught in her throat.
"Is...is it Odhran's work?"

Theora tilted her head as though smelling the
air. "No. It doesn't seem to be." She seemed
relieved, but also puzzled.

"Then what...?" began Calantha.

"Never mind." Theora shook her head quickly. "Talemeet is done and the village has settled. The Gatherer will come soon. And then," Theora sucked in her breath, "you must go. It's best you leave as quickly as possible. And not be seen leaving."

Calantha's head jerked toward the divining square.

"You will go in the back of a cart," said Theora. "With Kelwin, the gravedigger."

Calantha's eyes widened.

"Yes," said Theora. "No one will mark him. He travels often by night. He will take you part of the way, and then at dawn you will go on by foot. Openly."

"Openly?" Calantha's voice cracked.

"Yes." Theora bobbed her head. "You *must* act as though you have nothing to hide. Here." She handed Calantha a gray-green Herbroffe's dress. "Put this on. A Herbroffe at least may travel without question. And you'd best think of a new name."

Calantha nodded. She washed quickly in the basin in the corner, then put on the dress. It was too

big, but it would make her look older and the long
sleeves would hide the rope marks on her wrist.
Quickly, she braided her hair. She hesitated, then
doubled up her braid, as Freya did. That too would
make her look older.

As she waited by the fire for the Gatherer, a doubt
that had been niggling at the bottom of her mind
surfaced. Would this Gatherer have the right key? If
Gatherers had so many different ideas of where the
Sower lived, wouldn't they also have different keys?

She began to pace. "Why isn't the Gatherer here
yet?" she asked Theora. It was silent outside, long
past when everyone would be settled, let alone after
Talemeet.

Theora said quietly, "He had to return to his hut
and pretend to go to sleep. He will take the back way
here. There are strangers in our village. Yes." She
bobbed her head again.

Calantha stiffened. "Odhran's people?"

"Perhaps," said Theora. "I sense deceit. But there
is deceit in many people, for many reasons. Don't
fear, child. No one will mark Kelwin. I'll put a
hiding charm on his cart."

Under Theora's words Calantha sensed jagged worry. Had Odhran see her face? What if he knew where she was? Her nails dug into the palms of her hands.

Suddenly, Theora turned her head sideways. Calantha froze, heart racing.

There was a soft knock on the door, a pause, and then a double knock. Theora pressed her ear to the door, then quickly opened it.

An old man with a shock of gray hair entered, holding a cane in his hand. A young girl led him by his other hand. She was a year or so younger than Calantha, with a round, rosy face, and smooth brown hair tied at the nape of her neck.

Theora shut the door behind them and sealed it again.

"Greetings, Osric, Merlewinn. Osric, here is the child I told you of."

Calantha took the old man's outstretched hand. The Gatherer's blind eyes gazed into the distance as he held her hand in his warm, callused one, but Calantha sensed that somehow he saw her more clearly than most sighted folk.

"What is your name, child?" he asked softly.

"Calantha."

He nodded. "The story pods are woven deep into your being. It is well."

Merlewinn's deep brown eyes gaped admiringly at Calantha. Calantha flushed. No one in her village looked at her like that. Except maybe Beagan.

As they sat by the fire, the Gatherer said, "Calantha, go to the Eastern Mountains. That's where you'll find the Sower of Tales."

Calantha's breath escaped with relief.

He tilted his head. "Do you doubt it?"

"No, no. It's what Kasmira told me, only other Gatherers insist she lives elsewhere."

"Yes," he nodded. "Because they've tried to find her there and failed." His sightless eyes turned toward her. "But she is there. I know it. A Gatherer some five times before me found the way."

Calantha blurted, "But the key. Is yours the right one? You can't all have the same key."

Osric chuckled. "Oh, yes we can." His fingers searched until they found hers. "I give it to you, Calantha, with no hesitation. Here it is:

"If the Sower of Tales you seek to find
Unravel the knots that tangle your mind
Let the song of the story pods ring in your heart
Let go of all else, let the tales do their part."

Calantha sat still. "That's the key?"

The Gatherer laughed softly. "My child, how could the key to the Sower of Tales be anything but words?"

Calantha drew in a sharp breath. *Of course.*

Osric leaned forward. "Now repeat the words. Repeat them until they are knit into your being."

Stumbling at first, then steadily, Calantha repeated the key. She asked, her voice rising with panic, "But what does it mean?" She knew what he'd say, but it still dismayed her.

"Calantha, the key is passed down from Gatherer to Gatherer. It is for each to find the meaning."

"But I don't have time. I need to understand it *now* if I'm going to find her. You said other Gatherers have tried and failed—"

Osric said gently, "But some did uncover the meaning and find her. And you will, too."

Calantha gripped her hands together. Could she find the meaning? She, dusty, bumbling Calantha, mule; who her mother kept saying was *not* stupid. Could *she* find the meaning if older, more seasoned Gatherers couldn't?

The Gatherer reached for her hand again. Warmth flowed from his fingers.

"Calantha, I don't want to muddy your understanding with what I believe it to mean, because I might lead you astray." His fingers tightened. "But you hold the story pods in the core of your being and that's what matters. You will find the Sower of Tales. You must believe it." His voice trailed to a whisper. "You must."

Calantha's throat tightened; she sensed the anguish beneath Osric's strong voice. Perhaps because he couldn't see, the story pods were everything to Osric—his hope and joy, his reason to live.

She gripped his fingers, trying to give him strength. "I'll find her. Somehow. I will."

The Gatherer smiled and nodded. He reached into the pouch over his shoulder and took out a story pod. Tilting his head toward Theora, he asked,

"Is there time?"

Calantha looked pleadingly at her.

"Yes," said Theora. "Only just."

"Then let us share this tale," said Osric simply. I suspect you have sore need of it."

Calantha's body eased—she hadn't realized how tightly wound it had been.

As soon as Osric and Merlewinn left after the tale—a heartwarming one of a blind lad who saved his sweetheart from a giant—Theora turned to Calantha. "Kelwin will be by shortly. Now, for tomorrow. Have you thought of a new name?"

Calantha nodded, the glow from the tale fading fast. "Pyrena," she said. Her doll's name.

"Good. You'll say you're from Shantrig, to the south. It's far enough away; you're unlikely to meet anyone who'd know better. Kelwin will drop you at the juncture of the road from the south. Remember, travel openly. You have nothing to hide."

Calantha nodded jerkily.

Theora handed her a gray-green Herbroffe's gathering pouch. Inside was a wrap, a skin of water, and three bundles.

"Lorshcakes," said Theora quickly. "Some dried berries and ferthwen nuts. Yes. And story pods from the Gatherer for your journey."

Calantha's heart lifted. She knew by the familiar, blessed humming which bundle contained the story pods. Four of them, ripe with tales.

Theora said swiftly, "After Kelwin leaves you, take the road eastward toward the mountains. You'll come to a crossroads alongside a canyon. Be careful there; that's where Ulric and Odhran's men are most likely to be. Have your story ready. You're going to Lornfew to gather sneel grass."

"Oh, yes, for orange dye," said Calantha. Frensha had taught her that much at least.

Theora smiled and nodded. "At the crossroads, continue on eastward and go through the woods. There's a good trail; I've taken it many times, but it'll take you the better part of the day to get through, so stop there for the night. Beyond the

woods, the road continues east, but when you come
to a lake and the road splits, you must take the way
north."

"North?" Calantha's voice cracked.

Theora nodded vigorously. "Yes. It's the only
road around the lake. Go to the first village on the
lake—Lornfew. The Seer there, Onawa, will guide
you further. I'll send her word as soon as you leave."

Calantha glanced at the divining square.

Theora said quietly, "You're not alone, child. I'll
let all the Seers know as safely as I can. We'll do what
we can do to help you. And I've woven protection
and guards around you. Yes."

Calantha nodded, trying to ignore the pit of fear
inside her. Had Theora stopped the water in time?

Theora said swiftly, "I have one more gift for
you. At Xenyss' bidding." From her skirt pocket, she
took out a sheathed knife as long as her hand. She
drew it from the worn leather case to reveal a sharp,
pointed blade glinting wickedly in the firelight.

"Is it a charm of some sort?" asked Calantha.

"No," said Theora. "It is a knife."

Calantha stared at her. Then she sheathed the

knife and dropped it into her pouch. Her hand shook slightly as the meaning of Theora's words sank in.

Theora gripped her by both shoulders, her eyes blazing as though trying to send courage and comfort. "You will do. Yes. *You will do.*" She wrapped Calantha in a bony hug. "Strength go with you, child."

Calantha's eyes pricked. "My thanks, Sorcerer Theora."

Silently, they went to the door. It was dark, dark outside. The air was tight with waiting. Danger. And Theora's biting urgency to have her gone.

Calantha heard the clops of the horse before she saw it. Slow, steady clops. Then the dark outline of a large, shaggy horse pulling a cart drew beside them and stopped. A thickset figure sat on the front seat, stooped over the reins.

Quickly, Theora helped Calantha into the back of the cart and wrapped her in a blanket. Calantha felt a few hard objects being pushed against her, something like long tools, likely spades and forks.

The man at the reins, Kelwin, began to whistle—

a shrill, tuneless whistle—and the cart jerked to a start.

Calantha shivered as the cart jogged on—slowly, slowly, with the weariness of death. If only he would go faster; she needed to get away from the sharpness here. She pulled herself inward, and repeated the key over and over. What could it mean?

She sank into the tales for comfort.

CHAPTER ELEVEN

A hand shook her. "Quick now," a voice muttered. "Be gone."

Calantha fought her way out of the blanket, rubbing her face. She must have fallen asleep. In the gray pre-dawn light she saw a fleshy, wrinkled face with straggly hair bending over her. She gasped, then remembered. Kelwin the gravedigger. His eyes were pale blue and watery, but gentle. He smiled, showing discolored teeth.

She scrambled for her Herbroffe's pouch and climbed stiffly down from the cart. "My thanks," she whispered.

Kelwin pointed straight ahead to the road, then his whistling shrilled through the air again as the cart clopped on, turning down a road to the right.

Calantha watched him disappear, then, smoothing her hair and clothes, she began to walk. She was Pyrena. A Herbroffe. With nothing to hide. She slipped her hand into the pouch and touched the story pods. Warmth moved up her arm. Her fingers brushed against the knife and recoiled, then gripped it tightly.

Soon the light strengthened. The dim outlines of trees and bushes began to emerge, then gleam with color. Mist curled about the road and in the hollows of the gently rolling land; it was scrubby land, good mostly for pasture, with a few ripening story pods nodding here and there. The road was deserted, but Calantha kept turning around, her stomach strangely knotted. As the sun rose further in the sky, her uneasiness grew, in spite of the bright sunshine. Something was wrong. The air smelled gray, somehow. Heavy.

She slipped her hand into her pouch again, to touch the bundle of ripe pods. Her eyes scanned the roadsides for any signs of new story pods, but there were none. She clenched her jaw and, fixing her eye on the tallest eastern mountain with the crooked slope, repeated the key. What could it mean?

Her heart jolted as she rounded a shrubby curve and saw a cluster of people and a horse and cart coming toward her. She forced herself to walk on. Five people— four men and one woman. She couldn't sense anything from them over the thunder of her heart.

"Good day," said a tall man up front. He had dark hair and a crooked nose.

Calantha mumbled a greeting. Was there a sense of urgency about them?

"Where are you from?" asked the man.

"From...from..." Her mind had gone blank. "Shan-Shantrig," she said.

The woman in the cart smiled at her. She too wore Herbroffe's clothes. "Don't scare her so, Marnley," she said laughingly. "It's all right, child, we mean no harm."

Calantha looked down, pretending to be shy. *Oh, Sower of Tales, don't let them ask any more questions.*

The woman said, "You're a long way from home, child. Are you alone?"

Calantha flushed. "I...I set out with another

Herbroffe, but he…fell ill." Her thoughts flew ahead. "Searle. He…had terrible stomach pains. He stayed behind to recover, but the First Herbroffe," she swallowed convulsively, "she's difficult, so I had to keep on."

The woman clicked her tongue sympathetically.

Relief began to well inside her. They believed her. Calantha rushed on, caught up in the headiness of her tale. "It was the harwenberries. I told him they weren't ripe, but he ate them anyway."

The old man in the cart frowned. "Harwen-berries? 'Tis long past the season for them."

Flikketting lizards!

Calantha stuttered, "That's what I said, but he insisted." She smiled shakily. "And where are you folks from?"

"Farnthrip," said the man. "To the north."

The north. How close was it to Jaerlfin? Were they…? She sensed worry from them, and some-thing else, but she couldn't tell what.

The old man asked eagerly, "Have you seen any new story pods? There aren't any near us."

Calantha shrugged. "Oh, the story pods. They

stopped growing in our village too. But they'll start again, won't they?" She blinked stupidly.

"Let's hope so," said the dark-haired man. He waved and started up again.

It took a while for Calantha's heartbeat to steady and for her legs to stop shaking. She drew in a shuddering breath. She'd done it. Played a part. She was almost like a brave adventurer in a tale. Yes, if she pretended to be one, maybe she wouldn't drown in fear next time...she began to spin a tale in her head.

Soon the land became hilly, climbing upward around patches of twisted bushes and trees. She met two other travelers on foot, another Herbroffe, and a young boy who seemed to be in trouble—probably run away from his chores—but from neither of them did she sense any danger. Later, a group of Defenseroffes on horseback rode furiously past her in the opposite direction, a sense of urgency about them. She turned to stare after them, her heart thudding with foreboding.

It was midafternoon when, emerging from a dense sharo grove at the crest of a hill, Calantha saw a canyon in the distance over to her left. A whirl-pool formed in her stomach. The crossroads must be near. Odhran's men would be around.

Brave adventurer. She was a brave adventurer. But as she trudged down the hill and saw the large group of people sitting where the roads crossed, her courage twisted down the whirlpool. This wasn't a tale. She must keep her wits about her. The danger was real, *real.*

She wiped her hands against her skirt and walked on. Several people. Two carts. Men with unshaven faces sat beside one of the carts, with a fine gray horse tethered nearby. Too fine for a cart.

Alarm rang through Calantha, but she forced herself to look at them calmly. There were three women, a couple of old ones, and a plump middle-aged one with sharp eyes and crooked, protruding teeth, who sat against the tree near the gray horse.

A lanky youth, with pale skin and dark red hair straggling over sticking-out ears, lounged against another tree. He was just a few years older than her, but he eyed her suspiciously—could he be one of Odhran's men? She couldn't tell who traveled with whom, but she sensed something sharper here than what she'd sensed from the earlier travelers. Even through her fear, she knew it was more like that twisting she'd felt from the horsemen that day on the Green. There was intent here. Hidden intent.

"Good day," called out the plump woman with crooked teeth. "Where be you from, maid, and where be you headed?"

Calantha's mind went hazy. She made herself glance down, to seem shy again. Stumblingly, she replied that she was from Shantrig and on her way to Lornfew to gather the feathery sneel grass for her Herbroffe, who had an order from the weavery. She finished with her story of the troublesome Herbroffe with the stomach complaint.

The plump woman clicked her tongue, then asked casually, "And what be his name, your Herbroffe? If we see him, we can ask after him and tell him you be fine." Her eyes fixed on Calantha's face.

"Searle," replied Calantha, unhesitatingly. "You'll know him by his big, slow-witted face. His mother's always at him to keep his hair cut out of his eyes. If he'd listen, maybe he'd see better which berry is which."

The redheaded youth still watched her, a frown on his face, but the woman seemed satisfied.

The group began to talk among themselves. They seemed to be searching for the story pods, but Calantha hadn't heard of any of their home villages. Only the redheaded youth—Phelan, someone called him—didn't say where he was from. She couldn't tell if he was by himself or with one of the groups, but the way he kept looking at her made her queasy.

The plump woman who'd spoken before asked, "Well, maid, would you have any skill with story pods? We'd love to have someone accompany us to open a pod, if we don't make Talemeet." Her voice was innocent but her eyes were sharp.

Calantha's mouth went dry. Phelan was staring intently at her.

She managed to say, "No. I don't have time to think of story pods. Not with the harvesting my First Herbroffe expects."

The woman said something light, and the sharpness Calantha sensed from her dropped, but the redheaded youth still eyed her coldly.

"Well, I'd best be going," said Calantha. "Lyris, the First Herbroffe, isn't patient."

She saw the redheaded youth stiffen, then his eyes narrowed and fixed on her pouch. Calantha's heart thudded. *Go. She must go.* Even through her panic she felt his pointed disbelief.

Calantha jerked a curtsey and walked on, feeling eyes crawling on her neck. The others had believed her, but that redheaded youth, Phelan.... Despite herself, she looked back. Phelan and a few others were watching her. She made herself wave, then walked on, trying not to run to escape the prickling sensation on the back of her neck. In the distance ahead, partway up a hill, she saw the green smudge of the woods and lengthened her stride. By the time she reached them a half hour or so later, her legs ached and ached. She turned. No one behind her. But the road twisted around groves of trees; she could be followed and not know it.

Rubbing the back of her neck, she hurried into the woods. The road quickly narrowed into a track, with wide kerlnut trees and pale green brinlows pressing in on either side. Soon, the wind picked up, tossing the trees in gusts and starts. Branches rustled menacingly, as though shouting alarm. She nearly jumped out of her skin when a gray fox skittered across the road.

She walked on as fast as she could, taking swigs of water, munching on berries and nuts, not daring to stop. Again and again, she turned around, rubbing her neck. Putting her hand into her pouch, she touched the bundle of story pods and repeated the key of finding, repeated it as though it was a rope pulling her along. Then she spun out tales to keep herself going, ones she remembered and ones she made up.

Hours later, her head reeling with fatigue, she at last saw the trees thin ahead. Oh, thanks be to the Sower of Tales, she'd reached the end of the woods. Shelter. She needed some shelter for the night; even in the gloom of the woods, she could see that the sun would set soon. A dense sharo grove ahead to her right caught her eye. It would be a perfect place to hide. And to open a story pod.

The tops of the trees rustled noisily. She looked

behind again. Nothing. There was nothing there. Twisting her shoulders angrily, Calantha hurried into the sharo grove. The trees were large, with wicked thorns shoulder-high and higher. Weaving between the thorns, past some wide sharo leaves, Calantha found a small sheltered nook.

Dropping her pouch, she pulled off a few of the larger sharo leaves and used them to block the gaps through which she might be seen, fastening them in place with thorns. There. No one could see her now! She let out a deep sigh, sank slowly down to the ground, and closed her eyes. Green leaves wavered across her eyelids—jagged leaves.

When at last her breath steadied, she drank some water and ate a few berries, then opened the bundle of story pods. A tale! She needed a tale to dispel that mist of uneasiness curling about her. But one of the pods had burst open; the seeds drifted upward, murmuring words. Calantha watched them hungrily, catching hints of laughter. Oh, which tale had she lost?

Gently, she felt the other pods. A greenish one had strength—it would hearten her. The pink one was lively, and the gray pod soothing, with a slight lilt. She put the gray and pink ones back in her pouch. Courage. That's what she needed most. She drew in a deep breath, trying to steady her hands. Still. She must be still.

Suddenly, she sensed something across the back of her neck, like a slap of iron. She sprang to her feet and turned.

The leaves brushed aside violently. Red hair.

Grabbing her pouch, she ran, smashing past the sharo leaves. Her sleeve caught on a low thorn. She wrenched away and kept running.

He was shouting—she couldn't tell what over the roaring in her ears. Her foot caught in a root. She went sprawling and the green story pod flew from her hand. He was right behind her.

As Calantha scrambled to her feet, a flash of blue sang around her.

Xenyss.

The knife.

Grabbing it from her pouch, she unsheathed it and faced Phelan.

Chapter Twelve

Phelan backed off, crouching. He cradled the green story pod against his chest. "Whoa, easy now," he panted. "Easy."

"Leave me alone," gasped Calantha, "or I'll stick this right through you."

His eyes widened in alarm. She lunged slightly, hoping he couldn't see how her hand shook.

"Now wait, wait. Don't do that. I mean no harm." His breath was ragged. "Just put that knife away."

"Snarking bograts! How stupid d'you think I am? You were following me—"

"I wasn't. I didn't know you were in the grove; I was looking for shelter."

"Then why were you watching me? Why did you

chase me?" Calantha's eyes crackled. She lunged again with the knife.

Phelan scuttled backward against a sharo trunk. A wicked thorn grazed his ear and blood dripped down. He wiped his ear, his eyes still warily on her, then lowered his voice, "Please, please, just listen. I saw your story pod. I just...I just want to hear the tale."

She stared at him. He was lying. He must be.

Phelan's greenish-brown eyes were nervous yet pleading. "I swear it. Can...can you open the pod? I just want to hear the tale, that's all, then I'll leave you alone. I swear, by all the music in the wind."

Even through her terror, she sensed his desperation. He spoke the truth. But she'd sensed his suspicion earlier; she hadn't imagined that. It too had been real.

She held out her knife. "Just give me that pod and get out of here."

Phelan's face flickered with fear, defeat, anger. His mouth twisted as he flung down the story pod. "Take it then, you greedy..."

Hand pressed to his ear, he edged away, pushing

through the sharo leaves. He floundered through the undergrowth, thrashing like Eythun's mule had when it got caught in the threads drying on Frensha's line.

Calantha snatched up the story pod and stood still in the gathering dark. The pod hummed in her shaking hands.

Slowly, cautiously, she let her senses reach out—and caught the shriveled curl of his longing. He ached for the tale. It cut through the flailing and muttering, landing strong, hard, and bitter on her tongue. Her mouth puckered.

"Wait." The word was out before she knew it. Was she crazy? If only he didn't hear.

Silence. Then his voice, cautious, eager, "Can I hear the tale?"

Stupid, *stupid*. She should never have called him back.

She heard rustling, then Phelan stood before her in the spare light.

She drew in a crooked breath and pointed the knife at him. "If you give me any trouble..."

He held his hands out, palms up. "I mean no

harm. I swear it. I'm just an apprentice music maker. Look." He thrust his hand into his pouch and took out a flute. He lifted it to his lips and the music flowed—oh, how it flowed. It was jumpy, nervous, but he could play all right; it told of wanting, just wanting to hear the tale.

He lowered the flute and blinked rapidly. "It's not right. After I hear the tales, it's better. It's..." His voice trailed away.

Calantha stared at him, then at last nodded. "We need space to sit. And stillness, peace, to open it."

He jerked his head. "The clearing? Over there."

She followed him back to the grove and sat down opposite him, deliberately placing her unsheathed knife beside her.

He glanced at the knife, but said nothing.

Calantha cupped the pod in both hands and breathed deeply to collect herself. Her hands trembled.

"Can I do anything?" whispered Phelan. "Help in any way?"

She shook her head. She shouldn't have called him back; she'd never be able to open the pod with him sitting there.

Phelan looked steadily at her, then lifted the flute to his lips. Cool soothing music flowed, singing of green fields, deep flowing water, blue skies. Ease and grace. When he stopped, her hands no longer shook.

Calantha nodded her thanks, then closed her eyes and murmured, "Thanks be to the Sower of Tales, she who scatters the seeds."

Phelan whispered the words after her and her eyes sprang open in surprise. He'd spoken from the heart, she knew it. His eagerness for the tale reached out and met hers, in the seamless joining of Talemeet. She drew in a deep breath and, letting herself sink all the way into the pod, softly intoned the words of opening.

Slowly, the pod opened and the seeds circled their heads, glowing faintly in the dark. As the words reached them, Phelan leaned back against the ground and sighed.

A glorious tale, of a sailor seeking a mysterious isle and of his joyful adventures and success. At last the tale was done and the spent seeds circled their heads, changing color. Phelan sat up slowly, and lifted the flute to his lips. Lilting laughter, filled with color and joy, boldness and adventure, danced and rollicked through the air, echoing the tale.

Calantha's heart filled and filled. He'd played well before, but oh, now the music flowed from somewhere deep inside. When he finally stopped, Calantha watched the seeds circle above them once more before they rose upward into the sky—to return to the Sower of Tales.

Phelan put his flute away carefully. He looked hesitantly at her, then stood. "I'll...I'll go now. Try and find some other shelter..."

Calantha stared at him in the dim light. She sighed. "You can stay if you want. I don't care." He was no more one of Odhran's men than she was.

Phelan turned back, and flashed a crooked grin. "My thanks. Pyrena, isn't it?"

She nodded convulsively.

Phelan said, "I'll kindle a fire, then."

She hesitated. A fire would attract attention...but Theora had said she shouldn't hide.

Methodically, Phelan scraped together dry twigs

and moss, building a small pile before striking at his flint. He blew at the fire, feeding it with twigs, then larger pieces of wood. As she watched his red hair gleam in the firelight, the enormity of what she'd just done began to dawn on her—she'd let a perfect stranger see her open a story pod. What if he told anyone? And why had he looked at her so suspiciously at the crossroads?

At last, Phelan dusted his hands and sat back. Reaching into his pouch, he took out a lump of spicy cheese tied in a cloth. Carefully breaking off two pieces, he handed Calantha one. Calantha gave him a piece of her lorshcake and they ate in awkward silence, the ease of the tale gone. She tried to lose herself in the tale they'd just shared, but Phelan's eyes kept flickering toward her and she sensed his darts of curiosity.

All at once, her back stiffened and her heart began to pound. He knew something. Something about her—she felt it clearly. But what?

Phelan cleared his throat and asked hesitantly, "Pyrena, where did you learn that? How to open the pod?"

"I...my grandfather," she said quickly.
"He's...he's the Gatherer and when I was little, he
taught me. I don't do it often. It's just, I wanted to
be a Herbroffe and..."

He didn't believe her. His eyes were cold, disapproving.

She moistened her lips and said quickly, "Tell me
about yourself."

He looked at her steadily. "I'm just what I said;
an apprentice music maker. From Winthrop." He
paused, then added, "It's near Shantrig."

She froze.

"I go there often, to play with the master," continued Phelan evenly, but with a bite to his voice. "In
Shantrig, Herbroffes' bags are smaller than yours,
because they mostly harvest crawberries for red dye.
Oh, and I've met the First Herbroffe; he's a man,
not a woman, and his name is Chelford, not Lyris."

She reached for the knife.

"Look, don't start that again," he said sharply. "If
you don't want to tell the truth, don't, but at least
spare me your lies."

He dug the fire hard with a branch. As the flames

jagged upward, a poker of fear lanced through Calantha. She gasped, "You didn't tell those people back there, did you? What you just—?"

He snorted. "No! What do you think I am? I didn't like those people—they asked too many questions." He glanced at her, then away. "Look, Pyrena, whatever your trouble is, I don't need to know. I'll be gone tomorrow, anyway. I just want to get to the Eastern Mountains."

She started.

Phelan turned sharply toward her. His eyes narrowed. "D'you know about the Eastern Mountains? The Sower of Tales?"

Her mouth went dry. She tried to reach out and sense him and caught a powerful curiosity. It wasn't the same as she'd felt from Flenart at Councilmeet, but she couldn't be sure.

He watched her intently. "Are you going there too? Our Gatherer said something about a key. Do you know anything about it?"

She made herself shrug. "I don't know what you're talking about. I'm just going to Lornfew, like I said."

Phelan sat back abruptly, his mouth tight.

"Look, I really am going to Lornfew," she said quickly. "I said I was from Shantrig because...I can't tell you, but don't tell anyone. Please. Or about the story pod." She looked directly at his face. "It's vitally important."

Oh, flikketting lizards, she should never have said that. Now she'd given him a hold over her.

Phelan shrugged and said sarcastically, "What am I going to tell anyone? I don't know anything, do I?" Deliberately, he took his wrap from his pouch and snapped it open. He wound it carefully around himself, then lay down with his back to her.

Calantha's face flamed. Snarking bograts! How dare he be so scornful—and after she'd shared the tale with him. She snatched her wrap from her pouch and flung it around herself, then lay down, facing the fire, with the knife nearby.

She should never have called him back. He knew too much about her.

Cold. So cold. Eyes like javelins of ice, searching for her, sharp, piercing. She crouched, whimpering, covered her face with her hands. The eyes were turning toward her. Any minute now...no! They were ripping through her fingers, prying them apart. No! No! Her face was freezing, going numb. She screamed and screamed. Warm blue wrapped around her. Xenyss! Xenyss hid her face with a blue mask. "Out," he cried, a forceful, lighted presence. "Out. Begone!" He flung a ball of blazing fire at the eyes.

She woke up screaming, arms flailing.

"Pyrena. Pyrena. You all right?" Phelan bent over her, his face concerned, hair dishevelled.

Calantha sat up gasping, her heart threatening to explode. The ground was hard beneath her, wet with dew. She was in a sharo grove. It was dawn.

Phelan's words reached her as though through a cold, dark cloud. "...something's bothering you. Are you in trouble of some sort? If you tell me perhaps I can help."

She scrambled to her feet. "I'm all right," she said through clenched teeth. "Just leave me alone." She couldn't trust him; she couldn't trust anyone. She must go, go.

Phelan's face reddened. He sprang to his feet. "Don't worry, I don't want anything to do with you." He turned and began to methodically stamp at the ashes of the fire.

Calantha barely heard him. She crumpled up her wrap and thrust it into her pouch.

"Don't forget your knife," said Phelan bitingly.

Calantha grabbed the knife and pushed her way out of the sharo grove, rubbing at her face. Phelan's anger followed her, slivering through the numbness of the dream.

Calantha stumbled along the track to the end of the woods and, blinking hard, emerged into dazzling morning sunshine. She gulped in deep breaths of air, trying to pull in sunshine to clear the gray fog from her head. In the distance she could still hear Phelan stamping out the ashes of the fire in the grove.

A flash of blue washed through her, and a strange thought surfaced—should she have told him?

Snarking bograts! Calantha rubbed her face fiercely. Her task was too important; the last thing she needed was his smug, disapproving presence. She shoved the hair off her face and began to walk, looking around and around. No one in sight. Pulling out her water skin, she took a long swig. Oh, had those eyes seen her? She shivered despite the sun.

The lane began to widen as it curved around scrubby growth and rocks, through gently undulating land. As she walked on, her body began to warm up; at last, sensation returned to her face and the bright sunshine burned away the dark fog in her head.

Calantha pushed her mind into the tales, not daring to stop, not even to touch the few ripe story pods nodding along the way. As the land became hillier and rockier, she began to slow down, panting heavily.

Suddenly, she felt something on the back on her neck. She swung around. Phelan. Flikketting lizards!

He was gaining on her.

Calantha tried to walk faster, but Phelan still drew nearer and nearer. She was so preoccupied by his presence that at first she didn't notice the dark smudge on the road ahead. Then she saw the cloud grow bigger and her stomach plunged sickeningly. Two horses. Something keen and focused speared toward her.

She looked around wildly. Hide. She must hide.

No. Theora had said she mustn't. And there wasn't time.

She froze.

Phelan... He'd told her openly he was looking for the Sower of Tales. If he told them, they'd take him—Xenyss had said Odhran would try to stop anyone from finding the Sower—and what if Phelan betrayed her, Calantha? But even if he didn't...

The horsemen were nearing. Almost sick with fear, she ran back to Phelan and gasped, "Don't say anything about going to the Eastern Mountains. Or the Sower of Tales. Please. I don't have time to explain, just follow what I say."

He squinted at her. "What?"

"You don't understand," she said. "Please, just..."

The horsemen were alongside, pulling their horses.

Two men. Gray horses. Were they the horses she'd seen in Grenlea? She couldn't tell. One man was young, chubby; the other older, with sharp blue eyes. Both wore Herdroffes' clothing, but something was wrong, wrong. Darkness closed in at the edges of her vision, like a tunnel. *Oh, Sower of Tales, don't let them be looking for her.* Her mind reached to Xenyss and she sensed a faint blue mist over her face. The fear pushed back a little.

The older man nodded. "Good day. And where are you young people headed?" His voice was pleasant, but his eyes watchful.

Calantha glanced at him, then at Phelan. Phelan's face was tight, his eyes coldly resentful.

"My half-brother and I are going to Lornfew," she stumbled. "Searle, the other Herbroffe, fell ill so he...he is accompanying me." Calantha's voice faded.

Phelan glowered at her.

The older man looked keenly from her to Phelan.

Calantha stumbled on desperately, "The First Herbroffe wants sneel grass and it grows best near Lornfew."

The man didn't believe her; his suspicion was skewering. Should she run? She turned to Phelan, her eyes pleading.

Something flickered across his face, then he gave her a look of stabbing contempt. "I don't know why I have to get stuck with her. My stepmother insisted." He strode ahead, turning around to growl, "Are you coming or not? I don't have all day."

The chubby man snorted.

Calantha smiled shakily and started after Phelan, tripping over herself to catch up. Laughter followed her. The older man said, "Come on. You can tell they're brother and sister." The horses trotted away in the opposite direction.

When the men were out of sight, Calantha bent over double and retched. Phelan waited silently until she stopped. Her throat was raw, her breath stank, and her eyes streamed. With shaking hands, she wiped her face, then resumed walking. Phelan matched his pace to hers. His face was strained, troubled, but he said nothing. Unspoken questions hovered over them like a cloud of clonthip flies.

At last, Calantha managed to say shakily, "My thanks, Phelan."

He shook his head and muttered, half-ashamed, "I don't why I went along with you."

Calantha flushed. Her body still ached from the fright, from retching. "I'm sorry, but—"

"I know." His voice had an edge. "You can't tell me anything, and yet you want my help."

Calantha bit her lip.

Phelan darted a troubled glance at her. He hesitated, then said, "Look, Pyrena, I don't know what you're about or why you can't tell, but...but I know this has something to do with the story pods." He blinked rapidly. "If there's anything I can do to help..."

Calantha looked at him curiously. Slowly, she asked, "What do they mean to you?"

He let out a choking laugh. "D'you have to ask? My music! Didn't you hear, Pyrena? Without the story pods, it's just...just notes. Like words with no meaning." His voice was despairing. "But afterward, oh, the flute can tell stories."

Calantha stared at him. He meant it; he really cared about the story pods. She wavered; then a rock of reluctance turned awkwardly inside her. This was *her* quest. Not his. He might hold her back, or unintentionally betray her. Besides, there was real danger, and he didn't know that.

Phelan's face hardened. He shrugged, began to stride on.

"Wait." Calantha caught his arm. "Look, when I get to Lornfew, I'm supposed to find the Seer. If she says it's all right..."

Phelan looked at her, his face puzzled, resentful. Then he sighed and nodded. They walked on in silence but he didn't lengthen his stride to leave her. Calantha was surprised at the relief that washed through her.

They stopped once to eat, talking a bit more freely, but Calantha was careful not to give away anything. When they met another group of people, Phelan was convincing again as a reluctant brother accompanying his Herbroffe sister.

The sun was overhead, when, rounding a curve in the road, they saw a distant glitter of blue. The lake! As they neared it, the road split. Calantha looked around nervously as they turned north.

Phelan stared at her, his face puzzled. "It's all right," he said. "There's no one about."

She nodded, her stomach in knots. Had Xenyss covered her face in time? What would happen as they neared the northern lands? She walked on grimly, blind to the glitter of the lake and the beauty of the slender, white-barked leymore trees.

They came upon it unexpectedly, a little white-washed hut. On the porch sat a broad woman with a calm, wide face and deep brown eyes. She wore the pale blue robes of a Seer. Calantha's shoulders sagged with relief.

The Seer rose, eying them steadily. "I've been expecting you," she said to Calantha, in a deep, rich voice.

She stared at Phelan. Phelan flushed but held the Seer's gaze.

At last, the Seer nodded. "Come inside. Both of

you."

Calantha smiled uncertainly at Phelan as they followed the Seer inside. The large woman shut the door behind them. "I am Onawa," she said. "And who are you, with Calantha?"

"Phelan." He quirked an eyebrow at Calantha. "So that wasn't even your real name."

"I couldn't tell you," said Calantha. She turned to Onawa. "We met along the road and he helped me. I didn't tell him...I didn't know if I could trust..."

Phelan's face flamed nearly as red as his hair. His mouth thinned, but he said nothing.

Onawa's placid eyes looked over Calantha. "Didn't Xenyss say he'd send help along the way?"

Calantha's mouth dropped open slightly. Twice, Phelan had asked, "Can I help?" No—three times; the first time in the grove when she'd tried to open the story pod.

Onawa turned to him and said quietly, "Phelan, if you want to help, you need to understand that this is not a game."

Phelan's smile faded.

"There is danger at hand," said Onawa. "And it is all too real."

Phelan turned pale. He blinked hard, then said quietly, "If it's for the story pods, I'll help. I'll do anything. *Anything.* I can't imagine life without them."

Calantha's throat tightened. She knew it wasn't a lightly given promise. Smiling shakily, she said, "Neither can I."

CHAPTER THIRTEEN

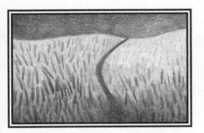

Calantha told Phelan and Onawa everything—about the dream in Grenlea; Xenyss; how she'd been kidnapped and what she'd overheard about Odhran; about her escape and what happened at Theora's. She even told them the key. Phelan and Onawa listened intently, caught in her tale. Phelan said nothing, but she saw a grudging respect grow in his eyes.

After providing them with fresh lorshcakes and fish stew, Onawa went out briefly to make arrangements for their journey. Phelan and Calantha ate silently, both caught in their own thoughts.

As they finished, Phelan asked, "Do you know what it means? The key?"

Calantha's mouth pinched.

He looked at her intently. "Don't worry. You'll find out. The main thing is to get you to the mountain."

Calantha tried to smile. Part of her wished she could just stay here for a while, safe in Onawa's hut, but she knew they didn't have time. Even now, Odhran's men might be searching for her. At least she wouldn't be alone.

She started as the door opened. It was Onawa.

"Phelan, how skilled are you with your flute? Can you play to calm animals?"

He nodded, his eyes puzzled.

"Good. I have a horse and cart. You'll cross the lake on a raft—Old Thornwood will take you—and you must play to keep the horse still. Best you avoid the road; there's too much activity in the village."

Calantha's heart sank. A raft, and Phelan to keep a horse from panicking? She blurted, "But why not go without the horse and cart? On foot?"

Onawa said placidly, "You'll need it on the other side—you'll say you're harvesting green heather for bedding." Her eyes radiated compassion. "And you need it for speed. With the horse and cart, you should reach the bottom of the mountain tonight."

Calantha glanced sharply at Phelan. He said earnestly, "I can do it. Don't worry."

Calantha nodded. There didn't seem to be much choice. Anyway, she'd rather face water than Odhran. She stared desperately into Onawa's warm, calm eyes, trying to shake the chilling memory of those other ones.

Onawa leaned forward and gripped one of Calantha's and Phelan's hands in each of her own. "You must work together, both of you. Remember what this is about. Calantha, don't let arrogance, or fear and anger blind you. This is bigger than you."

Calantha opened her mouth to protest, then clamped it shut. Arrogance?

Onawa continued, "Phelan, the same holds for you. This is bigger than *your* wants. Don't let disapproval or resentment hinder you."

Phelan flushed. He glanced at Calantha, shame struggling in his eyes.

Onawa said, "Phelan, you must see that she gets to the Eastern Mountains. Even if you cannot go on, she must."

Calantha turned shocked eyes to Phelan as the meaning of Onawa's words sank in. Would he back out?

He turned pale, but said crisply, "I understand. She was given the key; she has the best chance of finding the Sower of Tales. I'll make sure."

"Good." Onawa released their hands. "When you get to the other side, take the path due east until you reach a wide lane that skirts along the base of the mountains. You should get there by late afternoon. At the first sign of heather, you must stop and gather some. There are tools in the cart. Odhran's and Ulric's men will be about, you may be certain. You must be convincing."

Calantha nodded jerkily. Phelan flashed her a crooked grin.

"Follow the lane southward," continued Onawa "If you are asked, you are from Branwhip, to the far south. The lane curves around the mountains. From the south side there is another lane that ascends the highest mountain, but you must not go that way. That's where Odhran's men will be watching. You must turn beforehand. On your left, look for a small track going steeply up the mountain. It's your best chance. It will lead along the northern part of the mountain, to the eastern edge and from there to the top. Few people know it. It's steeper, but safer for now."

"Can the cart take that track?" asked Phelan bluntly.

"No," said Onawa.

Calantha's head snapped toward Phelan. He looked grim but resolute.

Onawa turned to Calantha and said, "Now, listen. The domain of the Sower of Tales is near the top. It is marked by a lone sharo tree."

Calantha nodded, pressing her hands together. Would she be able to unlock the key?

Onawa squeezed her shoulder then got up to bundle together food and water for their journey. She hurried them outside into the hot sunshine, where an old brown horse, harnessed to a cart, stood chewing grass. "I put a calming spell on him," she said, "but you'll also need the flute."

Phelan approached slowly, and raised the flute to his lips. Soothing music flowed, with strange little lilts. The horse quirked its ears and stood still.

Calantha thanked Onawa, then added quickly, "Will you let Xenyss and Theora know that I reached here?"

Onawa nodded, but she avoided Calantha's eyes. Something shifted uneasily inside Calantha, but there was no time for further talk. She climbed onto the wooden seat at the front of the cart with Phelan and took the reins. Phelan continued to play softly, the tune changing slightly, urging somehow. Onawa led the horse along the road then turned right, down a rough, grassy path to the lake.

At the edge of the lake, by a raft, stood a short grizzled man in ragged clothes, a long pole in his hand. He barely glanced at them as he led the horse onto the raft. It was a large raft, but it still dipped alarmingly as they rode on. Calantha gripped the edge of the wooden seat until her knuckles gleamed. She'd feel safer standing on the raft than sitting up so high on the cart. Phelan's soothing strains played on as the old man untied the rope and began to pole away from shore. The raft swayed and the horse snickered.

"Hold the reins tight," said Phelan, lifting his head from the flute before continuing to play.

Calantha gripped the reins in both hands. Steady, she thought, steady.

Phelan played on, as the raft swept further into the lake. Blue water, glittering wickedly in the sun, surrounded them. Phelan's flute reminded her of the tale of the girl whose dead mother's flute led her to safety across the raging river. On the raft went, and on Phelan played. Calantha kept her hands steady, not too tight, not too loose.

It seemed like an eternity before the opposite shore loomed closer. She looked at the Eastern Mountains. The highest one, with the crooked slope, towered above them. Calantha's throat tightened and her eyes blurred. All those times she'd dreamed of coming here to find the Sower of Tales, she'd never once imagined that it would be like this.

She started as the raft jerked with a grating sound. They'd reached shore. Safely.

Calantha let out a shaky laugh. Phelan kept playing as the old man jumped to shore with the rope and pulled the raft higher.

He tilted his head and motioned with his hands.

Nodding her thanks, Calantha tugged the reins and clicked. The horse clambered onto shore and the cart jolted and bounced over a rough track, eventually joining a smoother path leading away from the lake, up toward the mountains.

The path twisted and wound past patches of scrub and wind-bent trees—the odd story pod blowing in the wind—and at last met a wider lane running in both directions along the base of the mountains.

Calantha's back tensed. No one in sight, but there were too many trees and shrubs to see the way clearly. Phelan reached for the reins and turned the cart to the right, driving only a short distance south before abruptly pulling to a halt.

"Why are we stopping?" asked Calantha nervously.

"Green heather," said Phelan. He pointed to a mass of springy low gray-green shrubs.

"Let's go further," said Calantha, looking around. "I don't like the feel of this place."

Phelan's face tightened mutinously. "Onawa said to gather it when we first see it." He sprang down from the cart and tied the horse to a low shrub, then went around to the back of the cart. Tossing aside some arrac sacking, he took out two sickles and held out one to her.

Irritation rashed across Calantha's back. This was *her* journey; who was he to decide? Just in time, she remembered Onawa's warning and bit back the hot words that sprang to her lips. Getting down from the cart, she took the sickle and swung wildly at the heather.

A soft snort from Phelan made her look up angrily.

Phelan's face was wooden. "Here, like this." He bent down and swung in a neat arc, culling a handful of heather and flinging it onto the back of the cart.

Calantha made a small face and began to swing at the heather in earnest. Maybe it was best to have some heather in the cart if they were stopped, but she was not about to admit it. She gazed at a soft blue story pod in the distance and sighed. Still no new ones. Anywhere.

After a while the swinging became steady and they worked in silence. But Calantha kept stopping to look around; something about the air smelled wrong.

As she bent once again to her task, the slow clop of hooves rang through the air, along with men's voices. Horses, coming toward them. Five horses. She looked at Phelan, her face draining. Phelan's greenish-brown eyes blazed, as though sending her strength. He flashed his crooked grin, then resumed cutting heather.

Calantha bent over as well, her knuckles white around the sickle. Please, *please* don't let them be looking for her. She was too close to the Sower of Tales to be stopped now.

Nearer, nearer came the horses, casting long, dark shadows across the lane.

Casually, Calantha straightened up and looked around. Phelan whistled softly as he gathered another bundle of heather and carried it to the cart.

"Good day," he called out cheerfully.

The men stopped beside the cart. All strong and fit. Cold eyes. Menace—she sensed it strong and clear. Calantha's heart threatened to explode. Her hands shook, but she too gathered the heather she'd cut and flung it onto the cart.

One of the men, lean and stringy with a receding hairline, asked curtly, "What are you doing here?"

Calantha's mouth went dry. He must be confident that there were no Plainsfolk about to be so openly arrogant. Or were they searching for someone of her description? She ripped her mind away from the memory of those icy eyes and tried to speak. Her tongue seemed to be stuck to the roof of her mouth.

Phelan said sullenly, "Green heather. My half-sister is apprenticed to the Herbroffe and I got stuck helping her." He jerked a thumb at Calantha, his tone the perfect mix of resignation and resentment.

Calantha managed to mutter, "Well, it doesn't hurt you to tear yourself away from your precious flute just for once." She shook her head slightly.

Phelan glowered at her. "Let's just get this over with, all right?" Then, barely audibly, "It's the last time I—"

Before he could take three paces, the lean man moved his horse forward, blocking him. Calantha's heart lurched into her mouth. Every muscle in her body screamed to run, but she held still as Phelan flashed her a quick warning glance.

The man scowled at Phelan, then turned to Calantha. Cold, blue eyes, sharp and keen. "Where are you folks from?"

Calantha managed to indicate southward with her thumb and say, "Branwhip."

The man's eyes narrowed. "Branwhip. That's a fair distance to come."

"That's what *I* said." Phelan's voice was surly. "But she insisted that the heather is most fragrant to the north." He snorted slightly. "Fragrant!"

Calantha shot him a look. "Well, the sooner we're done, the sooner we'll get back."

The man asked, his eyes keen, "Did you see anyone along the way?"

"No one," said Calantha quickly.

She saw the man tense, and understood her mistake.

Phelan casually scratched the back of his neck. "Except for some men. On horseback, like you." He frowned. "And a horse and cart."

The man looked them over then moved his horse aside. His voice was silky. "I hear it's dangerous around these parts. Bandits."

Phelan muttered, "Well, we have nothing." He put his sickle down. "Unless, of course, they want fragrant heather." His voice held just the right amount of sarcasm.

The man stared at Phelan. "Tell you what. We'll escort you home. Make sure you get back all right."

"Don't trouble yourself," said Phelan quickly.

The man smiled. It wasn't pleasant. "No trouble. Just want to make sure you leave the mountains safely."

Phelan shrugged and went back to cutting heather. Calantha's head throbbed. They were suspicious. They wanted to make sure that no one went up the mountain. How would she get away with the horsemen watching?

Phelan barely whispered, "We'll manage. Don't worry." His eyes were strong, determined. Calantha flashed a shaky smile.

They filled the cart with heather while the men watched from a distance. When they were done, Phelan tucked some of the arrac cloth loosely around the heather but kept one large cloth on the wooden seat up front. Making a show of stretching, he climbed onto the seat with Calantha and called out to the men, "My thanks. It's a comfort to know we're safe."

Calantha heard the men mutter and laugh. As Phelan started the cart, she glanced back. Two of the horsemen were following at a distance.

"They'll see if I get off," she hissed.

Phelan whispered, "Just wait. I have an idea."

"We can't fight them," she said breathlessly.

His crooked grin was part bravado, part fear. "I know. I've apprenticed with my Defenseroffe. I know when it's possible and when it isn't. Here, hold the reins." He reached into his pouch for the flute and began to play. It was an easy, gentle tune, singing of rest at the end of the work day. Soothing, lulling.

Calantha gaped at him.

"Keep going," he said. "Not too fast."

Shadows lengthened as the sun sank lower in the sky. The cart bounced along slowly. Each time Calantha looked back, the men were there, only out of sight when they rounded a curve.

As they approached a deep curve with trees on either side, Phelan lifted his lips from the flute to say quickly, "The sacking. Wrap it around heather, like a body."

In a flash she understood. As soon as they were out of sight, she flung the reins across his legs and, grabbing some heather, wrapped the arrac sacking around it.

Not enough. When the horsemen came in sight, she dropped the arrac and faced frontward again.

On the cart bounced, on Phelan played, the horsemen keeping pace behind.

Calantha noticed a narrow track to their left, veering steeply up toward the higher slopes. Her heart raced.

"Is that it?" she whispered.

Phelan nodded. He lifted the flute long enough to puff, "Wait. Need more heather."

Calantha glanced back. The sun had just set, with screams of red; it would be dark soon. Would she be able to find the track again? As they rounded another curve, she quickly stuffed more heather into the sacking. The men on horseback had fallen back, lulled by the flute. On went the cart, on, farther away from the track. It was nearly dark when they approached a deep twist in the lane.

"Now," breathed Phelan.

Calantha squeezed his arm. "Phelan, my thanks. I—"

"Never mind," he lifted his lips fleetingly from the flute. "Just find her. Go!" His eyes were fierce.

As they rounded the curve, Phelan slowed the horse and reached over to grab the sack, pulling it on the seat beside him. Calantha jumped off with her pouch. She landed on her ankle, twisting it slightly. Rolling over, she bent double and hobbled toward some thick bushes. She crouched behind them, her heart hammering. Had they seen her?

The cart continued on, with Phelan's flute ringing in the evening air, still peaceful, lulling, and easy, but now with an added lilt—luring.

Calantha remained frozen behind the bushes, hardly daring to breathe, while the horsemen passed by. She heard one of them mutter, "Let's get closer, it's getting dark now."

Calantha's heart plunged. What would they do to

Phelan? What if they came after her? The trail of music grew fainter and fainter. She waited until she could no longer hear it or the horses' hooves, then limping, dodging behind bushes, she darted back along the lane. Hurry, she must hurry, find the path. Would she be able to see it?

She hobbled on in the growing dark. Surely she'd come far enough. Then, just as she was about to turn back, she saw it.

Crouching, trying not to put too much weight on her ankle, she stumbled upward along the steep track. It was getting darker now, deep shadows melting together, and the air had a growing nip to it. A flash of blue wrapped around her; she sensed Xenyss urging her on. She climbed upward as fast as she could, pulling on branches to spare her ankle.

At last, when she could barely see the path, she stopped. It was a moonless night. She couldn't risk falling or getting lost; she must stop. Nearby, to one side, she could just make out the shadow of a craggy overhang. She limped over and sank down onto the stony ledge.

At least with no moon, Phelan, too, would be

harder to spot. Hands shaking, she took the wrap out of her pouch and wound it tightly around herself. Oh, what would happen to him if they found she'd gone? Would they beat him, try to get him to talk? Take him to Odhran?

She blinked hard. She hadn't even thanked him properly.

Perhaps the only way to thank him was to find the Sower of Tales. Bring back the story pods. Calantha's chest began to ache. In two days there'd be no more story pods.

She ate the lorshcakes Onawa had given her, took a deep swig of water, then felt in her pouch for the pods. A bitter taste filled her mouth. She knew from the feel of it that the seeds had released in the cloth. Calantha lay down, her head just beyond the overhanging crag so she could see the stars. The rock below her was sharp and cold. Where was Phelan now?

She stared up at the stars. So many—pinpoints of light, blazing for all. Like the seeds of story pods, for all who cared to hear them.

Her throat tightened. What tales did the stars

hold? Did they keep the tales of the spent story pods? Did they see what happened to the people of Grenlea? To Phelan? Did they know what had happened to the story pods? Could they tell those tales, too?

Oh, Sower of Tales, I'm coming, I'm coming. Let me find you.

Tears seeped from the corners of her eyes and slid down the sides of her face. The stars blurred. Calantha pressed her hand against her mouth. She cried for the unheard tales, the loss of the story pods, the loneliness and danger of this strange place; she cried for her mother and family, for Kasmira and Xenyss, soft kind Xenyss; she cried for Phelan, who even now might be captured and beaten; and she cried and cried for the Sower of Tales. At last, hiccuping softly, she turned her mind to the story she had shared with Phelan, and to other tales. The smooth familiar flow dulled, then eased, the ache inside her. She repeated the key again and at last fell asleep, somehow settled by the steady compassion of the stars.

CHAPTER FOURTEEN

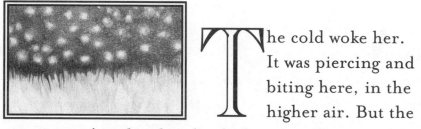

The cold woke her. It was piercing and biting here, in the higher air. But the stars weren't as bright, the dark not as impenetrable as before.

Calantha shivered and sat up, rubbing her arms and legs. Thanks be to the Sower of Tales, no dreams. Maybe the stars had guarded her, along with Xenyss. Today. Today, she must reach the top of the mountain.

She whispered the key.

If the Sower of Tales you seek to find
Unravel the knots that tangle your mind
Let the song of the story pods ring in your heart,
Let go of all else, let the tales do their part.

The stars were fading now, and she could see her hand in front of her eyes. Calantha folded her wrap and got up, putting her left foot down cautiously. Her ankle was sore but it took her weight, thank goodness.

At first it was difficult to see the track, and she moved slowly, stiffly. But as the dark horizon lightened, the path became clearer and her body warmed up. When it was light enough, she turned around to see how far she had come. Scrub and bushes below. No sign of the lane she and Phelan had traveled on. Where was he now?

A ripe pod danced nearby, just out of reach. She gazed longingly at it, but climbed on. At times she used her hands to pull herself over rocks; at times she slipped and caught herself on stray roots and twisted branches. As the sun rose higher in the sky, her ankle began to throb. She wiped her face again and again, her eyes flicking nervously downward. No one in sight.

On she went, trying to put as little weight as possible on her aching ankle. Where was that lone sharo tree? She repeated the key. *Let the song of the story pods ring in your heart.* Osric had said they were deep inside her. Was that enough? Was she supposed to say the key at the top of the mountain? *Oh, Sower of Tales, let me unlock the key and find you.*

By the time the sun was overhead there were no trees beside the path, just twisted, gray heather and other stunted shrubs. Stopping just long enough to drink from her alarmingly light water skin and to eat the berries Onawa had given her, Calantha pushed on. Knife-points of doubt began to scour at her. Why were there no story pods here? She hadn't seen any since the lower slopes. If the Sower of Tales lived here, shouldn't there be story pods?

She looked upward. Just rocks and shrubs and dirt. The mountain loomed above her dizzyingly. Below was an eerie uncomfortable silence; the air strangely empty. Askew.

A flash of blue wrapped around her. Drawing in a deep breath, Calantha continued upward, trying to ignore her throbbing ankle. She spun out tales of brave explorers, and the familiar hum and flow filled and strengthened her. Her hands and knees were now scraped and bleeding. There was nothing, no life apart from this mountain, the dust, the rocks, the scrub. Would she ever get to the top? When she closed her eyes all she saw were jagged rocks. She finished the last of her water.

It was late afternoon when she saw a wide blue-gray smudge higher up. Could it be a tree? She climbed for another half-hour before she dared to look up again. Yes, a tree. A huge sharo tree just above a jutting ledge. She licked her cracked lips and scrambled upward, murmuring the key. It seemed to take forever to reach the tree. At times, crags hid it from view, but at last, there it was, just above her. She scrambled over a large rocky overhang, gripping at crevices in the rock, not daring to look down. Slowly, she pulled herself onto the ledge.

Gasping, she lay in the deep, comforting shade of the sharo tree. She was here. She was here, at last! Face pulsing with heat and fatigue, she dragged herself to her feet, wincing as her ankle took her weight, and stumbled to the edge of the overhanging branches.

A plateau curved gently upward. Nothing on it but rock and rubble.

Calantha's mind went numb. She moistened her lips and parted the sharo leaves to walk through, then dropped down under the tree, her heart thundering.

A group of men. With swords.

She lay still for a while before daring to peer through the leaves again. The men were dressed as Plainsfolk, but the swords and spears in their hands...and the way they looked around....

The same menace she'd sensed from the men yesterday swamped over her. With piercing clarity she knew that they were here to kill. They paced, sharp-eyed, at the opposite corner of the plateau—it must be where the main path that Onawa had mentioned came up. Had others made it up here? Had anyone found the Sower of Tales? Or had they been killed? Calantha rocked herself, sick at the thought. If she said the key and the door opened, would they see her and follow? She closed her eyes in despair.

At last, she stood up, jaw clenched. She had no choice. She must say the words and when the door opened, she'd run as fast as possible...and hope she could get there first.

She drew in a ragged breath and began to whisper,
If the Sower of Tales you seek to find
Unravel the knots that tangle your mind
Let the song of the story pods ring in your heart,
Let go of all else, let the tales do their part.

The same rocks and rubble. The same men still
pacing at the far end of the plateau. No sign of a
door or opening. Nothing.

Calantha licked her lips and repeated the words
again.

Nothing.

The third time, she knew it wouldn't work. She
sank down under the sharo tree. Repeating the key
wasn't it. She'd known it all along, deep inside, but
she hadn't wanted to face it.

What could the words mean? She said them again
and in a twist of pain, she understood. A story pod.
She needed to open a story pod here. That's what
"let the tales do their part" must mean.

But she had none. Just the open ones in the cloth
in her pouch. She'd have to go back down the
mountain somehow and find a story pod. Maybe

more than one. What if Odhran's men were waiting for her? If they'd caught Phelan, they'd be swarming around...would she be able to run with her sore ankle?

Her head buzzed. She'd failed. She'd failed the Plainsfolk, failed everyone who'd helped her. Phelan's sacrifice was for nothing. The story pods would be lost because she was too stupid.... She buried her face in her hands. The first pod she'd opened for Talemeet would be the last. The Princess and the Pig.

Tears sprang to her eyes.

No.

She sat up fiercely and wiped her eyes. She was not going to cry. She must calm down, find a way. What would a brave explorer do? Her thoughts tripped into the tale of the one-legged boy who went through the labyrinth to find the treasure hidden in the mountain. She put her head down on her knees and, out of habit, for comfort, let her mind stream into the hum and flow of the tale, the steady fullness filling and filling her....

Her body jerked and arced. She gasped. The

humming of the story pods, but ten times stronger, dazzled through her. Her whole body pulsed and sang with the hum of the pods. Calantha lifted her head. Tingling, she stood up and peered through the leaves of the sharo tree.

Where before there had only been an empty, stony plateau, furrowed fields curved upward, filled with spent story pod stalks.

Calantha's breath caught in her throat. She pushed the leaves apart and started forward, then shrank back, eyes darting.

But there was no sign of the men, not a trace.

In a flash, she understood the key. She'd let go of all else; she'd let the tales do their part.

The men hadn't disappeared—*she* had.

She laughed chokingly. She'd found the domain of the Sower of Tales. She'd found it!

PART THREE

THE SOWER OF TALES

Does the Sower feed the tale
Or the tale feed the Sower?

Traditional Plains saying

CHAPTER FIFTEEN

onderingly, Calantha limped out from under the tree. The air was crisp and clear—and different. The sun shone with the same intensity it had earlier, but the humming of the pods pulsed everywhere. Gulping in deep breaths of air, Calantha let the humming work through her.

A narrow rutted track ran from the sharo tree and through a grassy field toward a wider lane curving upward along the sloping plateau. Calantha looked around uneasily as she hurried along the track toward the lane. The menace she'd sensed from the men was gone, but despite the humming, something wasn't right. The fields were desolate with gray and broken stalks, rattling emptily in the dry afternoon wind. Shouldn't the domain of the Sower of Tales be filled with ripe story pods?

Oh, Sower of Tales, had she come too late?

Partway up the lane, she saw a small crop of gray-green lorsha growing at the end of a field. There were patches of wild arrac as well, the long, narrow leaves gleaming dull red in the ditches and fields. But no ripe story pods.

Then she saw the colors in the distance—soft, blurred shades—and her heart leaped with relief. Ripe pods. A field full of ripe story pods! She could sense the deeper, joyful humming, even from here.

Limping along, she tried to go faster, the back of her legs aching from the incline. As she drew closer, she saw another field, next to the ripe pods, with more story pods growing in it, but in large patches of different heights—different stages of growth. Then, in a clearing at the end of the lane, she saw faded gray roofs. Four huts. And beyond them, a cluster of ruined huts, half-tumbled and broken down.

Calantha stopped, gasping. She raked her fingers through her tangled dusty hair and, wiping her face with her sleeve, continued at a slower pace.

As she neared the field of ripe pods, she saw three figures wearing red-green Gatherer's robes; they were struggling to cover some of the ripe pods with arrac cloth. Calantha's heart gave a strange flip. The Sower of Tales?

One of the figures—so small she looked like a child—turned and saw her. In a high, excited voice she shouted something to her companions, and all three came hurrying toward her. Calantha's eyes darted eagerly. Two women and one man. They were all old, the man slight and sinewy but bent and gnarled and nearly bald. Even the small woman was old, with untidy gray hair cropped short around her wrinkled face.

She ran up first to seize Calantha's hands, her face blazing with a smile that revealed crooked, yellowing teeth. "You found us!" she crowed, her blue eyes dancing. "Oh, thanks be to the story pods, you've come at last!"

The other woman, tall, slightly stooped, with mild brown eyes, beamed at Calantha. "Welcome, child," she said.

"Yes, and she is just a child," muttered the man,

rubbing his knob of a nose.

The small woman said fiercely, "Yes, but she's come, hasn't she? What's your name, child?"

"Calantha."

The small woman's eyes lit up as she turned to the others. "See! Didn't she say she'd come?" She grabbed Calantha's hand and pulled her along the lane. "Come quick."

Calantha winced as her ankle protested. "Are...are you the Sower...?"

The old man, struggling behind, snorted.

The small woman shook her head impatiently. "Of course not. We're her apprentices."

"What's left of us," the old man grunted.

The small woman rushed on, "I'm Musidora and this here," she pointed to the old man, "is Grelder. Don't mind him, his knees bother him. And that's Aelthea. Now hurry, will you!"

Aelthea? Calantha turned to look at the tall woman. Kasmira had mentioned an Aelthea, but...

"Musidora, slow down!" puffed Aelthea. "She's come a long way. She's tired. And look, she's hurt her foot."

Musidora clicked her tongue. "Ooh, never mind! I'll go on and tell her." She dropped Calantha's hand and ran toward the huts.

Aelthea smiled at Calantha as they continued at an easier pace. "Don't mind Musidora. We have waited long for you."

"Me?" Calantha's head spun.

"Aye, but we didn't think you'd be so young," mumbled Grelder.

Aelthea said sharply, "Well, what would you have her be? As old as us?"

Grelder muttered something inaudible.

As they continued along the lane, steeper now, Calantha had a vague impression of plots of vegetables and berries growing alongside, and even some sheep and cows in a far field. When they reached the clearing, Aelthea led the way toward the smallest gray hut. The old sharo thatch was cracked and worn, faded to a pale gray by the sun.

"Here she is!" Musidora's voice rang triumphantly as she came out into the hot sunshine. She was followed by another woman, tall, slender, in red-green robes.

Calantha gasped. Wrinkled brown face, wide gray eyes. Pointed chin, hooked nose, and wild, rough hair. The witch! The witch of her dreams.

The tall woman came swiftly toward Calantha, her gray eyes keen. "Calantha, thank goodness. I knew you'd come." She reached out a hand.

The Sower of Tales. At last! Calantha's throat constricted. Something, she must do something to honor the Sower of Tales. She tried to curtsey. She burst into tears.

As though from a distance she heard Aelthea cluck softly, heard Musidora's "Oh, my," and then she was being held by the Sower of Tales, sobbing against her shoulder.

"Calantha," murmured the Sower of Tales. "It has been too much, hasn't it?" Her hand traced soothing circles on Calantha's back.

At last, Calantha stopped and pulled away. "I'm sorry, so sorry. I didn't...it's just...there aren't any new story pods growing." Chest heaving, she asked, with all the pent-up anguish of the past days, "You haven't stopped sending them, have you?"

The Sower's eyes flashed. "No! I would never

abandon the people."

Calantha dabbed her cheeks with the back of her hands. "Then what's happened to them? Out there, Odhran's men..."

The Sower of Tales said firmly, "Come inside, Calantha; you're dizzy with fatigue."

Breath still shuddering, Calantha followed the Sower of Tales into the hut. Aelthea sat her down before the fire and Musidora brought her cups of water. Even Grelder handed her a wet cloth to wipe her face and hands. A fresh breeze blowing through the windows cooled her despite the heat from the fire.

As Calantha's eyes grew accustomed to the dim interior, she saw that it was a small and simple hut, like any Gatherer's, with few adornments except for wildflowers on the table. Deep blue skydrops. Aelthea handed her a large piece of lorshcake with soft curd cheese and harwenberry jam and insisted she eat it, while she bandaged Calantha's ankle.

"Better?" asked the Sower of Tales as Calantha put down her empty plate.

Calantha nodded, shamefaced. "I'm sorry,

I didn't mean—"

"No matter," said the Sower of Tales. "We all cry at times, it's part of life." Her tone really made it no matter. It reminded Calantha of Kasmira's, although Kasmira's rasping, cracked voice was very different from the fluid music of the Sower's—a voice like the wind swaying through the young leaves of spring, yet as old as the mountains. The voice of the story pods.

Calantha gazed hungrily at her. The Sower of Tales! Was she really seeing her at last? The Sower's face was wrinkled, softly creased, like a worn leather pouch, but she had strong, wild hair—dark, barely streaked with gray. Her large gray eyes were young and alive; wise eyes that knew joy and grief.

"It was you," said Calantha. "In my dreams."

The Sower of Tales nodded. "Yes, I tried to bring you to me. Before all this could begin."

"I didn't understand," said Calantha. "I thought..." she hesitated, but knew that she mustn't hold anything back. "I thought you were a witch."

The gray eyes filled with light. "I know!" cried the Sower of Tales. She laughed, like a burst of sun.

Then they were all laughing, even Calantha.

The Sower of Tales sighed. "Oh, it's good to laugh, we have sore need of it." Her smile faded. "Now tell me, Calantha. What is happening down there?"

Calantha's head buzzed with confusion. She'd expected answers, not questions. "But we thought you'd—"

"Calantha, I've had no news of the Plains since...for goodness sakes, tell me what's happening. When did the people realize that my seeds had stopped?"

Calantha tried to gather her scattered thoughts. "We didn't see it at first. Not until six days after they stopped." She moistened her lips. "I had a dream about the pods being gone, but I didn't realize—"

The Sower of Tales shook her head. "Never mind that—how are the Plainsfolk? What are they doing?"

"Searching," said Calantha. "Some of them. The Council sent out parties for news of the pods. And of you, your whereabouts. Other villages are searching too, but no one agrees about where you live, so..."

"But Kasmira knows!" exclaimed Aelthea. "I told her myself."

Calantha's head jerked toward her. "You're the same...?"

"Yes." Aelthea nodded, her eyes keen. "Kasmira was young, barely ready, but I had to come here... never mind. Go on, child."

Calantha drew in a deep breath. With the Sower of Tales questioning her, Calantha told them what had happened, and about the Councilmeet. When she related what Xenyss had said and done, a brief smile crossed the Sower's face.

"Ah, yes. Xenyss would see," she said.

"You know him?" cried Calantha.

"Of course I know of him," said the Sower of Tales. "I'll explain later. Go on, Calantha."

Calantha continued with how Flenart and Shraelyn had kidnapped her, what she'd overheard them say, and all that had happened since. Her voice faltered when she spoke of Phelan, and again as she told them, "King Ulric and Odhran's men are everywhere. They were out there on top of the mountain, too. With swords."

Calantha looked around at their uneasy faces and gripped her hands together. "Sower of Tales, what is happening to the story pods? Theora said the Great Liberation was ten years after the story pods began, and that she'd never seen the Essences without them. And Xenyss said you'd know what Odhran's after because only you know how the Essence of the story pods is woven into all the others." Calantha drew in a twisted, painful breath. "I came here to find out, and...and you will be able to bring the story pods back, won't you?"

The Sower of Tales flinched. Musidora groaned softly.

For a moment, no one spoke. Calantha turned icy cold, despite the warmth of the fire.

At last, the Sower of Tales said, slowly, "To answer that, Calantha, I must explain to you how the First Sower of Tales wove the story pods into the other Essences. And why." Weariness flickered momentarily in her eyes. "I am the third Sower of Tales, Calantha, and I came here over two hundred years ago, but the knowledge is passed down from Sower to Sower, as is the power to seed tales."

Calantha stared at her. Could the Sower of Tales really be that old? More than two hundred years?

The Sower of Tales continued softly, "The tale starts over six hundred and eighty years ago, when the First Sower of Tales was a storyteller, just one among others. Never mind how or where or why—it is much too long a tale. There weren't many story-tellers then, for it was a time of hardship and hunger. The Plains were part of the Kingdom of Jaerlfin, and the Plainsfolk lived in unbelievable poverty. Misery." The Sower drew in her breath sharply. "The tithes were harsh, the people were worked and taxed without mercy. Without justice." Her eyes were distant, almost as though she saw it all. "But when this young storyteller told her tales," the Sower smiled, "oh, she brought such joy. Such solace. For a while her listeners were lifted from their cares. The tales brought them comfort, and..."

"Respite," murmured Calantha, nodding slowly.

Musidora dug Grelder with her elbow and Aelthea said warmly, "Yes. Respite."

"And," said Calantha intently, remembering Talemeets, "maybe because of the respite there'd be a restoring of courage and…a chance to dream. To imagine." She looked up. "And to hope."

The Sower's eyes gleamed approvingly. "Yes, hope."

Grelder's shriveled mouth widened into a smile and he nodded, while Musidora thumped his shoulder and said, "Now will she do?"

The Sower continued, "So the young storyteller roamed the Plains telling her tales. Every settlement she visited longed for her to stay, because her tales eased their lot and gave such joy. Over time, she became famed for her tales, the best known. At last she decided, for many reasons, to go to the Place of Knotting—"

"She apprenticed *there*?" cried Calantha. "With the Sorcerers?"

Grelder snorted and shook his head. "How else d'you think she could weave such a far-reaching and elegant web?"

"Grelder!" The Sower frowned slightly, then turned back to Calantha. "Yes, she apprenticed with the Sorcerers. And she learned of the Essences— earth, air, water, fire, and the Essence of the human spirit—and how they are linked. She learned how to trace them, intertwine them, weave them, and feed them." The Sower's eyes were luminous.

Thrills coursed along Calantha's spine. Was she actually sitting here, across from the Sower of Tales, hearing about how the story pods began?

"She didn't at first have any intention of being a Sower of Tales. But the Plainsfolk wanted her tales. Needed them. And she couldn't possibly be in all places at once." The Sower of Tales turned to Calantha, half pleadingly.

"So she found a way to make the tales grow for all," whispered Calantha.

The Sower's smile flashed like a sunburst. "Yes, grow. That's just it. Tales grow, with a life of their own. Words and ideas are like seeds." A look of pure delight suffused her face. "You combine them in ways that are unexpected and lovely, and the result is a tale. She took a common plant—a weed, really, one filled with seeds—and she utilized it for her tales." Her smile slowly faded. "Of course, the Sorcerers had warned her that there is always a price to pay when the Essences are meddled with. But she never imagined—none of us did—that *this* might…"

"Always remember why she did it," said Aelthea softly.

Musidora nodded vigorously.

Calantha looked at them, then leaned forward, words tumbling out, "The story pods, they're every-thing to me. To many of us." She choked. "You don't know how much joy they bring."

The Sower's face glowed, and for an instant Calantha saw her as a young woman, filled with light and strength, hope and laughter. "My thanks, Calantha."

"It is them that forgot," said Grelder sourly. "Break the circle at your peril."

Calantha stared at him, bewildered.

"Hush, Grelder. It's not about blame," said the Sower of Tales. She continued, her eyes bright. "The First Sower did pay mind to the Sorcerers; she touched the Essences the least that she could. She harnessed the wind lightly, ever so lightly. She diverted the smallest bit in a loop, to carry her seeds to the Plains and to bring the spent seeds back to the mountain so that she could replenish them again

with tales. Like a circular seesaw—her seeds, sealed
with the tales, went from the mountain to the
Plains, and in turn the spent Plains seeds returned
to her." She shook her head slightly. "Just a small
diversion, so small. But whenever any new Essence is
knotted and woven into the larger fabric, the intent
of the weaver becomes tied to the changes." The
Sower looked steadily at Calantha. "And the changes
grow and shift with a life of their own. They become
enmeshed with the wider web. And they deepen and
strengthen those Essences that are similar. Alike."

Calantha's heart began to race.

The Sower of Tales drew in a deep breath.
"Calantha, the Essence of the story pods comes from
the oldest and the most powerful of all Essences—the
life-spark, the Essence of creation itself." Her eyes
blazed. "And so, over time, the Essence of the tales
enmeshed and interwove with all the other Essences
linked to that life-spark, strengthening them, too—
strengthening unity and love, joy and creativity and
hope."

Calantha stared at her. It was all falling into place
now. Slowly she said, "So the tales heartened and

brought folk together even more than they had before. Bolstered their dreams and hopes."

The Sower of Tales nodded. "Yes."

Calantha moistened her lips. "That's why the Plainsfolk were able to gain their freedom ten years later, whereas before..."

"Yes," said the Sower of Tales.

For a moment Calantha sat still. Then slowly she said, "The night before the seeds stopped, I had a dream." She told them about it, then continued, her voice uneven, "What I felt, the despair, the...the draining of life, of joy and hope, is...is that what will happen without the story pods? To everyone?" She looked pleadingly at the Sower of Tales.

A spasm of pain wracked the Sower's face. "Not all at once. But yes. Eventually."

Calantha's head spun. "But what can King Ulric and Odhran hope to gain?" She gasped. "They want us to weaken and despair. So they can take the Plains. But...they too will be caught in the despair, won't they? Won't they?"

Grief filled the Sower's eyes.

"Break the circle at your peril," murmured

Grelder again.

Calantha's eyes flickered momentarily toward him, then back to the Sower of Tales. Desperately she asked, "What is happening to the seeds? Where are they?"

The Sower of Tales stood up wearily. "Come. You will see for yourself. It is nearly time."

Musidora's face seemed to shrink as she placed a warm wrap around the Sower of Tales. Aelthea handed Calantha a faded red shawl, and the Sower of Tales led the way outside to a chilly twilight. The sky was clear, glowing like the deepest Essence of blue. Filled with dread, Calantha followed the Sower of Tales upward along the steep lane, away from the ripe fields. Even though the pace was easy, she was thankful for the bandage supporting her ankle.

Panting softly, the Sower of Tales stopped at last near the top of the slope and sat down on a large rock, motioning Calantha beside her. Calantha shivered despite her thick shawl. The air felt heavy; heavy with waiting. In the clear evening light, the ripe story pods gleamed in the field below. Her heart ached at the beautiful colors. She glanced at the arrac cloth covering part of the field.

"Watch," breathed the Sower of Tales, her energy spent. "Watch the ripe pods."

"The pods are about to release the seeds," said Aelthea, her voice a mixture of yearning and grief. She reached out and held Calantha's hand.

Calantha caught her breath. The pods were opening, the whole field of story pods. A cloud of milky blue-white seeds drifted upward. Then the humming grew stronger and words whispered and rustled, chattering with the wind, pulsing with the throb of the world, with Calantha's heart, the seeds rising, rising in song and delight, dancing upward into the sky.

Joy flooded Calantha.

"Now watch." The Sower's voice was harsh, ripping at the gladness. "They should spread out and scatter, so they can fall during the night onto the Plains. Everywhere."

Aelthea gripped Calantha's hand until it hurt.

The cloud of seeds drifted higher still and began to spread. Then suddenly, the movement changed. The dancing jerked and twitched, as though the seeds were being forced to follow another tune. The seeds weren't spreading anymore—something was wrong. Calantha sensed it like a foul smell, a bitter taste in her mouth. A scream in the song.

The mist of seeds came jagging together, jerking, as though fighting a tunnel of wind. They began to twist in a vortex, screaming for release. But slowly, inexorably, the tunnel of wind took them—toward the northern mountains. To King Ulric's lands.

Calantha's mouth felt like ash.

Musidora was weeping. "The last of them, oh, the last."

Grelder patted her awkwardly. "Not the last. We covered some. We still have those seeds."

The Sower of Tales sat still, her face stricken.

At last, Calantha managed to speak. "Odhran is taking the seeds."

"Yes," said the Sower of Tales. "It has been carefully planned. They will grow story pods for their own use. When despair fills the Plainsfolk, King Ulric will take the Plains."

Aelthea said softly, "Even if the Plainsfolk try to fight, they'll be weakened without the pods. The

King knows he will easily win."

Calantha gazed dully at them. Life without the story pods? No tales to sustain them? And the very Essence of life twisted, drained of hope. She began to rock back and forth.

Beside her, the Sower of Tales shivered slightly.

Musidora swiftly wiped her face and put her arm around the Sower of Tales. "Come," she said, fiercely. "You must rest. You're all worn out."

In the looming dark, they headed silently back down the path. As though from a great distance, Calantha noticed the first evening stars beginning to glimmer in the deep blue sky. The beauty stabbed and stabbed at her heart. How could there be any beauty in the world after what she'd just seen? Her head felt bruised.

As the Sower entered her hut, Aelthea pulled Calantha toward the one next door. "The Sower of Tales must rest now. Come, you can help me prepare the evening meal."

CHAPTER SIXTEEN

I nside the hut, Aelthea slowly coaxed the fire to life and lit the lorsha torches on the wall. She put her arm around Calantha, who stood staring blindly at the fire.

"I know," whispered Aelthea. She held Calantha close for a moment. "Come, now. Help me cut arrac for the stew."

Her head in a storm, Calantha followed Aelthea to the table in the corner and sliced the white arrac root and red leaves, barely aware of what she was doing, then chopped some herbs, while Aelthea added them to the pot along with some beans and other vegetables. As the stew began to simmer, the mellow smell of arrac eased through the fog encasing Calantha. Dully, she became aware of her chest aching. Her mother's stew smelled just the same.

Aelthea touched Calantha's back gently. "Go and rest, child; you're all worn out." She pointed to the bed in the corner.

Calantha lay down, her body rigid. She'd never sleep, never. As though from a great distance, she heard Aelthea humming as she sat rocking by the fire. Dimly, she recognized the tune—it was the moon song that Kasmira used to sing to calm her when she was little. Slowly, her eyes drooped...

Someone was shaking her gently. Calantha woke with a start.

Aelthea smiled and smoothed Calantha's hair. "Come now, wash. It's time to take the stew to the Sower's hut."

At the basin in the corner, Calantha washed, repeatedly splashing cold water over her face. Dread still pounded through her, but thank goodness her head wasn't as numb as before; that awful gray fog was subsiding. Surely, surely the Sower would know how to stop Odhran; she was the one who sowed the tales. She knew how the wind was harnessed.

Calantha followed Aelthea, who carried the stew

pot wrapped in layers of cloth, to the Sower's hut.

Inside, the Sower of Tales sat at the table near a cheerful fire. She, too, looked more rested. Grelder fed wood to the fire, coaxing it higher, while Musidora bustled about setting the table, bringing lorshcakes and some butter.

The Sower of Tales smiled warmly. "Calantha, come. We'll eat first and talk after. I know you have many questions, but," she grimaced slightly, "we won't foul our food with dark matters."

Calantha thought she'd never be able to choke down the food, but surprisingly, she ate well, even mopping the bean-and-arrac stew with the last of her lorshcake. Despite herself, the peace of the hut, the gentle humming that pervaded the air, worked its way through her, lightening and heartening her. Grelder ate silently, glancing at Calantha every now and again, while Musidora chattered on about the sharo thatch she must make to mend the roof of the Sower's hut.

Calantha looked up. "Sharo thatch?"

"Yes." Musidora made a face. "It's my task, but oh, I'm such a poor hand at it."

"My mother's been trying to teach me how to make sharo thatch," blurted Calantha.

"Ah, yes, Luvena," said the Sower of Tales, her eyes gently amused. "She's most, er, dutiful, isn't she?"

Calantha stared at her. How did she know? Oh, wasn't *dutiful* just the right word for her mother! A crack of laughter escaped her.

Musidora chuckled, her eyes twinkling. "So, have you learned, Calantha?"

Calantha grinned widely. "Not very well."

"Yes," said the Sower of Tales. "You can put your mind to anything, can't you, my Calantha? Even *not* learning sharo thatch."

Calantha's mouth dropped open slightly. How did the Sower know? Then they were all laughing, laughing.

At last, Calantha wiped her eyes and turned to Musidora. "I tell you what; I'll learn properly. And then I'll come back and help you make sharo thatch."

Musidora nodded, but her smile slowly faded and the air grew tight again. Silently, Aelthea and

Grelder cleared the dishes, then moved the table against the wall. The Sower of Tales pulled Calantha along to sit by the fire.

The others soon joined them, but for a while no one spoke. Calantha sat still, her eyes fixed on the leaping flames, her hands clenched in her lap, but only seeing the seeds streaming to the north.

The Sower of Tales sighed faintly. "You saw what's happening to the seeds."

Calantha drew in a ragged breath. The thoughts burning in her mind ever since she'd seen what had happened to the seeds burst from her mouth. "Sower of Tales, you know how the wind is harnessed. The seeds are yours. Can't you stop it?"

The Sower's face seemed to turn gray.

Grelder broke the silence, his voice scouring like rough bark. "Break the circle at your peril."

Calantha turned to him. A spark of anger lit inside her then arced into full flame. "Yes, you keep saying that. But it's just a children's game—what does it have to do with the seeds?"

Grelder recoiled slightly.

"It may be only a game now, Calantha," said

Aelthea quietly. "But the meaning goes back to the start of the story pods. The Plainsfolk understood, then, that you break the circle at your peril."

Musidora's voice was unexpectedly ragged. "Think on it, child. The circle is about how the seeds flow. And it's why Odhran has been able to do this now...."

"Aye," muttered Grelder, but in a softer tone. "Because they weakened the circle."

"*Who* weakened the circle?" Calantha turned to the Sower of Tales, foreboding building inside her. "I don't understand."

The Sower's hands were still in her lap. "My child, think on how old I am—and only the third Sower of Tales after all this time."

Calantha jerked out, "I did wonder. But I thought it must be something the first Sower learned at the Place of Knotting and then passed on."

The Sower of Tales shook her head. "There isn't enough skill to tap those Essences of life for so long."

Dimly, Calantha began to see. "The circle?" she whispered.

"Yes," said the Sower of Tales.

"Give and take," muttered Grelder.

"Sowing and reaping," said Musidora.

Calantha stared at the Sower of Tales. "Is it something to do with what we give you?"

The Sower of Tales smiled faintly. "It was the simplest way. The Plainsfolk wanted the tales. Needed them. In return, to keep it flowing…"

Grelder began to sing in his cracked old voice,

I send Tales, my people, to give you heart
I send Tales, my people, to strengthen your will
But who will stoke my spirit?
Who will nourish my skill?

"The lament of the Sower of Tales," said Aelthea softly. "The song is forgotten now."

Musidora nodded, her eyes very bright. "At Talemeet, the Gatherer would sing it, and all the people chorus the response." She began to sing in a low, sweet voice, and Aelthea and Grelder joined in,

"We will stoke your spirit, O Sower
Our hearts will seed your skill

Send us tales, O Sower
And we shall quicken your will."

As the soft strains of the lament faded, a spark crackled in the fire.

Calantha's eyes pricked. "So that's why the seeds change color at Talemeet, after we hear the tales. They...they bring you strength from us."

Aelthea nodded and Grelder looked at her with grudging approval.

Calantha said wonderingly, "That's how you knew about me. And Xenyss. About all of us. Because the seeds also bring you...news of us." Her breath caught in her throat.

The Sower of Tales sat still.

Calantha murmured almost to herself, "Kasmira said that long ago, all villagers gathered for Talemeet. They honored the tales." She looked up. "That stillness. The...the togetherness, we don't hold it long enough, do we? We don't mull the tales, we don't..." Her mouth shook.

"You have become complacent about the tales," said Grelder.

"Odhran noticed that the circle was weakening," said Aelthea softly. "He watched and waited. He diverted the wind at its weakest point and twisted the circle."

Calantha's head began to pound. "Is Odhran also stealing the spent seeds from the Plains? From all the story pods that open in the Plains?" Her voice dropped to a whisper, "The seeds that should return to you?"

"Yes," said the Sower of Tales. "He is taking those too."

Calantha said dazedly, "So that's why you don't know what's happened in the Plains since the seeds stopped. And..." Terror speared through her.

"Yes," said the Sower of Tales. "Without the seeds from the Plains, I don't have the strength to stop him." She paused. "And because Odhran has learned to drain the Essence from the Plains seeds, he is growing stronger."

Calantha felt cold fingers crushing her heart. She forced out the words, "What...what will happen? To you? To the story pods?"

Silence. Silence.

The Sower of Tales sat back. "Change is part of life, Calantha. Everything that has a beginning must also end."

Calantha's face twisted. No more story pods? No more story pods? And the Sower of Tales...

She felt Musidora's hands on her shoulder, and Aelthea stroking her back; heard even Grelder murmuring sympathetically.

The Sower of Tales leaned forward and took Calantha's hands in both of hers. "Calantha, the danger is far greater than the loss of the story pods. Or even my death."

The look in the her eyes chilled Calantha to the bone.

The Sower of Tales continued unflinchingly, "Calantha, the seeds I scatter hold the Essence of the tales—the power of the Sower of Tales to create worlds. It is the oldest, most powerful Essence of all. The first Essence of creation itself. Odhran does not yet have the skill to drain my seeds, even if he has drained the seeds from the Plains. He cannot drain my seeds while I, the Sower, still have some small strength left. But without the Plains seeds

I will grow weaker."

With all her being, Calantha wished she didn't have to hear any more.

The Sower of Tales continued, "In time, Odhran will be able to drain the power of my seeds. Calantha…" For the first time, the Sower's voice faltered, "Calantha, if he succeeds in draining my seeds, he will be powerful beyond stopping. He will seize the Plains, seize King Ulric's kingdom. The circle will be destroyed past mending, and the story pods will be no more. Odhran will be master of all, and the world he will create will be one of horror. To serve him and him alone."

Calantha gazed at her as though through a black mist. She dropped her face into her hands, shaking uncontrollably.

The Sower's voice cut through the maelstrom in her head. "Calantha, there is hope. There is still hope. You must believe it."

Calantha looked up, her face stricken. "What hope is there?" She felt as though her body had shattered apart.

The Sower said gently, "Why do you think

Odhran has expended so much effort to try to stop anyone from finding me? Why do you think he's been trying to discover who you are?"

Calantha stared at her. "I don't understand..."

The Sower of Tales leaned forward and gripped Calantha's arm. "My child, think on it. He has been draining the seeds from the Plains. He must have sensed your strength and skill, enough to direct his divinations toward you—enough to fear that you were the one most likely to find me and thwart his plans."

"Is that how he knew about me?" gasped Calantha. "Every time I opened a story pod I gave myself away?" Her eyes widened. "Phelan and I shared a tale. Does he know about him, too?"

The Sower of Tales shook her head. "No. Odhran is much too new at reading the Plains seeds—he's unlikely to have gleaned many particulars at first. But he would not have directed his divinations toward finding you if he didn't believe that you posed a real threat to his schemes."

The roaring in Calantha's head grew. "But what can I do?"

The Sower of Tales said firmly, "You have already

done much, Calantha. You found me."

Grelder said, trying to speak gently, "If only we had more time…"

The Sower of Tales shook her head impatiently. "What is done is done. But Calantha, Odhran has not yet managed to drain my seeds. And you are here. That is where our hope lies."

CHAPTER SEVENTEEN

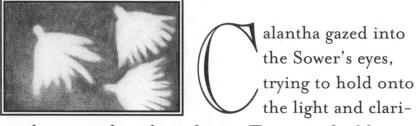

Calantha gazed into the Sower's eyes, trying to hold onto the light and clarity, the strength and steadiness. Trying to find hope. The Sower of Tales reached out and took Calantha's hands between her own. Slowly, warmth began to flow through Calantha.

Aelthea stood up, touched Calantha's shoulder as though to give her heart, and silently brought five mugs to the fire. She crumbled a reddish herb into each of them before pouring in boiling water from the kettle. "Drink this," said Aelthea firmly. "Every bit."

Wrapping her hands around the mug, Calantha tried the scalding hot brew. Loosethorn tea. The same as Theora had made for her. Slowly, as she sipped the tea, the fog of fear in her head began to recede. She glanced at the others—at the Sower, whose gray eyes turned every now and then toward Calantha in concern, and the apprentices, all old, but somehow filled with endurance, and united in their love of the Sower, their love of the tales. And their love of the Plainsfolk.

Calantha's eyes pricked suddenly. All the times she'd dreamed of coming here, she'd never once imagined that the Sower would need *her* help. The Sower had had no sustenance from the Plains for nearly half a moon now, and yet there was no complaint in her eyes; just courage and acceptance.

Something strong and peaceful sank deep into Calantha and settled into place. She finished her tea, then got up to put away her empty mug, along with those of the others.

Sitting down again, she turned to the Sower of Tales and said in a low voice, "Tell me what to do. Just tell me what to do. I can let the Plainsfolk know. If we fight now, take the pods growing there, we'll get your seeds back and—"

The Sower of Tales put her hand over Calantha's

clenched ones. "My child, there isn't time. Jaerlfin Castle is in the mountains behind JaerlzGate. It is difficult to take at the best of times, and now with the twisting of the Essences, it will be impossible."

Calantha moistened her lips. "Then should I take seeds from here to the Plainsfolk? We can plant them, be heartened..."

The Sower of Tales said gently, "Calantha, the only way you can help the Plainsfolk is to prevent Odhran from draining my seeds. If he succeeds in doing that, nothing and no one will stop him."

Calantha began to melt again with fear. "But how can I stop him? He...he's a Sorcerer." Despite herself, her voice cracked.

Musidora rubbed her arm. The Sower of Tales looked at her steadily. "Calantha, our one saving is that the seeds fall on all, even there on King Ulric's domain."

"How does that help us?" choked Calantha. "They don't deserve it...."

"Yes, they do," said the Sower of Tales passionately. "The tales are for all. Even Odhran. It must be that way. And strangely, it could be Odhran's downfall. Odhran does not hear the tales much, and King Ulric rarely now, but his son Roarke does, and often. He is still young enough to be ignored, yet old enough to see what his father cannot." The Sower of Tales laughed suddenly. "Roarke is greedy like his father and he hopes one day to be a seller of tales."

Calantha's head snapped up with surprise.

"The tales are for all," snorted Grelder. "They always have been."

Musidora nodded vigorously.

"But how does that help us?" repeated Calantha.

The Sower's eyes gleamed. "Calantha, the seeds bring me fragments of those who hear the tales, so I know what others do not. I know that King Ulric is so greedy to take the Plains that he is like a serpent swallowing its own tail. I know that Odhran plays that greed well—to keep Ulric's eyes fixed fiercely on the Plains and blind to the danger at his very own shoulder. The danger to his kingdom. Don't you understand? What Odhran fears above all is that his true plans will be uncovered before they are accomplished, while he can still be stopped. If he drains the Essence of my seeds, he will be too powerful to stop, but until then...Calantha, that's why Odhran tried to stop anyone from coming to me."

"But what can I do?" cried Calantha again, gripping her hands tighter.

The Sower of Tales lowered her voice. "You must go to King Ulric, and warn him that his kingdom is in danger. You must convince him of Odhran's true plans so he can stop Odhran; you must convince the King to release my seeds before Odhran learns how to drain their power."

Calantha's stomach twisted sickeningly. Go there? Toward those eyes? She said through numb lips, "Why would King Ulric listen to me? Why would he believe me? I'm just a—"

The Sower of Tales said quickly, "Calantha, remember, the seeds bring me news of my listeners. I can tell you something of King Ulric that few know. It may convince him that you speak the truth, that you do indeed come from the Sower of Tales."

Calantha stared at her.

"Listen," said the Sower of Tales. "When Ulric was small, he had many nightmares. To comfort him, his nursemaid made a toy lion. He called the lion Sighurd, and each night Ulric told Sighurd the tales he'd heard from the story pods. The seeds brought me his eagerness to share them with Sighurd. But when his father, King Kendrick, found Ulric taking Sighurd to bed, he was enraged at such weakness in his son. He had Sighurd destroyed." The Sower of Tales drew in a quick breath. "Ulric did not listen to the tales much after that, but whenever he did, I felt his keen hurt and sorrow." The Sower of Tales looked deep into Calantha's eyes. "If you tell him that the Sower of Tales sends a tale for Sighurd, he may be jolted long enough to listen."

Calantha's heart sank. She was supposed to convince King Ulric by mentioning a toy from his childhood?

The Sower of Tales said softly, as though she heard Calantha's thoughts. "He loved that toy, Calantha. Never underestimate the power of love to cut through greed and anger. It is the most powerful tool."

Calantha longed to believe it—that King Ulric's

old bond with a probably forgotten toy might open him up to listening to her. She drew in a painful breath. "Tomorrow. It's the last day.... How long before Odhran can...tap your seeds?"

"I don't know," said the Sower of Tales. "My strength fades each day. We have a few seeds that we've saved and planted, and we will continue to harvest those story pods and use their Essence. But without the Plains seeds I will weaken further, and as that happens, the veil that separates us from your time will also weaken; then Odhran's men may be able to enter and finish their work. When I die, Odhran will easily drain my seeds. Calantha, there is not much time."

Calantha tried to quash the pain and fear roiling inside her.

The Sower of Tales said, "It is dangerous, Calantha, I won't lie to you. Odhran grows stronger each day from the Plains seeds. The Seers and Sorcerer Theora may have been able to mask your identity from him so far, but he will soon be able to see who you are. For all we know, King Ulric may already be in his grasp—I cannot tell, he is so consumed with greed and rage. It's a faint chance, I know, but it's our only one. We must stop Odhran from draining the power of my seeds."

"You are our one hope, child," said Musidora. "We can no longer go forth into your world; we are too old. We would die instantly."

Calantha looked up. "The circle?" Her voice choked. "Will it ever be whole again?"

The Sower of Tales hesitated, then said, "If my seeds are released, the story pods will start to grow again in the Plains. Your Seers and Sorcerers will eventually undo the knots Odhran has tied in the wind. I don't know how long that will take, but when they do, the seeds from the Plains will start to come back to me, and in time, the circle may mend. But if Odhran drains my seeds…Calantha, he must be stopped, he must. For the sake of all the Plainsfolk."

Calantha gripped her hands together until her knuckles gleamed.

The Sower of Tales closed her eyes as though to gather her strength, then leaned forward and took Calantha's hands in both of hers. They were now warm, tingling with a familiar humming. "Calantha, there is one other thing that you must do if you cannot release the seeds."

Calantha shrank back.

The Sower's grip on Calantha's hands tightened and her eyes blazed. "It's the one way of ensuring that Odhran will never drain my seeds. Calantha, if you cannot release my seeds, then you must destroy them. *Burn them*."

Calantha snatched her hands away and covered her mouth. Musidora gasped and Grelder's face twisted with grief. Aelthea wept softly.

"You must!" The Sower's voice was fierce. "We will die, yes, and the circle will be past mending, but it will stop Odhran. At least then the Plainsfolk will have some chance. In time they will learn to overcome the despair, and regain their freedom. But if Odhran drains my seeds, nothing will stop him. Even if the Sorcerers at the Place of Knotting can be persuaded to interfere with our world, they will be unable to help."

Tears seeped down Calantha's face. She pressed her hands against her mouth, but couldn't hold back the anguished sobs.

"Promise me!" said the Sower of Tales. "Promise me."

Calantha felt something inside her shrivel and die, but somehow, she managed to nod.

Musidora, her own face wet, handed Calantha a handkerchief. Calantha wiped her face, blew her nose. Only the Sower's eyes were dry, her face sad but serene.

Softly, she said, "It is much to ask of you, I know. And too much to take in. Calantha, I wish I could have taken more time before burdening you with this, but time is running out. You must leave tomorrow. The sooner the better."

With every fiber of her being, Calantha wished that she could wake up from this nightmare, be in bed beside Freya, have nothing worse to deal with than her mother's scolds, Freya's scorn—even the dreaded sharo leaves, the offering of service, and Julissa. Oh, if only she could go back to being that careless, bumbling girl in the Plains.

She gazed into the fire, seeing an earlier time— one of cruelty and pain, the Plains under a vicious regime, the will and soul of the people snapped.

And no story pods to comfort and hearten them, no story pods to unite them in delight. No hope. Fear the only way of life.

"I'll go. I'll do it. I'll stop him somehow." Her voice sounded harsh, strange to her own ears.

Aelthea's hand came down comfortingly on Calantha's back.

The Sower of Tales said, "Never despair, Calantha, no matter what happens. Within each tale are all the seeds. And within each seed are all the tales. If only one seed survives, then maybe in time..."

Calantha nodded, clenching her jaw. She was not going to cry again.

The Sower's voice rose slightly. "And remember, Calantha, that even if the circle is not restored, the tales will always be—"

"The circle *will* be restored," said Calantha fiercely. "The story pods will return. They must."

The Sower of Tales smiled faintly and sank back in her chair. For a while they all sat in silence. Then Musidora got up and whispered something in the Sower's ear. The Sower of Tales nodded.

Musidora smiled as she brought a ripe story pod, a deep blue one, to the Sower of Tales. At the mere sight of it, a tiny spark of hope fluttered in Calantha's heart. The ache inside her began to ease.

"We all have need of this," said the Sower of Tales.

As the Sower took the story pod in her hands, Calantha sensed a collective sigh and the seamless coming-together of a Talemeet. The story pod glowed within the hands of the Sower—she needed no words to open it—and slowly, slowly, the petals curled back and the milky blue-white seeds rose, circling their heads.

The tale! Calantha listened with all her heart to the tale of a carpenter who searched despite all odds for the magic wood needed to make a wand to vanquish an evil wizard.

When it ended, they sat in deep silence, savoring the tale, while the seeds circled above their heads.

Then Musidora asked, "Does anyone have a tale to tell?"

Aelthea sighed. "I think we're all done in."

The seeds continued to circle above them, drawing in color—fainter than in the Plains, Calantha saw—then flowed over to the Sower of Tales, hovering above her head. Something like light streamed into her from the seeds through the top of her head. Her face began to glow faintly and then her whole body. When at last the color of the seeds had drained to a soft blue-white, the seeds drifted down to the Sower's lap. She seemed less tired.

Calantha started. From her pouch, she took out the cloth containing the two broken story pods and handed it to the Sower of Tales. "They opened of their own accord, they didn't circle us…"

Musidora said excitedly, "No matter; they still bring some strength."

The Sower's eyes shone as she untied the cloth. The seeds, paler shades of colors than those from a Talemeet, flew upward, circling her.

"Come," said the Sower of Tales. "We will share this."

Grelder shook his head.

"No," said Aelthea. "You must stay strong."

"For the good of all," said Musidora fiercely.

The Sower of Tales sighed and nodded. Once

again, the Essence of the seeds streamed down into her, and when the seeds were blue-white once more, they drifted into her lap with the others. She gathered them all into a red-green arrac sack.

"So little sustenance," murmured Aelthea.

Musidora asked eagerly, "What do you see?"

"Unrest," said the Sower of Tales. "Fear and turmoil. The dissolution continues. But at least we can plant these tomorrow." Her smile flashed.

Aelthea said, "You must rest now. Let the seeds do their work."

The others stood to leave while Musidora hovered around the hut, tidying up.

"Come," said Aelthea to Calantha. "You'll stay with me."

"Sleep well, Calantha," said the Sower of Tales. Her eyes suddenly filled with amusement. "Don't dream of witches."

Grelder snorted with laughter.

"Hush now," clucked Musidora at the Sower of Tales. "Save your strength."

Outside, the night sky sang with stars. Calantha drew in deep gulps of the dark chill air, wishing it was courage she was gulping in.

Grelder sidled up to her. "We'll take care of her," he said gruffly. "Make sure she keeps going as long as possible."

Calantha nodded. She said in a hard, bright voice, "I'll stop him. I will. I'll release the seeds. I'll bring back the story pods for all." She thrust the other promise she'd made to the Sower of Tales into a deep, dark hole in her mind.

Grelder said nothing, but his eyes held a hint of grudging admiration. And pity.

Chapter Eighteen

Calantha slept in Aelthea's hut on a low cot by the fire. For a while, she went over the tales as always; then, as the flames died and the embers glowed, her mind turned reluctantly to what lay ahead. When she'd left Theora's, she'd believed that her only task was to find Sower of Tales—but now it seemed that the hardest part was yet to come. She must go north, to JaerlzGate, to Odhran. She wrenched her mind away from the thought of those icy eyes and sank into the tales again. She must hold them, hold them as long as she could.

It was early, the light barely whispering in the sky when she stirred.

Aelthea was already up. "Quick, wash and eat.

There is something you must see." She smiled warmly but wouldn't say anything more.

Calantha splashed hurriedly in the basin of chilly water and ate the coarse lorsha porridge Aelthea had made. The sky was lighter now, dawn scenting the sky. Her ankle felt much better, but Aelthea insisted on applying fresh salve and re-tying the bandage firmly.

"You'll need it for your journey," she said. "Now come. You're about to see something that few people have seen. It will fill you with heart." Aelthea's face shone as she opened the door.

Wonderingly, Calantha followed her outside. It was chilly but fresh. Peaceful. There was no sign of the heartache and dangers that lay below in the Plains. The dewy pink sky was clear and full of hope.

Despite everything, Calantha's heart lifted. At least for now she was still here, in the domain of the Sower of Tales, with the familiar humming pulsing through the air. She drew in a long, crisp breath. She would just *be* here while she could. She wouldn't think of anything else. Not yet.

She followed Aelthea down the lane into the field

with the patchwork of story pods at different heights. Aelthea's steps quickened as she walked past the story pods, deep into the far end of the field, which was bare.

The Sower of Tales, Musidora, and Grelder were already there, at the edge of a large plot of freshly furrowed soil. The Sower of Tales smiled at Calantha, her face bright and joyful.

She took a red-green arrac sack from Grelder and slung it across her shoulders, then began to walk along a furrow, her apprentices following in a ragged line, each touching the one ahead.

Delight shivered and coursed through Calantha.

The Sower of Tales dipped her hand into her sack and, bending over, began to sow the seeds, murmuring words as she sowed, with the apprentices also murmuring softly behind her, their faces glowing with joy. Something faint that was almost light streamed from the Sower's hand into the seeds. On they went, the Sower's hand never faltering, swooping in smooth arcs to scatter the seeds, the lips moving, the Essence of the tales streaming from her hand into the seeds. Calantha couldn't make out the words, but she sensed them flowing like a river, a song, a blessing. A promise. Her heart filled and filled until she thought it would burst.

It wasn't long before they finished. The Sower of Tales stood still in the peaceful morning light. She looked drained but happy, her eyes clear and serene. Musidora and Aelthea seemed uplifted too, and even Grelder seemed lightened, the lines on his face eased.

As they turned to came back to Calantha, it suddenly dawned on her that this morning's sowing must be just a small, small part of what they would normally do. When the seeds from the Plains came here, they must have sown entire fields.

The Sower of Tales smiled. "Calantha. Are you ready?"

Calantha drew in a deep breath and nodded.

Silently, the Sower of Tales led the way out of the field, onto the lane, then downward to the lone sharo tree.

Calantha glanced back at the huts with the worn sharo thatch, and the cluster of ruined huts behind, trying to hold the image in her heart. She knew without asking that there had once been many more apprentices.

She blinked hard, then lifted her chin. "Remember, Musidora, when I come back, I'll help you make new sharo thatch for your huts."

Musidora smiled quickly and nodded. But she didn't meet Calantha's eyes.

As they reached the sharo tree, the Sower of Tales turned to Calantha. "Aelthea will take you partway down the mountain. There is a tunnel that will bring you close to the bottom. Few know of it. But first, Calantha, as in all the tales, I have three gifts for you."

Her eyes twinkled as she beckoned to Musidora, who handed Calantha the pouch that she had left last night in the Sower's hut. Looking inside, Calantha saw Xenyss' knife, a water bottle, and two bundles.

"Food to sustain your body," said the Sower of Tales, "and story pods to sustain your heart."

Calantha's hand warmed at the familiar humming.

"And the third gift." The Sower of Tales gently touched Calantha's cheek. "The third gift, my

Calantha, you already have."

Calantha blinked, puzzled.

The Sower's voice rang with elation. "It is in your heart, Calantha, remember that. And what is in your heart, no one can take away. You will always have the tales to sustain you, no matter what." The Sower of Tales paused, then said, "Use this gift well, Calantha. It can be your strength *and* your weakness."

Calantha stared at her. What could she mean? How could the tales ever be her weakness?

The Sower of Tales put her hand over Calantha's heart and a sudden burst of heat and well-being flooded Calantha. "And remember, as long as the tales are with you, so a part of me will always be there, too."

Calantha's throat tightened painfully as she nodded. The Sower of Tales looked deep into Calantha's eyes. "Listen. Within each tale is every seed. And within each seed are all the tales. As long as even one seed survives, the story pods may live again. And as long as you hold the tales—"

Calantha burst out, "I'll succeed. I will. And I'll

come back." She tried to still the shaking of her lips. "I'll come back and be your apprentice. I pro—"

The Sower of Tale put her fingers over Calantha's mouth. "Don't make that promise, Calantha. Not now. If you come, I'll welcome you; but there may be reasons why you cannot return."

Calantha's eyes flickered. If she failed...?

The Sower of Tales shook her head. "No. Not that. You are fully worthy of this task. Believe it. But there may be other reasons." Her eyes bored into Calantha's as though trying to convey something.

Calantha wanted to insist that nothing would prevent her from coming back, but something made her stop.

The Sower of Tales wrapped her in a long, warm embrace. "May the strength of the tales go with you. And my blessings. I will always keep a thread of mind tied to you."

"Aye, and I will, too," said Musidora, hugging her.

Grelder smiled a surprisingly sweet, gap-toothed smile, and awkwardly patted her back. "And I," he said.

The Sower of Tales smiled once more, like a sunflash, her eyes flooding with light. Then she turned and walked away with Musidora and Grelder, her robes fluttering with each step.

Calantha watched and watched, her heart following the Sower of Tales until she was gone from sight. She dashed her hand across her eyes.

"Come, Calantha," said Aelthea.

Calantha drew in a deep breath and followed Aelthea to the sharo tree. Aelthea ducked under the low branches and strode to the side where Calantha had come up, then scrambled down onto a ledge.

Calantha started. There was an opening in the rock face. It hadn't been there when she'd come up, she was certain.

"It is still in our space," said Aelthea briefly. "When you reach the other end, you'll be back there again. And you must be careful."

Taking Calantha's hand, she led the way into the darkness of the cave.

"Steps," she whispered, her voice echoing softly.

They were soon engulfed in absolute darkness. Calantha kept one hand on the side of the rock wall, the other on Aelthea's shoulder. It was silent except for the sound of their breathing and their footsteps tapping downward.

Was the darkness less impenetrable, or was her mind playing tricks? No, there was gray ahead. Then, a few more steps around a curve, she saw light.

Aelthea stopped. "This is as far as I can go, Calantha." She touched her face gently, then engulfed her in a long hug.

Calantha clung to her. Aelthea smelled fresh and grassy, of the story pods, just like Kasmira.

"Remember me to Kasmira," breathed Aelthea. "And may the tales always sustain you." One last grip, then Aelthea was gone, her footsteps tapping upward, fading, fading.

Calantha fought the urge to run after Aelthea. When she could no longer hear her footsteps, she drew in a shaky breath and, squinting, moved out of the cave into the morning light.

PART FOUR

THE SEEDS OF HOPE

If you snatch their stories you snatch their souls.

Sorcerer Odhran

Greed feeds on itself like a serpent swallowing its tail.

The Sower of Tales

CHAPTER NINETEEN

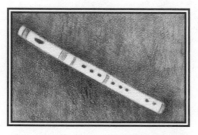

Immediately, Calantha felt the difference in the air. No humming, arcing, or singing, as in the domain of the Sower of Tales, but ordinary air. No, worse. It was like being wrenched, thrown into discord; the air reeked with distress. The skewing of the Essences had worsened.

Calantha twisted her shoulders to shake off the discomfort and looked around. No one in sight. She was on the eastern side of the mountain, perhaps halfway down, surrounded by rocks, scrubby heather and wind-bent trees, all bathed in golden morning sunshine.

She began to climb down. There was no path to follow, so she clung to branches, rocks, and tufts of coarse sneel grass. After a while she glimpsed a faint trail over to her left and made her way toward it. She wasn't sure if it was the same path that she'd taken up the mountain; it was steep, and her knees and toes ached from the incline going down, but it was easier than fighting through the brush. Luckily Aelthea's bandage supported her ankle so well that it hardly hurt at all.

She stopped suddenly and looked around. She'd felt something stirring.

Not a sound.

She waited for a moment, trying to catch her breath, then shook her head and continued down, trying to make as little noise as possible. But as she approached a large clump of twisted shrubs, she heard a faint whicker.

A horse. Odhran's men! Calantha crouched behind the bushes, her legs limp. She must turn back, find another way!

Looking around frantically, she spotted a large rocky crag to her left. From there she might be able to see where they were. And how many of them.

Slowly, carefully, she edged over to the rock. Gripping tightly with her fingers and toes, she climbed up onto the crag. She lay panting on the top, then pulled herself to the edge to peer down.

A brown horse! One of the horses ridden by the two men who'd followed her and Phelan the day before yesterday; she was almost certain.

Then she saw the man, his head wound in a cloth.

She dropped down, head flat against the rock. Was it Flenart? If it was, she'd have no chance of talking her way through.

Hardly daring to breathe, she peered again at the figure below. The head-covering was oddly tied. Was it arrac cloth? If only she could stop her panic and sense that figure; all she could catch were traces of worry. Waiting and watching.

Then the man below suddenly turned his head. She darted back, but not before she'd caught a glimpse of hair escaping the cloth. It took a few seconds to register—red hair. Eagerly, she peered over again. Yes. Red. The figure clicked softly to the horse and began to move.

Calantha scrambled to her feet, rushing down the side of the rock, not caring how much noise she made.

He crouched low, facing her, stick uplifted.

"Don't, don't, Phelan, it's me. *Me*."

Phelan's face broke into a joyful smile. He flung
down the stick and rushed forward, hugging her.

Calantha half-laughed, half-sobbed, "You got
away. Oh, thank goodness, you're safe."

Phelan put his hand over her mouth. "Shh," he
whispered. As the arrac cloth around his head partly
slipped off, Calantha saw the cuts and bruises on his
face. And the swelling above his left eye.

Quietly, Phelan led the horse down the path,
stopping under a rocky overhang. It was where she'd
stopped for the night on the way up; from here they
could see down the mountain. No one in sight.

Phelan turned eagerly to her, his voice low. "Did
you find her?"

"I thought they'd kill you," whispered Calantha.
"How did you get away, and with their horse?"

Phelan shook his head impatiently. "They set
upon me near Branwhip, but luckily some
Defenseroffes came by. One of Odhran's men got
away but the Plainsfolk caught the other. There's talk
of fighting, Calantha. The Plainsfolk were headed

for Maernlea because the Seers have been spreading the word that Ulric and Odhran are behind the disappearance of the story pods." Phelan looked strangely at her. "And they said a village was attacked. They wanted me to join them, but I took this horse and stayed the night in Branwhip, then came here to wait for you. Did you find her?"

"A village attacked?" Calantha gaped at him. "Which one?"

Phelan reached out and shook her. "Did you find her?"

Calantha nodded. "Yes, and it's worse," her breath caught. "Much worse than you can imagine." Quickly, she told him everything, repeating things as he questioned her.

His mouth was grim when she finished. "All right. We'll go north."

Relief gushed through her. She wouldn't have to face the journey alone. She said shakily, "My thanks, Phelan, for coming for me."

He flushed, but said gruffly, "Thought you might need help. Anyway, it's for the story pods. Couldn't just leave it to *you* now, could I?"

Calantha grinned, then sobered. "You said a village was attacked. Which one?"

Phelan didn't meet her eyes. "Shernthrip. Burnt down, the men said."

"Shernthrip?" Calantha's voice cracked. "When? I was just there."

"Two days ago," said Phelan grimly. "Early morning, they said. Men on horseback. They torched the village, then fled back north. The Plainsfolk seemed convinced they were Ulric's men."

Calantha pressed her hand against her mouth. The morning after she'd left with Kelwin. Odhran must have seen where she was. "They wanted to get me," she whispered in anguish. "Did...did you hear what happened to Sorcerer Theora? And the Gatherer?"

"The Sorcerer escaped." Phelan's voice faltered, "But they said the Gatherer died in the fire. And many others."

Osric. No more. What about Merlewinn? Calantha's eyes stung and stung. "Onawa must have known," she whispered. "Why didn't she say anything?"

"Likely to spare us," said Phelan gently. He put a steadying hand on her back. "Calantha...we should go."

Calantha wiped her eyes fiercely, and drew in a long, sharp breath. She mustn't give way to grief; there wasn't time. "All right. Which way do we take?"

"The same lane we came down, but north," said Phelan. "It's the quickest."

"But those other horsemen. Won't they...?"

"If luck holds, we'll be fine," said Phelan quirking his crooked grin. "I told the Defenseroffes in Branwhip—they said they'd start patrolling."

Calantha nodded and silently they left the overhang. As Phelan untied the horse and led it down the mountainside, Calantha followed blindly. Shernthrip burned, and Osric gone.... A taste of what life would be like with Odhran.

Something hardened inside her. The other promise she'd made to the Sower of Tales, to burn the seeds, crept out from the dark hole into which she'd thrust it.

At last, they reached the wider lane at the base of

the mountain, the one on which they'd been
stopped by Odhran's men two days before. Phelan
looked around, then swung onto the horse's back.
He reached his hand down to Calantha and pulled
her up behind him.

The horse circled nervously, then Phelan whispered, "Hold on." He dug his heels hard into the
sides of the horse and it leaped forward. Calantha
clutched him as trees, shrubs, and heather rushed by
in a blur. It was almost a relief to be moving fast,
after the painstaking walk down the mountain.
Thank goodness Phelan knew how to handle the
horse. She concentrated on holding on tightly, and
keeping a watchful eye out.

The lane was deserted, and to her relief, they met
no one except for a patrol of Defenseroffes, some of
whom had already met Phelan in Branwhip. The
patrollers briefly questioned Phelan as to whether
they'd seen anyone suspicious, then waved him and
Calantha on.

As they continued northward, the terrain grew
rougher and the vegetation sparser, but even
though they saw no one else, not even more

patrollers, Calantha sensed a growing uncertainty in the air. Tension.

At last, Phelan slowed the horse to a canter, then a trot. "Larchend," he panted. "The last village of the Plains before we get to Ulric's lands."

Peering over his shoulder, Calantha saw in the distance the blue-gray roofs of a village. Her back stiffened. The unrest in the air was almost overwhelming here. Silently, they trotted past empty fields and houses and at last onto the village green.

It was swarming with people. In one corner, near what seemed to be the smithy, a group of men were gathered, some in gray Defenseroffe's clothes, examining weapons. They looked grim and purposeful.

As Phelan and Calantha rode by, a few of them turned to stare. A large, bald Defenseroffe called out, "Where are you youngsters headed?"

Calantha tightened her grip on Phelan. Of course, they'd be suspicious of all travelers. What if they wouldn't let her and Phelan pass?

"Greetings," replied Phelan easily. "We're just headed to..." he muttered something inaudible and

pointed vaguely to the far end of the Green where
two roads diverged, one to the north, the other
northwest.

The bald man looked at them keenly, then
Calantha sensed his interest in them wane; thanks be
to the Sower of Tales, she and Phelan were too
young to be deemed suspicious.

He nodded and said tersely, "Be quick, then.
And stay clear of the north. You young folk
shouldn't even be out and around; there's trouble
brewing."

Phelan nodded and waved, keeping the horse at a
steady pace across the Green. As they neared the
roads, Calantha saw guards and barricades further
along on the northbound road.

"Flikketting lizards," she hissed, "will they let us
through?"

"Not without questions," grunted Phelan. He
half-turned and grinned. "Never mind; I'll find
another way."

Continuing at an even pace, he headed down the
northwest road and past the last of the houses. As
soon as they were out of sight, Phelan turned the

horse northward onto a track between two fields.

Calantha looked around nervously as they criss-crossed a succession of fields, but luckily no one saw them. At last they reached the northbound road—well out of sight of the village and the barricades. As Phelan swung the horse onto the road, Calantha heaved a sigh of relief. They were really on their way now.

The land soon grew rockier, with low scrubby vegetation and windswept trees. Calantha scanned the landscape watchfully, her stomach tight with unease. There would be no Plainsfolk patrols here to help them if they encountered Odhran's men. She glanced at the northern mountains looming threateningly in the distance. The Sower's face flashed into her head. Somehow she must find a way to see King Ulric. She must.

The sun was hot overhead when at last they came upon a stream by the side of the road. Phelan pulled the horse to a stop to let it rest and drink. Calantha groaned as she dismounted. She ached in parts of her body that she hadn't known existed. Stiffly, she bent down and drank her fill. A few spent story pod stalks jutted into the air amid the coarse grass, with a couple of ripe ones swaying nearby. Eagerly, she began to reach for a ripe pod, then stopped. There wasn't time.

Phelan looked at her and grimaced slightly. "The last day," he said.

Calantha's eyes flashed. "It won't be the last. Don't you say that!"

Phelan turned red. He started to say something, then stopped, his mouth tight.

Calantha splashed cold water onto her face, then turned to Phelan. "I'm sorry," she said. "It's just—"

"I know," said Phelan. "We're getting closer to Ulric's kingdom; there'll be more of his men about. We'll need to make some plans."

Calantha shrugged defiantly. "Well, it doesn't much matter if we're captured, does it? After all, we want to go to Jaerlfin."

A gleam of approval shone in Phelan's eyes. "I hadn't thought of that. I thought we'd have to fight...." He flushed and shook his head sheepishly.

Calantha grinned. "Actually, it might be best to just let them take us." Her face sobered. "Phelan, if anything happens to me, you must go on and tell—"

"Nothing's going to happen to you," he said harshly.

"We don't have time to pretend," snapped Calantha. "Odhran sent men to Shernthrip after me. If he knows I've been to the Sower of Tales, he may have instructed his men to kill me." She faced him squarely. "If that happens, then you must go on. You must tell King Ulric, and convince him of the truth." Her eyes blazed, and somehow, she forced out the words, "And if you can't, then Phelan, you must burn the seeds."

He stared at her, his face losing all color. Then he nodded abruptly. "Come on, let's get going."

It became eerily quiet as they rode further into the desolate mountain terrain.

Calantha whispered, "Where does King Ulric's land start?"

"I don't know," said Phelan over his shoulder. "Plainsfolk keep clear of these parts. They're dangerous."

The land grew rougher and wilder; each time they rounded a blind curve, the pit in Calantha's stomach deepened. The horse plodded on, weary now. Calantha couldn't help looking at times for new story pods, but she saw none.

They saw the men at a distance, along a straight stretch of the road. A large group of men. Even from here they could see the scarlet-and-gray livery. They must now be in Jaerlfin.

"This is it," said Phelan.

Calantha gripped his waist and peered over his shoulder. In the harsh glare of noon, she saw the glint of metal, and her mouth went dry.

Phelan slowed the horse to a walk and headed steadily for the men. Quickly, Calantha straightened the arrac cloth around his head—no need for the red to show.

About a dozen men stood grimly across the road. Calantha scanned their faces. Were any of them the men they'd seen the day before yesterday? None seemed familiar.

Closer they trotted, closer.

Phelan called out, "Good day. We have a message for King Ulric."

Calantha's heart raced. Unexpectedly she felt a

thread of clean blue from Xenyss, strengthening her. With all her force, she willed the men to part; just move aside. The three men in the center looked puzzled, then began to move.

Phelan trotted on toward the gap between the men. His voice was cheerful and careless. "My thanks."

Calantha fixed a smile on her face. Would it work?

They were almost past when a voice called out, "Halt!"

Calantha's heart threatened to explode. Phelan pulled the horse to a stop and half-turned it. The men quickly surrounded them.

A tall, sinewy man with cropped hair, cold, gray eyes and a face as tight as a whip, seemed to be the leader. "Who are you?" he snapped. "From whom do you bring a message?"

Calantha's mind went blank. The men were suspicious, taut.

Phelan said quickly, "From the others, along the side of the mountain. One was taken by Plainsfolk."

A few murmurs broke out. Another man—thin,

nervous, with strange shifting eyes and mottled skin—said, "We know that already. Swernlip came yesterday. He said he'd been after two young people when they were attacked by Plainsfolk. He managed to get away."

The leader's eyes narrowed, "Who are you? Don't recall seeing you ever."

Before Calantha or Phelan could speak, a stout man with flabby jowls and bulging eyes grabbed hold of the bridle. "Take that turban off," he cried.

Phelan tried to snap the bridle loose, but the men set upon them, pulling them off the horse. Someone snatched the arrac cloth off Phelan's head.

The large man with bulging eyes said triumphantly, "Red hair. Didn't Swernlip say the boy he'd been following had red hair?"

Their arms were grabbed and held tight.

The leader, the tall man with the whip-like face, said, "All right. Who are you? Where are you headed?"

Calantha's eyes darted over the harsh faces. "We're from the Plains," she said. "But we spoke the truth. We do have a message for King Ulric."

Someone, she couldn't see who, wrenched her arms. She cried out.

"From whom?" snapped the tall man.

Calantha said through gritted teeth, "My message is for King Ulric alone. It's of the utmost urgency. If you don't take us there at once, you'll be in grave trouble." She gasped with relief as the man holding her arms loosened his grip.

"We don't take orders from children," growled the leader.

The man with the mottled face turned to them. One eye seemed to be slightly off, staring in a different direction from the other.

The stout man with the flabby jowls scoffed, "What kind of people are you Plainsfolk to send children as messengers?"

Calantha said harshly, "I tell you, it's urgent. We must speak to King Ulric. Why would we come here if it wasn't important?"

Phelan added quietly, "What harm do you think we could do, anyway? We're young and unarmed."

The man with the strangely wandering eye said to the leader, "Best take them to the King. He might want to question them as to the Plainsfolk's movements."

Another man said quickly, "What if it's a trap to divert us?"

"We don't have time to stand around all day," said Calantha loudly. "Are you going to take us to the King or not?"

The leader nodded at the horse and the bag across Calantha's shoulder. "Search those," he snapped.

Calantha's heart leaped to her mouth. The knife. The story pods.

Someone went through the horse's saddle bags and found nothing but food, while another man yanked the pouch off Calantha's shoulder and turned it upside down.

The stout man with bulging eyes picked up the knife. Then he opened the bundles. An uneasy murmur arose as they saw the story pods.

The stout man looked keenly at Calantha and Phelan, then turned to the leader. "Take them to Odhran."

Calantha's heart lurched. "Our message is for King Ulric," she cried.

"The King will be displeased if you don't take us to him first," said Phelan. "Our message is for him alone."

The man with the wandering eye turned toward them curiously.

The stout man scowled at the leader. "The Sorcerer's instructions are clear. Anyone with an affinity to the story pods must go to him."

Another man licked his lips nervously. "Who would you rather displease—Odhran or the King?" Dread emanated from him like a chilly mist.

As the men eyed their leader and the stout man, Calantha felt some vital power shift; the stout man with bulging eyes now seemed to be in charge.

Looking straight at the leader, the stout man said, "The Sorcerer would be most..." he paused, "...displeased if he heard that you had disobeyed his orders, Mandreck."

The two men stared at each other.

The leader, Mandreck, turned away first, as though he'd tasted something foul. "Take them to Odhran, then. We'll stay here, keep guard." He nodded to the thin man with the mottled face and wandering eye. "Justhorn. You go along with Beswinn."

Calantha looked despairingly at Phelan. The stout man, Beswinn, prodded them to mount their horse, while others held the reins. Phelan struggled but was hit hard across the mouth. Beswinn climbed onto a gray horse on one side of them, and Justhorn a roan horse on the other, each gripping ropes tied to the reins of Phelan and Calantha's horse.

"Should we jump?" whispered Calantha.

"No," jerked back Phelan. "We'd never get away. Let's at least get to the castle..." He turned his head and tried to smile, but his body sagged.

"Quiet," shouted Beswinn. "Or I'll tie you up and sling you across the horse like baggage."

Calantha sensed an oily smugness about him—he could hardly wait to take them to Odhran. Her mind began to go numb at the thought of those eyes. She must reach the King first, she must.

A burst of blue washed over her and somehow she managed to pull her frightened thoughts together. At least they were going to Jaerlfin. They hadn't failed yet.

CHAPTER TWENTY

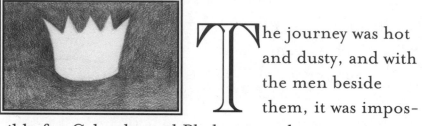

The journey was hot and dusty, and with the men beside them, it was impossible for Calantha and Phelan to exchange more than a few words. They stopped only once, to water the horses; Calantha and Phelan were given a meager trickle of water, which just left them wanting more. As the afternoon wore on and they neared the northern mountains, the terrain grew steeper and steeper.

Calantha eyed the harsh peaks closing in around them; the jagged line in Xenyss' divining square sizzled across her mind.

It was late afternoon when she saw a large settlement in the distance, the largest she'd ever seen. JaerlzGate. The town nestled at the base of a moun-

tain, and above it, like a cold gray slash, loomed a
large castle with stone walls, battlements, and tur-
rets. Jaerlfin Castle. King Ulric's seat.

The air of foreboding was overwhelming here,
like a painful tightness in the air, but under it...
Calantha frowned. The story pods? Yes, there were
story pods growing here, in or near the castle, she
was sure of it. And the seeds of the Sower of Tales,
too! Her heart raced as she raked the castle, trying to
sense where the seeds might be. The harsh stone
front gave nothing away.

On they continued, slowing to a walk as they
entered the streets of JaerlzGate. Calantha had never
seen a place so large, or such houses. They were
built of stone and brick and most of the roofs were
tiled with flinty stone, not sharo thatch. Some of the
houses were over two stories high, with large windows.

But there was little green growing here; no flowers, and only spare tufts of nervous grass. And few
people in sight. The horses hooves clicked ominously
as they rode through a large square cobbled with
stone. The only people they met scurried out of the

way, bobbing their heads, averting their eyes. No one smiled. Worry and fear—even through her own turmoil, Calantha sensed the grimness, the furtive shrinking and hiding.

Pity and horror struggled inside her. Oh, how could they live with so little joy? Was it always like this, or was the loss of the story pods starting to be felt here as well? She swallowed convulsively. If she couldn't stop Odhran, would it be like this in the Plains?

No. It would be worse.

Then they were past the town, and the road zig-zagged steeply toward the side of the castle. The front of the castle towered above sheer, brutal rock. A large balcony jutted out from the lower part of the castle, facing a rock platform some distance below, with a narrow track leading to it from the village. It was the place where the King might greet his subjects, Calantha guessed—and at a safe enough distance that troublemakers were kept outside the castle.

A group of soldiers passed them going down. A short man barked out, "Hurry. We have news that

Plainsfolk are coming this way. We prepare to fight."

Phelan stiffened, then turned his head to look at
her. She stared at him, her heart sinking. How
could the Plainsfolk fight here? The Sower of Tales
was right—JaerlzGate was impossible to take.

On they went, along the winding road up to the
castle, and at last to the moat. The drawbridge was
up, but when Beswinn called out, it jerked down. A
yawning iron gate opened beyond, like a beast's maw
preparing to devour them.

They trotted across the drawbridge, the horses',
hooves clopping on the wood, and in through the
gate. Calantha looked around frantically. The hard
gray stone of the castle was cold and unpitying; the
urgency in the air, sharp like a knife. How could
they get away from Beswinn and Justhorn and reach
the King? There were throngs of scarlet-and-gray-
clad soldiers here in the cobbled courtyard, their
weapons glinting in the sun. Phelan's face was grim,
too, as he turned this way and that.

They trotted on through the courtyard, the
hooves of the horses clicking doom, and stopped at a
large wooden door around the far side of the castle.

Beswinn and Justhorn dismounted.

Calantha's knees buckled as she was pulled off the horse. As Justhorn reached out to steady her, she suddenly wrenched away and began to run, with Phelan staggering behind her.

Beswinn roared something, and he and Justhorn caught them easily. Beswinn shook Phelan like a dog with a rat. "Where did you think you'd get to?"

Calantha gazed despairingly at Phelan as they were dragged back to the door.

"Get a rope—tie them up," roared Beswinn.

Their arms were yanked behind their backs, tied tightly, and they were led into a bare, chilly chamber with a stone floor. Calantha's eyes widened, trying to see in the gloom. A steep staircase went up along the side of a dim, gray hall. She shivered and shivered. Phelan's face was pale and frightened. He knew just as well as she did—there was nowhere to run.

Two women, dressed in drab gray and brown, scuttled by, each intent on some task. They looked at them curiously and bobbed respectfully to Beswinn, who seemed to have puffed out even more.

"Stay and watch them," he ordered Justhorn. "I'll

find the master. He'll be most pleased with me." A
smug smile flickered on his face as he started up the
stairs.

Justhorn scowled and shifted.

Calantha's mind began to melt with panic. She
must get to the King before those cold eyes got her.
Desperately, she stared at Phelan to root herself,
then wrenched her mind toward the Sower of Tales
and Xenyss. Clean blue washed over her.

The panic began to recede and a small idea dewed
in her head. She'd managed to convince Flenart and
Shraelyn to drink water and to sleep. Could
Justhorn offer a keyhole of hope? She let her mind
tiptoe toward his.

Resentment. Yes. It was strong. And restlessness,
uncertainty. Was it possible...? He'd wanted to take
them to King Ulric. If he was loyal to the King,
maybe...

She drew in a deep breath. Softly, she said to
Justhorn, "It's best that you take us to King Ulric;
he's waiting for our message. He'll be most displeased not to get it right away. After all, he is the
King. It's what Odhran would wish, too."

She stared at him and in her head sent out the strongest urging she could—*go to King Ulric, go to King Ulric.* She felt the humming of the pods and a thin blue strength from Xenyss adding to the power of her mind and her head began to throb.

Justhorn's eyes flickered. It was difficult to see where he was looking, with his left eye staring at them and his right somewhere else.

He blinked hard and turned toward the staircase. Then his mouth tightened and he muttered, "King Ulric is master here still, no matter what some may.... Come along, then." He began to lead them down a chilly gray passage.

Hardly daring to breathe, Calantha followed him. She felt Phelan staring at her—curiously at first, and then with growing elation—but she didn't dare return his glance; she kept her mind on urging Justhorn. Soon they approached another hall, much bigger than the one before, and with a curving staircase so wide it would have fit five of the previous one.

Up they went, following Justhorn. As they approached guards, Justhorn said curtly, "Important message for King Ulric, we must see him at once."

Calantha caught fleeting glimpses of wider passages, better lit with more torches, and walls covered with tapestries. At last they stopped at a huge, wooden door. A lion's head was carved in the center, mouth open in a roar, showing jagged teeth.

Justhorn spoke to the guards, who opened the doors. They entered a wide, luxurious room, bright with large windows. A guard on the inside listened to Justhorn and cried out, "King Ulric, an urgent message for you."

As Calantha let her mind drop from Justhorn, she saw him blink and shake his head, then look alarmed. Calantha had a blurred impression of several men standing at the far end of the room, around a massive table. A tall, heavyset man turned and came forward. A young boy, about ten or so, with unruly brownish-gold hair and a peevish expression, scurried alongside.

King Ulric was square and strong, with a long face, deep-set eyes, and a fleshy, pouting mouth. A small scar on his temple puckered his left eyebrow upward into an angry slant. He was richly dressed in brown and gold silk, with gold ornaments about his neck.

"What is it?" he snapped. His green eyes were cold.

Calantha's mouth went dry. She sensed a hard determination in him, a greedy, intractable stubbornness fuelled by cold, cold anger. How could she possibly reach him? He had a heart like stone.

Phelan spoke first. He said loudly, "King Ulric, she brings you a message from the Sower of Tales."

King Ulric's eyes narrowed. "What nonsense is this?" he barked.

Calantha kept her eyes on King Ulric, willing him to look at her. She had a vague sense of heads turning in their direction, and the boy's head jerking toward her.

She began to speak quickly, her voice low and earnest, "King Ulric, it is the truth. I've been to the Sower of Tales. She has a message for you. You and your kingdom are in grave danger."

The King turned to the guards and roared, "Who let this Plainsgirl into my presence? Take her away."

As the Guards came forward and seized Calantha,

some of the other men in the room, soldiers and courtiers, drew nearer.

"You must listen," shouted Calantha. "The Sower of Tales sent me with a message for you, a tale for Sighurd!"

The King, about to turn away, swung back. His eyes flickered with incomprehension and surprise, then lanced into fury.

The door behind them flew open. A thin voice said, "Here is my prisoner. What lies is she feeding you, my lord?"

A cold wave washed over Calantha.

"She's telling the truth," cried Phelan. "Listen to her."

Calantha started to scream, "Odhran is after your kingdom. He plans to drain the seeds from the Sower of Tales to gain their power. You must stop him, release the seeds. You must. Listen to me, in the name of Sighurd...."

But the King's eyes were filmed with rage. He couldn't hear her. A strong, thin hand grasped her shoulder and swung her around.

Calantha's shoulder went numb as she stared at

the white-robed figure flanked by Beswinn and others. Sorcerer Odhran. He was not much taller than she was and his face was thin, his hair scanty and weak. But she knew those pale blue, chilly eyes. They bored into hers. Cold. So cold. Calantha's face went numb, and then her mind. *She must not speak, not speak, not speak.* She tried to tear her eyes away but couldn't.

As though through a tunnel, she heard Odhran say smoothly, "This is the girl who I had divined might be troublesome to our plans, my lord."

His eyes flickered away, and the numbness receded. Calantha gasped, tried to shout, "He's lying, I tell you!" But the words came out garbled, and as the icy eyes turned to her again she felt a surge of powerful darkness. Her mind went blank. *Must not speak, nothing to say, nothing, nothing, nothing.*

From a distance, she heard Phelan shouting, "Hear her, at least. Why do you think Odhran is trying to stop—" Then his voice too was silenced.

Odhran bowed to King Ulric. "I'm sorry, my lord, that you've been subjected to this...mockery." His eyes swerved to Justhorn.

Even through her numbness, Calantha could see that Justhorn was terrified. He was perspiring heavily, licking his lips.

Odhran continued, "I specifically ordered these captives brought to me, so that you would be free to plan your campaign."

King Ulric barked out, "Then make sure your orders are followed. D'you think I have time to listen to every lunatic from the Plains?"

Odhran bowed obsequiously. "Of course, my lord."

The boy next to him asked, "Father, who is Sighurd?"

Calantha fastened her eyes on the King, pleadingly.

The King's face shuttered darkly. "Nobody. Be quiet, Roarke."

"Rest assured, my lord," said Odhran. "I shall take care of this matter—and whoever is responsible for this outrage."

Justhorn began to babble, "M-my lord, she said she had a message of import for you, that only you must hear. I meant to serve you well, I meant no..."

The Sorcerer chuckled dryly. "It shows their desperation, my lord, that the Plainsfolk think to sway you with this nonsense. The Sower of Tales indeed! Just as well I came. This girl is likely a witch. You can see the influence she cast over Justhorn."

Justhorn nodded vigorously. Calantha tried to open her mouth but couldn't.

The young boy next to King Ulric was still staring at her, his pale green eyes curious. He tugged his father's sleeve. "Did she really come from the Sower of Tales?"

"Roarke, don't interrupt your elders," snapped King Ulric.

Roarke's face hardened. It made him look just like the King.

"Go, go," shouted King Ulric. "Take them to the dungeons."

"My lord," said Odhran swiftly, "it might be useful to question them."

A look of mild distaste crossed the King's face. He waved his hand dismissively. "Very well. Do with them whatever it is you do with these creatures."

Tears of strain welled in Calantha's eyes. If only

she could speak. She stared pleadingly at King Ulric, then at the boy's dark-lashed eyes.

Roarke shrilled, "Stop looking at me like that. Make her stop!"

Odhran said sharply, "Turn your eyes away, Master Roarke. My lord, she's trying to bring your son under her snare." His eyes flickered briefly onto Roarke, who frowned slightly, then shook his head.

King Ulric thrust Roarke behind him and roared, "Stop prating, man. Take her away. What do I pay you for? And don't go far, we'll need you to divine the Plainsfolk's whereabouts for our campaign."

Odhran bowed low. "Yes, my lord." His face never wavered, but even through the numbing fog, Calantha sensed his throbbing anger. The King seemed oblivious to it. Was he so blinded by his own importance and authority that he couldn't see Odhran clearly? Perhaps the Sorcerer counted on that.

Odhran turned to leave and flicked his fingers, a sharp, hard click. "Justhorn, you come, too."

Roarke peered around the back of King Ulric, at

Calantha. She made a wild lunge but was dragged out with Phelan, surrounded by Odhran's guards. Arms still tied, they were trotted along passages that turned and wound, up and down so many flights of stairs that Calantha knew she'd never be able to retrace the way. Phelan's shoulder bumped against her as they were driven along. His eyes echoed her despair. She knew that the numbing fog that still froze her tongue held his, too. Dimly, she noticed Justhorn's hands shaking, fear radiating from him like a stench.

At last, well into a gray and dusty part of the castle, Beswinn opened an iron door and led them into a dank, bare chamber.

The door banged shut behind them. Odhran strode to the only chair, a wide wooden one, and sat down, his arms regally outstretched.

Calantha found her mouth could move now. Her knees nearly buckled as, at a nod from Odhran, she was released by the guard. Odhran ignored her, and turned his eyes to Justhorn.

Justhorn was swallowing convulsively, his eyes shifting wildly like an animal in a snare. He stammered, "Master, she cast a spell on me. It's as you said, she's a witch..."

Odhran's voice was cold and clipped, very different from the glib fluidity with which he'd addressed the King. "Few people are skilled enough to make you do what you don't want to do. She certainly isn't; she can only see people's leanings, and persuade them deeper." His voice grew colder. "You must have already been so inclined."

Justhorn babbled, "Master, I swear..."

Odhran's eyes narrowed. "My orders are to be obeyed, Justhorn. Unquestioningly. It seems that you need a reminder." His pale eyes bored into Justhorn.

Justhorn turned purple. His hands went to his throat and he began to choke.

"Stop it," screamed Calantha. Phelan shouted too, and lunged forward. Both were held back by guards.

Odhran smiled faintly as Justhorn fell to his knees, then collapsed on the floor, making gasping, strangled sounds. Abruptly, he jerked. Then he began to breathe again, with sobbing rasps. A pungent wetness spread around his legs.

"Perhaps you will now remember that I am not to be disobeyed," said Odhran.

Calantha had a dazed impression of Phelan's white face, and the fear emanating from the other guards. Beswinn's smile was triumphant, but also frightened.

Odhran flicked his fingers. "Oh, get up, man, get up."

Justhorn struggled to stand, trying to hide the wetness with his hands. His face was red and his eyes streamed.

"Next time I will not be so patient," said Odhran. "Next time, it will be your wife and daughter, and you will watch."

Something in Justhorn's eyes died. He sobbed hoarsely, "Master, I will do as you say, anything, anything, just spare them...I beg you...."

Odhran's thin mouth creased into the barest smile. "Well, fortunately for you, I feel charitable today." His eyes flickered to Calantha and Phelan. He waved his hand dismissively at Justhorn. "Oh, go and clean yourself up." He turned to the other guards and said, "Let this be a reminder to all of you that my orders are to be obeyed." His voice hardened as he emphasized every word, "And without the slightest deviation. Go and wait outside. Beswinn, Marlshorn, you stay."

The guards murmured, some saluted as they left. Marlshorn, a beefy man with an expressionless face, stayed behind with Beswinn.

Nausea swamped through Calantha as Odhran settled back in his chair and brought his hands together, steepling his fingers. She stiffened her knees.

Odhran's cold eyes looked her over from head to toe, then settled on her face. He raised a scanty eyebrow. "Well. You don't seem to have much to say anymore."

Calantha said half-sobbingly, "You won't succeed. You won't."

He smiled thinly. "On the contrary, I will. Having you here is the final proof. Oh, you've led me a merry chase, I'll grant you that. But here you are at last." His eyes glinted. "How kind of you to pay me a visit and save me the trouble of another Shernthrip."

Calantha's heart threatened to explode. *Oh, Sower of Tales, help me*, she thought.

CHAPTER TWENTY-ONE

N ow," said Odhran quietly. "Just what did your precious Sower of Tales tell you? Did she really believe that the King would listen to you if you mentioned Sighurd?" His voice dripped scorn.

Calantha spat out, "She told me all I need to know to stop you." She would not let him see how frightened she was.

His eyebrows shot upward. "Stop me? Do you really think you can? How?"

Calantha cried, "It isn't just me. We know you're behind this—the Seers, the Sorcerers, the Plainsfolk—that you've tampered with the Essences. They'll come and fight. The Seers will undo the knots you've tied in the wind. They'll stop you."

Odhran's thin mouth curved into a smile of real amusement. "Well, how unfortunate for you that they don't have the time. Do you know how long it has taken me to tie those knots in the wind? It has been slow and painstaking, but a labor of love. And now I can reap the rewards of my labor. I grow stronger every day, thanks to the seeds that you kind Plainsfolk insist on sending me. It will be no trouble to keep your simpleton Seers at bay until all the story pods are gone. No trouble at all. And once I drain the power of the Sower's seeds, no one, *no one* will stop me." Odhran's voice rang with quiet elation.

"You're too late, Odhran," shouted Phelan. "King Ulric will wonder about Sighurd. He'll—"

Odhran's eyes glinted. "Really, you are pitiful. Who do you think informed his father that his precious son slept with a toy? Who do you think stoked Ulric's anger when Sighurd was destroyed? I honed it like a knife to my needs; but delicately, carefully, so he hadn't the faintest idea. It'll be child's play to convince Ulric that you Plainsfolk divined of Sighurd solely to humiliate and mock him." Odhran snapped his fingers. "Sighurd, indeed!"

"Others heard the truth," cried Calantha. "They'll realize—"

Odhran chuckled dryly. "The truth. How touching. And stupid. You didn't tell them anything that I haven't already. The skill of deception, you see, is to veer from the truth as little as possible. King Ulric and his courtiers know that I plan to drain the seeds of their power." Odhran again put the tips of his fingers together. "I told him myself. I told him it's necessary in order for me to sow the seeds for new story pods. For him, of course, and his sons, and his sons' sons; so they can always be Sellers of Tales. It appeals to his greed and self-importance—something else I've coaxed and fanned, along with his anger. As you already know, the true skill of influencing others is to work with what you already have." His eyes glittered. "By the time Ulric or anyone else learns the truth, it will be much too late."

Calantha shouted, "You won't stop us. We'll bring the tales back. Somehow, I'll bring them back."

Odhran gazed at her as though looking inside her

and also past her. "Ah. You *do* plan to be a nuisance, don't you?" He shook his head. "The old Gatherer here, too; I thought I had him well under my grasp, but...such a pity I had to get rid of him." His eyes focused and bored into hers. "Now let me see..."

She felt a stab of pain in her head, like cold, cold iron. With all her force, she dragged her eyes away and turned them toward the floor.

A soft laugh escaped Odhran. "Don't be tiresome. Do you really think that will work? There's no one here to distract me. I can..." the words came slowly, "make...you...do...anything."

Calantha felt her face being dragged upward, her eyes being turned toward his. Her stomach twisted and cramped. Hate—she was drowning in a filth of hate.

"Leave her alone," yelled Phelan. He lunged toward Odhran, but Marlshorn caught and held him.

Calantha screamed inside, *Xenyss, oh, Sower of Tales, help me!*

The Sower's words rang in her head—*what is in your heart, no one can take away.* A thread of blue seemed to guide her to the faint humming deep inside her. Calantha grasped the thread and followed it. Yes, the humming of the pods was always there inside her, her love of the tales, clean, pure, a spark of hope and joy. She channeled her whole being into that humming, and the chilly poison around her began to fade.

Odhran's voice held grudging surprise. "You're stronger than I thought. Good! It will be even more of a pleasure to break you."

Phelan shouted, "You feeble little rat, can't you get any satisfaction other than hurting people?"

A flicker passed across Odhran's face. He turned to Phelan and glared. Phelan gasped and collapsed in a limp heap on the stone floor.

Calantha tried to run to him, but was jerked back by Beswinn. "What have you done to him?" she screamed.

Odhran said coldly, "What I will do to you will be far less pleasant."

Calantha's face twisted as Beswinn restrained her. Was Phelan still alive? It was her fault if he...

Darkness swooped down on her—a cold, grasping

mist. Her head was being turned again, to Odhran.

The humming. She must cocoon herself, stay with the strength of the story pods, no matter what.

The chilly darkness receded again. As though through a haze, she heard Odhran's voice purr with satisfaction, "Well, well! You're going to be more useful than I imagined. Much more useful."

Stay with the tales.

Through the humming she heard Odhran's dry laugh. "I thought I'd only have to kill you, but the Essence of the pods is strong within you. Yes, you may be just the tool I need."

Calantha's heart jolted, but she stayed with the humming, sinking deeper into it.

Odhran came close to her. Calantha shut her eyes.

"That power you cling to, the Essence of the Tales, will give me just the added strength I need to break open the seeds from your precious Sower of Tales and drain their power."

Calantha felt an icy shard thrust into her mind. She shrank deeper still into the heart of the humming; she was safe here, oh, safe. As the humming grew within her, she felt the numbing cold being pushed back.

Odhran said coaxingly, "Come now, Calantha. Give me that Essence and I will reward you. You will tend the pods for me, be my Gatherer; we need a new one anyway. Come to me and you will always have tales to sustain you."

Calantha shuddered.

"You can't hold out, Calantha," crooned Odhran. "When you're hungry and tired, when the circle weakens and despair fills you, you will lose. Tonight, I will drain the last of the Plains seeds, and I'll be that much stronger, and you will be that much weaker. It's only a matter of time. If you come to me now, you'll save yourself considerable grief."

Calantha's face twitched, but she kept her eyes downward and stayed with the humming, strong in the humming. Dimly, from the corner of her eye, she saw Phelan stirring. Slowly, he sat up.

Odhran clicked his tongue. "You're making this much more difficult than it has to be." His voice became hard and creamy. "I wonder how long you'd hold out if you had to watch your companion being...shall we say, corrected by me? He's a flute player, isn't he? Now...how would he play with broken fingers?"

Calantha's stomach twisted, but she made herself stay with the humming within her. She felt the bitter-cold poker again, trying to lance through, and being pushed back.

"Very well!" Odran's voice was laced with anger. He motioned to Marlshorn, who picked up Phelan. "Cut his arms free. Hold out his hand."

"No, Calantha," Phelan cried, his voice strong with conviction and rage. "No matter what!"

Odhran turned to him, his eyes flashing. Phelan screamed. Calantha shut her eyes and turned her head away. But not before she saw the smallest finger of Phelan's right hand twist and dangle crookedly.

As though from a great distance she heard Phelan gasp, "No, Calantha, don't, don't!"

Tears seeped from Calantha's eyes. Her heart felt like it had shattered into pieces, but somehow, somehow, she managed to cling to the humming inside her.

Odhran said pleasantly, "A glutton, isn't he? Very well. Another—"

A sharp rapping at the door interrupted him.

"What is it?" snapped Odhran.

The door creaked open and a frightened voice called out, "Forgive me, Sorcerer, forgive me. The King requests your presence right away."

Calantha, peering through her tears, saw Odhran turn pale with rage. "Very well. Wait outside. I'll be right there." He turned to Calantha, his voice sharp. "Today, tomorrow, it's of no consequence. I've waited long enough; I'm a patient man. Maybe Theora told you of my perseverance. Sooner or later, I will take your power, and I'll leave you an empty, broken husk." He clicked his fingers. "Take her away. And him, too."

Beswinn asked, his voice hushed, "Yes, master. To the dungeons?"

"Don't be a fool," cried Odhran. "There are too many people about, and your lord and mine likes to meddle there. Take them to the usual place for our special guests. Lock them in separate chambers. Don't give her any food or water." His voice grew sharper. "But give the boy plenty; I want him strong enough to scream."

Beswinn and Marlshorn, along with other guards,

dragged her and Phelan along more passages and up stairs that wound on and on. Calantha caught glimpses of Phelan's face, twisted with pain, and that awful dangling finger. She stumbled and fell, her arms still tied behind her back, but guards pulled her on.

At last, a door was opened and she was flung into a small, empty chamber. The door shut behind her and the key clicked with finality. She heard the guards' footsteps go further, some voices, then another door being slammed shut.

As the sound of footsteps receded into silence, the coldness of the stone floor seeped into her.

CHAPTER TWENTY-TWO

Alone at last, Calantha wept and wept. She kept seeing Phelan's dangling finger, hearing his agonized scream.

Waves of despair washed over her. She'd failed. She hadn't been able to get through to King Ulric, let alone convince him; she couldn't have, even with more time—Odhran had made sure of that. She had no hope of finding the seeds, to release them—or even to destroy them. She'd failed the Sower of Tales, she'd failed Kasmira, Xenyss, Theora, the Plainsfolk who had helped her, and all who'd died in Shernthrip because of her. And she'd failed Phelan most of all; Phelan, who might never again be able to play his flute....

Her stomach heaved. Bile, sharp and bitter, filled

her mouth. How long would she be able to keep Odhran at bay, if he hurt Phelan again...?

Oh, she'd rather die than be Odhran's tool. How could she bear to live if it meant seeing the Plainsfolk beaten with despair and cruelty, the circle broken, and knowing that she'd been the cause? How could she live without the story pods? Without even the humming inside her?

When she was all cried out, she struggled to sit up as best she could with her hands still tied behind her back. Her arms and shoulders throbbed and ached, but somehow she managed to wriggle backward until she leaned against the wall. Facing the door. If Odhran came—no, *when*—she must be ready to defend herself.

Hiccuping softly, she looked around. The room was bare, with a couple of high windows; they were too small for her to climb through, even if she did manage to get untied and up to them. Besides, where would they lead?

The tales. She'd stay with them as long as she could. Hold them as long as possible. The Sower of Tales had said that what was in her heart no one could take away, but if Odhran succeeded... She shuddered. She went over every tale that she remembered, tales that nourished and heartened her, tales that made her shiver with delight, tales she'd made up. As the humming within her deepened, Calantha suddenly became aware of another humming close by. She closed her eyes and tried to concentrate. Her heart leaped. The Story Pods. They were growing somewhere in the castle! And the Sower's seeds were here too—she could sense their deeper, richer humming. But where were they? And how could she reach them?

She fell asleep, at last, and awoke later when the windows were black with night. Escape. She must escape. She sat up, trying to free her arms, and began to shout. Her voice echoed, mocking her. Then she heard a distant shout. Phelan—it must be him. She couldn't make out any words, but at least he was nearby and able to call out. How much pain was he in? After a while the faint shouts tapered away. A flash of blue wrapped around her, and comforted, she sank back into the tales.

When she awoke again, her cheek pressed against

the cold stone floor, the windows were gray, and a dim, stingy light filled the chamber.

Calantha struggled to sit up. She tried to break her arms free, but couldn't budge them. Twisting backward, she leaned against the wall. This would be the first day with no new story pods growing in the Plains. Her heart filled with dread. The Plainsfolk would have harvested the last of the pods, and they might keep for a few days at best, but then...

What was that? Shuffling at the door?

Odhran!

There it was again. The doorknob twisted furtively. She straightened up, her stomach knotting. She couldn't sense him, but it had to be Odhran, hoping to catch her unawares. She must be ready and stay with the humming.

She heard faint jingling, then the sound of a key scraping furtively into the keyhole and being tried. The door was pushed, but didn't open. Calantha heard a muffled oath.

Hope flared within her. "Who's there?" she cried. "Help me. Can you help me?"

Silence. Except for the beating of her heart.

She heard more keys being tried, then, at last, a key clicked and the door slowly swung open. A head crowned with tawny gold hair peered around the corner. Roarke. He stared at her, his pale green, dark-fringed eyes fascinated, yet fearful.

"Please," she said desperately, "you must help me. I spoke the truth yesterday. I did." She willed him to enter, to listen, and saw his eyes widen with fear.

No. He'd felt her urgency; he was leaving. Oh, how could she hold him? Her head cleared; the Sower of Tales had said Roarke listened to the story pods...

Turning her eyes downward, she said quickly, "Wait. I won't look at you, I promise. But if you like, I can tell you a tale."

The feet froze outside the door.

Calantha's mind darted through the tales she knew and loved, the ones she'd made up. *Oh, Sower of Tales, help me find the right one to hold this boy.*

And then, like a flash of sun, she knew which tale. Somehow, she'd weave in the gaps.

"I have a tale just for you," she said softly. "And it's about the Sower of Tales."

Out of the corner of her eyes she saw the door open wider and the feet turn, then stop.

Calantha tried to moisten her lips. Odhran might come at any moment, but she must go gently so as not to frighten Roarke. She drew in a deep breath and let herself sink down, down into the quiet place within her, the heart of the humming. "Once," she began, "long, long ago, there lived a young woman who told tales. She dwelled in the kingdom of a rich and vain king. Now this king owned all the lands that he could see, but yet he wanted more. He treated his subjects with disregard and cruelty, working them without mercy. The young woman was just a poor serving girl, and her only solace as she worked was losing herself in tales. Oh, in the tales, she could be anyone, go anywhere; she could be free...."

Calantha saw Roarke's feet, shod in red leather, take a few tentative steps toward her. She didn't look up. "The young girl didn't really want to share her tales with others. She was the poorest of the servants, the most despised; but one day, when she found a poor young page weeping after he'd been unjustly whipped, she tried to comfort him with a tale. A tale of a young page who became a prince. As she spoke, she saw a spark of hope gleam in the page's eyes. Soon he was enthralled in her tale, and she knew that for a while he had forgotten the pain of the whip that had raised ugly red welts on his back. For a while, he was lost in wonder."

As the humming of the tales grew within her, Calantha felt her words strengthen and flow like a silken river. Roarke's red feet waded closer and closer.

"When the tale ended," continued Calantha, "the page was thrust back into his harsh life. But he remembered how that young woman had helped him and he returned to her for more; and he told others, and soon they too clustered around her for tales. And she told them tales of adventure, tales of hope and delight and wonder. She told tales, for back then, there were no story pods."

He was sitting down now.

Slowly, she raised her eyes. His face was deeply curious but wary. "Don't look at me," he cried. "Just go on with the tale."

Immediately, she lowered her eyes. "There were no story pods and no one had ever dreamed of such a wonder. But the young woman's fame grew and grew, and at last she began to wander the Plains, bringing solace to the folk who toiled in the harsh, hot sun for a harsh, cold master who wanted more and more, but was never satisfied." Roarke shifted slightly.

Calantha went on. "In time, the fame of the storyteller was such that each village longed to have her stay with them, so they could hear her tales. They begged and tried to entice her to stay. Others told tales too, but oh, no one told them as she did, no one with the same heart and love. She was worn with wandering from village to village. She despaired that she could not be in all places at once."

Calantha looked up at Roarke. "So, what do you suppose she did?"

"What?" asked Roarke.

Hope sparked inside Calantha, but she said quietly, as though simply answering his question, "Why, she'd heard that there was a place where Sorcerers learned to twine Essences. And so she went there.

But first, she had to reach the coast at the southern-
most part of the land. It was a long, hard journey,
but somehow, she got there. Of course, she had
many adventures along the way."

"What adventures?" demanded Roarke, his dark-
fringed eyes wide. "Tell me."

Calantha smiled and shook her head. "No, no,
those are other tales, and maybe later I'll tell you,
but for now, let's see what happens to our storyteller
as she goes to the Sorcerers. She travels across the
seas, into rough and dangerous waters—"

"Did she go alone?" asked Roarke eagerly. "How
could she?"

"What do you think?" said Calantha.

Roarke blinked, then scowled. "How should I
know? It's not my tale."

Calantha nodded. "Well, it's not my tale either,
but I'll tell you what I think happened. The young
woman went on a ship that was bound for distant
lands and she worked for her passage. The journey
was dangerous, and they were set upon by pirates."

Roarke's eyes gleamed.

"But that's yet another story, for another time.

For this tale, all you need to know is that she found the Isle. That in itself took many, many moons, for it was no ordinary Isle. It was the Isle where the Sorcerers dwelled and it is called—"

"I know," cried Roarke. "The Place of Knotting! Odhran's spoken of it." A shadow crossed his face.

"Yes, the Place of Knotting," said Calantha. "And it is so called because it is a place outside of our time, a place where other worlds knot into ours."

Roarke's eyes widened with amazement. "Other worlds?"

Calantha nodded eagerly, her own insides squirrelling with the delight of the tale. "Yes! A place of coming together. Imagine the tales of other worlds, the endless, endless tales!" Her eyes shone.

Roarke gaped at her, his mouth partway open.

Calantha's mind tripped ahead, weaving the tale. "So here came our storyteller. Imagine how she loved to explore the worlds. Imagine how many more tales she learned. She knew hundreds and hundreds, but now she learned even more. And moreover..." Calantha paused and lowered her voice.

"What?" cried Roarke.

"She learned how to knot the Essences together. She learned to do what she had come to do. She learned how she could spread and share her tales, spread them on the winds, so she could send hope and solace to all the people."

"How?" Roarke's pale green eyes sparkled.

"Oh, it was so simple," said Calantha. "Perfect. The simplest things often are the most perfect. She found a plant—a weed, really, with many, many silky white seeds that spread with the wind..."

On she continued, describing how the Sower of Tales went to the highest Eastern Mountain and harnessed the wind. Then, remembering what she'd seen, Calantha described how the Sower of Tales sowed her seeds. As Roarke listened, entranced, Calantha sensed the tale joining her to him; sensed the unity between them grow and strengthen. Softly, she finished with, "And so, that is how she became known as the Sower of Tales."

Roarke let out a sigh of deep contentment. "Is it true, then?"

Calantha nodded. "Yes, it is. It may not all have

happened just like that, but it's true. And," she paused, "as in all tales, there's more."

Roarke sat up. "Tell me," he cried, rubbing his hands together. "Oh, I'm so glad I found you."

"It was clever of you," said Calantha. "How did you find me?"

He grinned. "There isn't a corner of this castle I don't know, no matter what Odhran thinks. I felt a sort of..." he frowned, "I don't know, a sense of story pods, this way. Not the ones Odhran's growing, but others."

Calantha's heart leaped, but she said nothing.

Roarke's face grew sullen. "I've missed the tales. Our Gatherer's been gone for a while." He blinked hard. "I think Odhran had something to do with it, only Father won't listen." He sighed, then looked up, grinning. "But at least I found you, and I was right. Your tale is just like that of a story pod."

Calantha started. Her tale like a story pod tale? She half-grinned. "Well, it's *about* story pods, anyway." Then her face sobered. "And now, I come to another tale, if you care to listen. It's a tale of many, many years later. Of a king who had plenty, but who sought to have more."

"Like that first king?"

Calantha nodded. "Only this king also had a young son and a sorcerer. One day the sorcerer came to him and said, 'Sire, I have a plan for how you can expand your kingdom. There is a way in which, if we can take all the story pods...'"

A hard gleam came into Roarke's eyes. His mouth tightened into the peevish expression she'd seen when he'd been with his father.

"Are you starting your lies again?"

Calantha forced herself to look at him calmly. "Why don't you listen, and decide for yourself?"

His eyes narrowed. He was edgy now. "Are you a witch like he said?"

Calantha's chest constricted, but she said softly, "What do you think?"

"How should I know?" he said sullenly.

"Well, why don't you think it over? You seem to be able to think clearly enough."

He frowned at her, as though turning over a new idea.

"All right," he commanded. "Go on with your

story. But," he raised a grubby finger. "Don't look at me, all right? I know that's how Odhran does things. When he looks at you."

Calantha grinned. "See, you *can* think for yourself."

He grinned back, then ordered, "Now look away."

Calantha looked down, and continued with her tale, keeping the words flowing from that deep, quiet place inside her, the place of truth. And she told the story of how Odhran really wanted to gain control of the kingdom, of how she went out on her quest, and then came to the north kingdom, and was taken prisoner. She saw Roarke tense at times, when she spoke of the greed of the king, but he made no movement to leave. He listened to her tale.

When she finished, she kept her eyes down. Silence.

At last Roarke said tightly, "What happens next? After that girl and her friend are captured."

Calantha looked up. She said simply, "That depends on you."

He stared at her with frightened eyes.

"Is it true?" he whispered, almost to himself.

"What do you think?"

"You keep asking that, but how should I know?" He shifted angrily, uneasily. His pupils were dilated and his dark, curly lashes blinked up and down.

Calantha felt an unexpected pang of pity. He was young, so young, only a few years older than Beagan, and she could sense his turmoil and fear. How could she help him to see the truth? Softly, she said, "What does it feel like in your heart? And in your stomach?"

Roarke frowned. Hesitantly, he closed his eyes as though to think, feel. Then his eyes flew open and he gasped, "It's true, isn't it?"

"Yes." Calantha clenched her jaw. She wanted to shout at him to hurry up and free her—Odhran might even now be on his way, or his guards—but she knew she must still tread warily.

Roarke's face seemed to shrink in terror. "What can we do?"

Calantha moistened her lips and tried to speak quietly. "Untie me. The only way to stop Odhran is to stop him draining the Sower's seeds. We must

release them, or…" her voice broke despite herself,
"or destroy them. It's the only way to keep your
father's kingdom safe." She hardly dared breathe.
Would he do it? He was used to listening to others.
Would he listen to her now, or would the fear of
flouting his father be stronger?

Roarke hesitated, looked into her eyes. He was no
longer a young prince, but a frightened young lad.

Calantha spoke as she would to Beagan. "Roarke,
I'm sorry; I know it's hard, but…if you care at all
about the story pods, about your father's safety, you
must help me."

"You're not a witch," said Roarke slowly. "When
you look at me, I don't feel that fog like with
Odhran, even though I feel your wanting."

A grin flashed across her face. "See, you are
clever. Now untie me, Roarke. Please. We must get
away and find the seeds."

Without hesitation, Roarke came toward her.
"Hold still," he said. "I have a knife."

From his pocket he took out a small, sharp knife,
and, unsheathing it, cut her free.

CHAPTER TWENTY-THREE

Calantha gasped as she tried to move her arms. They seemed to be frozen behind her. Forcing them forward, she began to rub them with Roarke helping her. She winced as the flow of blood stung agonizingly through her arms.

She pulled herself to her feet. "Quick, now. We must find Phelan—he's locked nearby. And then we must find the seeds."

Roarke nodded. "Is he the man who was with you?"

"Yes, we must hurry, before..."

She sensed his stabbing fear even as she saw it leap into his eyes. Swiftly, they went to the door. Heart in her mouth, Calantha looked out. No one.

"Where is he?" hissed Roarke.

"I don't know," she whispered. She didn't dare shout for Phelan. As Roarke locked the door behind the empty chamber, she darted to the other doors around her, calling softly.

Roarke joined her. "Are you sure he's here?"

"Yes," she snapped. She bit her lip. "I'm sorry. I heard him last night, but it was faint." She looked quickly over her shoulder. What if Odhran came? She must get to the seeds, but she couldn't leave Phelan, she couldn't.

They turned a corner and Calantha's heart sank at the number of doors along the passage. She knocked at one door, then another. Her heart leaped as Phelan's voice cried out, "Calantha? Calantha, I'm here."

Almost sobbing with relief, she beckoned Roarke and he came running. She bit her tongue while he tried key after key.

At last, one key turned and the door opened. Phelan stood by the door, his face pale, his red hair tousled. But his arms were free. Immediately she saw his hand—he'd tied the broken small finger to his adjacent fingers with a strip of cloth torn from his shirt.

She grabbed him by the shoulders. "Phelan, are you all right?"

"Yes, yes, I'm fine." His good hand gripped her arm. Calantha saw an empty tin plate and a skin of water on the floor behind him. She shuddered as she remembered why Odhran wanted him fed, then reached for the skin, her mouth aching. Unstoppering it, she drank and drank.

"Come on," she cried. "We must find the seeds."

But Roarke held back, his face suddenly abashed as he looked at Phelan.

Calantha said, "Phelan, this is Roarke. I don't know what I'd have done without him. He's helping us."

Phelan bowed slightly to Roarke. "My thanks," he said. "You are a wise prince, worthy of being the next King."

As Roarke puffed up and flashed a smile, Calantha glanced gratefully at Phelan.

"We must go. Roarke, which way? You mentioned the story pods that Odhran's growing, but do you know where the *seeds* are?"

Roarke nodded.

Calantha could have hugged him. "Oh, Roarke, thank goodness. Take us there, the fastest way."

"What about guards?" said Phelan tersely.

Roarke gave him a look of scorn. "I know every part of this castle. I'll get us there without running into any guards."

Calantha grinned at Phelan over Roarke's head.

Roarke locked the door after them, and, finger to his lips, led them along a dingy passage, then around others, twisting and turning without hesitation. At last, he headed down a gloomy, gray passage that seemed to end at a solid stone wall flanked with columns on either side. Flashing a proud grin, Roarke bent down to twist the center of a small stone flower carved in the left column.

The stone wall swung inward, revealing a narrow staircase.

Panting slightly, Roarke led the way through, shutting the stone wall behind them. To Calantha's surprise, it wasn't pitch dark. Somehow, a faint light seemed to reach them.

"Which way?" asked Phelan.

"Down," said Roarke.

"Where are the seeds?" cried Calantha.

Roarke gleamed with importance and excitement.
"Above the Great Balcony. That's where Father
addresses the villagers below. There's a parapet
above it and I've seen them, large arrac sacks with
the seeds. That's where Odhran's growing the story
pods, too, in big containers." His smile froze and
he blinked hard. "There'll be guards. Lots of them.
And...and Odhran's chambers are right beside the
parapet..." His voice caught. He was a young boy
again, not the swaggering leader he'd been earlier.
"Maybe we should go to my father first...?"

Calantha's nails dug into her palms.

Phelan said, "We don't have time to convince
your father, even if we could. You saw what happened yesterday."

Panic clawed at Calantha's throat, but she tried to
speak softly. "Roarke, we must get to the seeds and
release them. It's the only way."

Roarke stood frozen. Calantha sensed his con-
flicting feelings toward his father, the love mixed

with resentment and apprehension. And his growing terror as he realized what was at stake.

"Roarke, please," she whispered. "For the story pods."

Phelan gazed at his face. "And for your own sake, Roarke. For the good of your kingdom."

It was just the right thing to say. Roarke squared his shoulders and nodded. Calantha bent down to hug him. As he looked into Calantha's eyes, something vital passed between them. Trust—and a dropping of pretense.

"Roarke," she said, "if we can't manage to do it, if we're stopped and you can't convince your father to release them, you must try to burn the seeds. You must. Promise me you'll do it."

He stared at her, his face wavering with hope, fear, and dread.

Her eyes stung, but she said fiercely, "It's the only chance we have. If Odhran drains the seeds..."

Roarke's face hardened. "I promise," he said.

"Come on," said Phelan. "Let's go."

They began to hurry downward. *Oh, Sower of Tales, let me find a way to save the seeds*, Calantha pleaded silently, as she followed Roarke and Phelan.

The stairway wound in a tight spiral. Exhausted as she was from lack of food, the circular motion soon made Calantha's head spin, but she kept pace behind Phelan and Roarke. At intervals, they passed small windows in the deep stone walls, and through them Calantha saw how high they still were.

But as they continued downward, even through the turmoil, she began to sense the humming within her sing in chorus with the other humming. They were nearing the seeds! Oh, if she could only release them, the ordinary winds would disperse the seeds, and pods would begin to grow again in the Plains, grow everywhere. Once the Seers and Sorcerer Theora untied the knots in the wind, the Plains seeds would return to the Sower of Tales and restore her strength. Hope began to spark inside Calantha.

At last Roarke stopped, panting. "The parapet is out there. But there'll be guards. There always are. Handpicked by Odhran."

Phelan looked at Roarke's scared face and said, "I'll go look around."

"No," Roarke's face pinched. "It'd better be me. You wait here."

Calantha caught his hand. "We'll all go." She needed to be out there, with the seeds.

Roarke shook her off, his face pale but determined. "No. I might be able to distract the guards. If they see you..."

"But—" Calantha started.

Phelan gripped her shoulder. "Calantha, if we're caught now, we won't get another chance."

Calantha bit her lip and nodded.

Silently, Roarke bent to twist the center of another flower at the bottom of a column.

The stone wall swung toward them. With a frightened backward glance, Roarke eased through the doorway, shutting it behind. They heard his footsteps edge stealthily away.

Minutes passed. Calantha pressed her hands together. What if Roarke got caught? Or gave them away? They were so near the seeds.... Phelan's face was taut in the gloomy light. She reached out and gripped his good hand. His fingers tightened around hers.

At last, they heard footsteps running.

Calantha turned to Phelan, her heart racing. Was Roarke being chased? Leading guards to them?

The stone wall swung open and Roarke's alarmed face came around.

"They're gone!" he cried.

Calantha swayed.

"What d'you mean they're gone?" snapped Phelan.

Roarke gasped, "They're not there. The guards, too—no one's on the parapet. I went right to the edge and looked over down to the Great Balcony." He swallowed convulsively. "The arrac sacks are there. On the Great Balcony. It's swarming with guards and soldiers. Father's addressing a group of Plainsfolk below."

Plainsfolk. Calantha's heart jolted.

Roarke continued, "I went partway down, saw two guards on the way. I asked...one of them said Father ordered the sacks to be moved, so he could keep an eye on them." He choked.

"He believed us!" cried Calantha. "Is he going to release the seeds?"

Roarke shook her arm. "No!" he shouted, almost sobbing. "The guard said that the King, my father, wants Odhran to drain the Essence of the seeds at his bidding, in front of him."

Calantha felt the blood drain from her face. "He can't believe..."

Phelan said grimly, "Calantha, he's driven by greed. Forgive me, Roarke, but he doesn't realize the danger. He must think he'll be able to control Odhran."

"We have to get there," gasped Calantha. "We must convince him—you must convince him of the danger, Roarke. Take us there. Now. Hurry."

Roarke's face was ashen. "Down some more. But Father's chambers are behind the Great Balcony and we'll have to get past...come on."

Roarke raced downward again, around several twists of the stairs, then jerked to a halt beside another stone wall. He held his finger to his lips.

Calantha's heart threatened to explode. They were closer to the seeds; she could sense them. Oh, she must reach them, she must! She froze as they heard voices outside.

"Guards," whispered Roarke. "I'll go distract them."

Phelan nodded.

Again, Roarke bent and twisted the center of a carved flower low on a pillar, and the stone wall swung inward. Roarke ran out. They heard his shrill voice, the deeper voices of men, then the running of feet.

Roarke's head reappeared. "Let's go! I sent them around the corner."

Calantha and Phelan darted behind him onto a rich passage with ornate wooden doors. Calantha saw the backs of two guards running in the opposite direction.

Roarke panted, "It's longer this way but there usually aren't guards here...."

But as they rounded the corner, a guard stood at attention.

Everything happened fast.

The guard shouted, "Stop!"

Roarke cried, "Run, this way, run!"

Calantha heard the guard yell, "Intruders, Plainsfolk, help, help!"

Roarke grabbed her hand and swerved down another passage with Phelan behind.

Like an arrow, Roarke darted past more guards. One of them grabbed at Calantha, but she managed to wrench away as Phelan butted him and Roarke kicked his shin. They raced along another passage, and, at last, headed straight toward the wide doors opening to the Great Balcony. Tugged by the seeds, the deep, joyful humming, Calantha had only a blurred impression of the throng of people on the Great Balcony. Somehow, she twisted past the guards with Roarke and sped onto the balcony, with Phelan behind.

As guards turned toward them, Calantha saw King Ulric at the balustrade of the balcony and heard him shouting to the people below, "...and I will sell them for a fair tithe. I am now the Seller of Tales. The seeds have come to me alone, and my Sorcerer shall..."

On top of the wide balustrade stood pots of story pods, all in different stages of growth. Below them, against the balustrade, were a row of arrac sacks. The seeds, the seeds—she felt the blessed humming!

She ran toward them, but was jerked back by a guard. Through the balustrade she glimpsed a small group of Plainsfolk below, a blue robe, a tilted head. Xenyss! A rush of blue wrapped around to greet her, and she thought she heard him call her name. As she struggled against the guard, Roarke shouted, "Father, Father!"

King Ulric turned, his face like thunder. Roarke shouted, "Father, release the seeds. Listen, you must listen." King Ulric's eyes flashed as they fell on Calantha.

Calantha lunged forward, crying, "Don't let Odhran drain the seeds—he'll take your kingdom. The Sower of Tales sent me—"

"Father, it's true," cried Roarke.

Phelan, too, was being held back by guards. He shouted, "Listen, just listen..."

Past the King, Calantha saw the white robes of the Sorcerer snap around as he swooped toward them.

Roarke suddenly gasped. He was turning purple.

Odhran cried, "My lord, kill her. She's strangling your son!"

Somehow Calantha managed to wrench away from the guard holding her. She caught Roarke in her arms and tried to shake him to breathe. His eyes were frantic as he gasped for air.

She screamed at King Ulric, "In the name of Sighurd, it's Odhran who is hurting Roarke. Make him stop!"

Odhran came toward her, shouting, "My lord, stop her before she kills your son."

A thin voice rang out from the crowds below. "Odhran!"

Calantha felt the sizzle of something hot arc toward Odhran. He turned, his face ugly with rage, and staggered backward. It was enough to break his concentration; Roarke was breathing again, gulping air. Through the balustrade, Calantha saw Xenyss' blue figure, head tilted upward. He'd diverted the Sorcerer.

Calantha helped Roarke to stand. He gasped, "Father, believe her, she tells the truth."

Odhran swooped to the balustrade and a streak of fire peeled from his fingers. Calantha screamed, "Xenyss!"

The fire hit Xenyss square in the chest. He was falling, falling.

Odhran turned to her and Roarke again.

Calantha flung Roarke away from her, toward his father. Grief and rage tore through her. Xenyss. Lying still. Xenyss, *Xenyss*.

She felt an iron band catch her throat, felt Odhran sinking onto something inside her, pulling ferociously, ripping and tearing toward the humming within her.

Blinded with grief and rage, without knowing how, Calantha gathered herself into a furious whirlwind, and channelling all the strength and power within her, turned to fight Odhran.

Odhran tottered backward.

Yes, she could do it. He'd killed Xenyss. Xenyss! She hurled her hatred and fury at him. Odhran fell back further.

Then, through a mist of red, she saw Odhran smile. A burning cold poker pierced her. No! Too late she realized her mistake—her anger had given him a passage to enter.

With all her strength, she wrenched away from

her fear and hatred, and collapsed into the pure, cool light of the tales, her love for her family, Xenyss, the Sower of Tales. Oh, she must stay true to the Essence of the tales, that spark of creation; the Sower of Tales had woven it out of love for the Plainsfolk—love, not hatred or anger at the then King. She must never betray it.

She clung to the humming, but the icy burning poker wormed closer, closer. He was stronger today...her face and body were going numb...she couldn't move.

Odhran's voice scratched through the mist, "Stay back, my lord, I'll deal with this creature once and for all. I'll keep your son safe, and then I'll drain the seeds in front of you, in your service."

She heard Roarke scream, then Phelan's voice, and more shouting.

Calantha stumbled back. As she lost all feeling in her limbs, she fell down on her knees. Odhran's bone-chilling greed bored closer and closer toward the humming. From a great distance, she heard Phelan shout her name. Through a thickening mist, she saw Odhran stumble as Phelan, wrenching free of a guard, rammed the Sorcerer. Odhran pushed Phelan away, his eyes still fixed on Calantha, but the brief distraction was enough.

The Sower's face dazzled into her head.

With all her force, Calantha screamed, "Burn the seeds, burn them, burn—"

The Sorcerer's grip seized her throat again, strangling off her words. But behind him, through a blur of pain, Calantha saw Roarke snatch a torch from a holder against the stone wall and heave it at the arrac sacks against the balustrade. A few of them lit and caught.

The band across her throat loosened and the icy poker retreated as Odhran turned, his eyes livid. As Roarke reached for another torch, Odhran flung his arm toward him.

Calantha screamed.

Something sizzled from Odhran's hand and hit Roarke's right arm just as he thrust the torch into the arrac sacks. Roarke leaped into the air and fell to the stone floor.

The King raced to his son and caught him. He looked up, his face stricken, naked fear in his eyes.

At last, he understood the threat. "Guards, seize Odhran!"

The burning icy force on Calantha jerked away, then was gone. She collapsed as Odhran turned to face the guards rushing him. They reeled backward, as though scorched, then more guards advanced on him—among them Justhorn, his mottled face grim with fury and determination.

Calantha tried to stand, but her feet were frozen, her hands still numb. Somehow, she pulled herself onto her hands and knees and managed to crawl toward the sacks.

The seeds, if only she could save some. The King's men would deal with Odhran now; the danger of him draining the seeds was past. Not all the sacks were burning—oh, she must save what seeds she could, she must restore the circle. A guard grabbed her.

She screamed at King Ulric, "Let me go! The seeds, we must save some or the circle will be broken beyond repair...."

But the King was still hunched over Roarke.

Sobbing, struggling against the guard who held

her, Calanatha saw Phelan break free and run toward the sacks.

A scream of rage tore through the air. Calantha turned and saw Odhran, cornered at last by the guards, their swords and spears pressed against his throat and body.

Odhran's mouth twisted. His eyes flashed fury and hatred as they swung from her to the King. "Live in despair, then," he shrieked. "Ulric, you most of all."

Fingers outstretched, he flung his hands toward the balustrade as though hurling something.

"No!" cried Calantha.

Fire arced from Odhran's fingers to the story pods and sacks of seeds against the balustrade.

Calantha screamed and screamed as the story pods and seeds burst into flames. "Save the seeds. Save what you can, save them." She could feel the humming of the seeds fading, fading.

King Ulric seemed to wake to the danger. Still cradling Roarke, he shouted, "Guards, save what seeds you can."

Released at last, Calantha dragged herself somehow to the blazing sacks alongside Phelan. Still on her knees, she tore through the flames, her hands numb, oblivious to the fire, her body pulsing with the humming within her, trying to pull the seeds to her. She grabbed and grabbed at singed seeds, slapping out the fire with her bare hands, against her legs, reaching for more, the seeds burning, burning. With all her heart she called to the humming, trying to hold it—and at last, a few seeds, some still on fire, turned and came toward her as though drawn.

The smell of burned flesh filled the air.

PART FIVE

THE SONG OF THE STORY PODS

If the Sower of Tales you seek to find…
from the Key to the Sower of Tales

Chapter Twenty-Four

A handful of seeds. A handful of precious blue-white seeds. Calantha grasped at the thought of them as though to a lifeline while she drifted in and out of consciousness over the next few days, with her body screaming in pain and Odhran's chill burning hard and cold within her.

At first she was only dimly aware of being in a large chamber in Jaerlfin castle with Theora tending to her, plying Essences to heal the outside burns and the deadlier chill inside—a different burn from those on her hands, arms, chest, and legs, and harder to heal.

Calantha didn't want to be awake. The grayness of sleep was almost better than the grayness pressing the air. The last of the story pods was gone; the dissolution had begun. She'd sleep and sleep and never wake up—if it weren't for the nightmares. Dreams of fire, fields of story pods blazing, blazing, words and tales turning to ash, with pain clawing the air.

And worst of all, dreams of the Sower of Tales shrouded in mist, walking away from Calantha, growing fainter and fainter, until she disappeared over the crest of a hill. Calantha could never move in her dreams, or even call out to the Sower of Tales; she could only watch, as despair and grief shredded her.

She shivered uncontrollably. Would she ever be warm again? Even the roaring fire in the grate and the soft bed with layers of blankets didn't seem to warm her. The chamber, richly furnished and with warm tapestries on the walls, had wide windows, but still it seemed gray and gloomy. It was near Roarke's chamber, Theora had told her. Phelan, who was also injured, was nearby.

"Calantha, it's time to change your bandage," said Theora.

Calantha kept her eyes tightly closed. She

couldn't bear to look at Theora. Her face was lined and her eyes weary. She must also feel the collapsing circle, be bowed by it. How could she work to restore the circle with that weight upon her? She and another Seer from the Plains, Laveda, were here at the castle, tending to the injured; they'd been on their way to Jaerlfin, and they'd stayed when the King had frantically begged for help to save Roarke's life and to bind Odhran.

He was in the dungeons, Theora had told her, along with some of his personal soldiers. She and Laveda had tied and knotted the Essences to hold Odhran from escaping—for he was still a Sorcerer, and dangerous. Later on, he would be sent to the Place of Knotting, so that the Sorcerers there could deal with him and hold him safely. The King had wanted to kill Odhran, but Theora had stopped him, hoping that Odhran might still reveal how he had manipulated the Essences of the wind. But he'd told them nothing.

Theora spoke again, her voice firm. "Calantha, you must sit up. Yes."

The blankets were lifted, and Theora's arm went

around her. Calantha's body tightened in anticipation of the pain. She gasped as Theora helped her to sit.

Sitting up exhausted her. She pressed her bandaged hands against the soft pouch tied loosely around her neck. The seeds. Oh, thanks be to the Sower of Tales, they still hummed. They still held the Essence of the tales.

Theora, trying to hearten her, had told her that others too had managed to save some seeds, a few here, a few there. Many were burnt and others singed, but some were untouched. Calantha clung to the hope of those seeds—surely the Sower of Tales must live, if those seeds lived. And she clung to the faint humming of the tales still within her. Odhran hadn't managed to steal it, but oh, how his chill burned and burned inside her.

Theora helped Calantha swing her legs out of bed. Gently, she began to unwind the bandages around Calantha's thighs. Calantha caught her lip between her teeth as the bandage stuck. Theora eased the bandages off with warm water. Closing her eyes, Calantha retreated to the faint humming deep inside her. She must hold on to it any way she could, keep away from the defeat in the air. Its heaviness sapped all strength. She sat hunched over as Theora soothed dignes lotion onto her legs, murmuring healing words, then straightened so that Theora could tend the burns on her chest.

"You are mending. Yes," murmured Theora.

Calantha opened her eyes and whispered, "The circle. Have you restored the Essence of the wind yet?"

Theora sucked the air in through her teeth. "We're working at it, child. Laveda and I, as well as the other Seers in the Plains."

"When?" asked Calantha. She sensed the doubt from Theora, the constant burrowing worry.

Theora hesitated, then said gently, "It takes time to unravel the knots, child. It took Odhran years to tie them. Yes, so they wouldn't be detected."

Time? Calantha's chest tightened painfully. They didn't have time. With every passing day the Sower of Tales was fading, disappearing. Oh, if only she could go there to the Eastern Mountains, find the Sower of Tales and hold her somehow until the wind was restored.

Theora gently touched Calantha's cheek and began to remove the bandages around Calantha's arms and hands. Calantha drew in a hissing breath.

Softly Theora said, "Roarke asked about you again today. He, too, is recovering. Yes. The King will barely let him out of his sight. He's a devoted father now." Theora bobbed her head. "And Phelan keeps asking and asking after you. His burns are healing as well. Yes."

Calantha retreated back into herself. She didn't want to think of Phelan or Roarke, of their hurt and pain—hers were already too much. Sinking into the humming, she forced her mind into the tale of the three-legged mouse who, despite her injury, saved enough lorsha, grain by grain, for the winter.

"Calantha." Theora had finished tying fresh bandages around her hands. "Is that better?"

Calantha nodded. The dignes balm and Theora's healing Essences had eased the burns.

"Now try to stand," said Theora. "The sooner you move, the better."

Calantha's eyes widened.

"Yes," insisted Theora. "If you are to heal."

Calantha drew in an unsteady breath. Theora was right. She must move, if she ever hoped to go there, to the Eastern Mountains, to the Sower of Tales.

She braced for the pain she knew would come and, with Theora's help, slowly pulled herself to her feet. Her head swam dizzily and she broke out in a sweat. Biting her lip, she stood still, waiting for the waves of pain to subside, then lifted her foot to take a step. Her thighs and knees screamed fire.

The chair. She'd walk to the chair. Gritting her teeth, Calantha took another step, then another. Gasping, she collapsed into it.

Theora tucked the blanket around Calantha's knees. "Yes, you will do." She flashed her quick smile. But Calantha could still smell the concern from her, the weight of worry.

"I'll bring your food now," said Theora. "And something that will do you more good." Theora smiled and left abruptly.

Slowly, Calantha's heartbeat steadied. She'd moved. If she moved every day, she could soon be

on her way. She touched the pouch around her neck
again, the pouch of seeds. For the first time since
the burning of the seeds she began to think of what
she might do next. She wouldn't be able to walk to
the Eastern Mountains, not for a while, but with a
horse and cart...surely Roarke would supply her
that. As for the seeds, she'd leave them with the
Plainsfolk. Give them to the Gatherers. They'd plant
them when Theora and the Seers untied the Essence
of the wind. Once the story pods began to grow, the
Plains seeds would return at last to sustain the Sower
of Tales. Then she would cast her seeds to the Plains
again, and the story pods would return. They *must*
return.

She didn't notice until Theora had placed two
bowls of arrac-and-lamb stew down on the table,
along with fine lorshcake, that someone stood
behind her. Phelan.

Calantha shrank back. No. She didn't want anyone looking at her, to feel burdened by their concern. She couldn't bear to sense Phelan's loss and
pain either—not on top of hers.

Phelan came closer. "Calantha," he said.

Unwillingly, her eyes turned upward.

His face was pale. His shorn red hair made his ears appear to stick out even more. Part of his scalp was burned and his hands were heavily bandaged. Calantha's chest squeezed. His hands!

Phelan's greenish-brown eyes stared calmly at her. There was grief in them, but no pity, either for her or himself. No lament. Slowly, the roiling in her chest receded and something settled. Yes, Phelan understood. After all, he'd shared the unthinkable with her.

"Phelan," she said.

He flashed a shadow of his crooked grin, and, sitting down, struggled with the spoon until he managed to grasp it in his bandaged hands. Slowly, he lifted the spoon to his lips.

"Aren't you going to eat, then?" He quirked his eyebrow.

She nodded. Up until now, Theora had fed her. Fumbling, she tried to pick up the spoon. Again and again it fell.

She flushed. Phelan was watching her. She kept her eyes fixed on the spoon, and at last managed to lift some stew to her lips. Her head began to clear as she ate.

Cautiously, she let her senses tiptoe toward him. Concern, wariness, fatigue, but under it, something hidden. A pit of grief. His hands—oh, she couldn't go near that. Calantha snatched her mind away and retreated again to the humming.

Over the next few days her burns healed slowly—even though the chill inside her lingered like a well of frozen air, despite Theora's plying of the Essences. And the dreams still tortured her. Dreams of fire, of tales devoured by Odhran.

But it was the dream of the Sower of Tales that drove her to walk farther and farther each day. She must mend, and as quickly as possible—in her dreams, the Sower of Tales always left her, and Calantha could never move, still held back by some awful weight. She couldn't even call out to the Sower of Tales, though she ached and ached to follow her.

She only half heard Theora's daily news of Roarke, and shut down when Theora murmured that he longed to see her. But Phelan came to eat with her every evening. In a way, his presence strengthened her—maybe it was his doggedness, his unpitying calm—but sometimes it felt like a reproach. A reminder that it wasn't just her loss. Her sacrifice.

As they ate together one night, Phelan told her that the King had met with some of the Grand Council from Maernlea, to call a formal truce with the Plainsfolk. He had to, Phelan said wryly, in order to get the assistance of the Seers for his son and the others injured. He added, "But it takes time for word of the truce to reach all corners of the Plains. I've heard that Defenseroffes are yet wary of strangers, in case they're Ulric's men. So skirmishes are still breaking out."

Calantha froze. The armed swordsmen at the top of the Eastern Mountains—would they still be there? What if the veil guarding the Sower's domain had fallen? The chill inside her spread like a freezing mist. Could that be what her dreams meant?

Phelan's voice broke her thoughts. "How is Roarke today?" he asked Theora, who was burning loosethorn in a bowl and murmuring words to sweeten the air and speed the healing.

"Better," said Theora. "He is out of danger, yes. But he'll never hold a sword in his right hand again." She shook her head and sucked in the air between her teeth. "Perhaps that is no bad thing. Yes. It might presage a true and lasting peace between Jaerlfin and the Plains."

Calantha pulled herself inward again. The Plains, fighting, none of it was her concern anymore. She just had to reach the Sower of Tales.

As they finished the meal, Theora said softly, "Calantha. Roarke asked again about you." She hesitated. "He longs for a tale from you. He says his attendants barely remember any and they don't know how to tell them."

Calantha's mind shuttered darkly. She was too cold. The humming was too faint; she couldn't give it away. She must keep it to heal, save her strength for her journey.

Phelan scraped his chair back and stood in front

of her. He crouched down so she couldn't avoid his face. His eyes were worried, but his voice earnest. "Calantha, you still have the tales inside you. Can you not...?"

Calantha hunched down and turned her face away.

"Calantha, if I could..." Phelan held up his hands, then let them drop.

His words hit her like a lash. "Leave me alone," she cried.

Phelan stood up and turned away, then came back, his face stricken.

Calantha began to rock back and forth.

"Hush, Phelan," said Theora. "The chill came close to her heart."

"But she's alive, isn't she? And she has her gift. She has it still."

His anguish slivered through the cold and pierced her to the heart. His hands, oh, his hands. How his flute had soared in the sharo grove after hearing the tale, and quieted the horses on the lake; oh, how joyfully, how recklessly he'd enticed the horsemen on the Eastern Mountains.

Calantha wrapped her arms around herself to stop shattering apart. So much lost—Phelan's hands and Xenyss; Xenyss gone, falling, his blue eyes startled; the story pods lost, the seeds burned; and the Sower of Tales, oh, the Sower of Tales still walking away, away....

Calantha's face wrenched.

No! If she started to weep, she'd never stop. With all her strength, she pulled herself inward to the humming and held herself there until the bleeding inside stemmed.

Theora said softly, her voice thick with tears, "Calantha, we stopped Odhran in time, we did. Xenyss' sacrifice was not in vain. We will undo Odhran's knots in the wind and plant the seeds we saved. The circle will mend in time. You must never give up hope."

Hope. Yes. She must hope. She would reach the Sower of Tales and hold her somehow....

Why was Phelan still standing there, as though trying to pull her to her feet? Why was he waiting, as though he expected it of her?

Calantha sat like stone. Then under her grief and

anger, a knot suddenly loosened. Maybe Phelan waited because he believed in her. Believed she could do what Roarke wanted. Unexpectedly, the Sower's face flashed in her head, saying passionately, *The tales are for all. It must be that way.*

Calantha drew in a deep breath. She stood up, leaning on her stick. "All right. Take me to Roarke."

CHAPTER TWENTY-FIVE

Slowly, Calantha followed Phelan and Theora to Roarke's bright, well-lit chamber. At the doorway she paused, dismayed, wishing she hadn't come. The chamber was crowded with courtiers, servants, and soldiers.

Roarke sat in a deep chair by a blazing fire, wrapped in heavy blankets, his right arm bandaged and slung across his chest. One glance at his face—blanched and worn, with dark rings under his eyes—and Calantha knew that he too struggled against Odhran's chill. His father, the King, sat beside him, his face strangely pulled, head drooping, eyes downward as though consumed by something within him. He looked years older.

Roarke's face lit up when he saw Calantha. He waved his good arm. "Calantha. At last. Come here, sit by me."

Calantha quailed at his eagerness as she sank into the chair quickly vacated by a courtier. She was exhausted even from that short walk.

Roarke asked after her, but the King said nothing. He barely glanced at her, although the scar above his left eyebrow tightened. Calantha could sense the anger still pulsing from him, the devouring rage and regret. And blame. There was grayness pressing at everyone.

Roake looked eagerly at her, his face thin with unspoken want.

Calantha glanced at Phelan. His greenish-brown eyes were tired but steady. Quietly expectant. Somehow, they strengthened her.

She drew in a shaky breath. Sinking into the humming deep inside her, she managed to gather the strength to draw it out past the chill. "Once," she whispered, "there was a young prince who longed to run away and fight pirates."

Roarke's eyes sparked, and color rose in his cheeks. As Calantha's voice steadied and strengthened with the tale, the chatter at the periphery of the room dried. The courtiers and attendants drew nearer. King Ulric's head never lifted, but Calantha could tell that he listened—the anger from him subsided to a simmer.

Calantha spun out the tale as best she could; it was an old one, and she had to make up parts she couldn't remember. When at last she stopped, Roarke sighed deeply. The air had lightened somehow, and even Theora's face was brighter. Phelan quirked his crooked grin, then dropped his head and stared at his hands.

Calantha sat back, drained. The burns were biting again. But surprisingly, she hadn't noticed the pain while she'd told the tale.

Theora clucked. "You're tired. To bed with you. Yes." She hurried to help Calantha.

Roarke touched her gently in thanks as she went by. Some of the attendants murmured their thanks as well, but a soldier standing by the door hurriedly turned his face away.

Through a haze of pain, Calantha recognized Justhorn. Justhorn, whom Odhran had tortured and humiliated in front of her and Phelan. His mottled face was bruised and burned from his attempts to capture Odhran, but it was shame that she sensed pulsing from him. Shame because she had witnessed his humiliation.

She paused, but she didn't know what to say. Besides, she didn't have the breath.

Alone in bed, exhausted, she sank cautiously into the humming inside her. Oh, thanks be to the Sower of Tales, it was still there. She lay motionless. Was the humming stronger? Yes, it was. It was steadier, firmer, less thready. And she'd found her way to it with greater ease past the chill!

Something deep inside her unknotted. Telling the tale had strengthened the humming, not depleted it! She should have known that; oh, she should have known. She sank into a deep and restful sleep.

But she awoke gasping, her face wet. The Sower of Tales. Still walking away, away. Only this time Calantha had been able to call out after her, *wait for me, oh, wait*, and had even taken a step toward her. But the Sower of Tales never stopped, never even looked back; she just walked on and disappeared.

Calantha wiped her face and blinked at the window where faint light was stirring. It was dawn. She'd slept through the night! For the first time, she hadn't woken with the pain.

She gained strength faster then, hope driving her. Each day she moved farther, and she forced herself to eat. Each evening she went to Roarke's chambers to tell him tales. Her voice was steadier, and she could sit longer now, and tell more than one tale.

Roarke, too, strengthened and grew brighter each day. All the courtiers, even Theora, seemed more rested after the tales, more hopeful. The air felt less gray, less twisted. And even though Calantha was always spent afterward, the humming inside her slowly deepened and the chill receded.

Now in her dreams she was able to walk after the Sower of Tales; she was getting closer, even though that weight still held her back. But no matter how hard she tried, how much she called, the Sower of Tales never slowed, never once turned around. She always disappeared over the crest of the hill.

One afternoon, nearly a moon after the burning of the seeds, Calantha sought out Roarke in his chambers.

Her burns were healing. She still had some bandages on her hands but they weren't as thick, and scabs were growing over parts of her arms, legs, and chest. She hadn't asked Theora, but she was sure she could travel. When Roarke's attendants were occupied, she quietly asked him for a horse and cart for her journey the next day.

Something like fear and dismay flashed across Roarke's face, but he agreed immediately. He even insisted that two soldiers should accompany her, in case of trouble along the way. Then he sat back, suddenly quiet, his face downcast and almost as peevish as when she'd first seen him.

Calantha's heart fluttered uncomfortably. She hurried from his chambers, dreading what he might ask her. Outside, in the corridor, she closed her eyes with relief.

At last, she was going! Tomorrow she was going!

She touched the soft pouch of seeds around her neck. She'd leave them with the Gatherers in the Plains. The king was guarding the seeds his soldiers had saved; she didn't know what he planned for them, but it was unlikely that any would reach the Plainsfolk. Hers would, though. Every one. And when the wind was restored, the Plainsfolk would plant them and grow story pods again.

Then Roarke wouldn't need her anymore....

She'd take the North Plains road tomorrow. It wasn't the fastest way to the Eastern Mountains, but she must leave some seeds with Kasmira—after all, Grenlea too would be bowed with the weight of the collapsing circle.

Calantha bit her lip. How difficult would it be to leave her family again? She shook her head. No matter. She'd stop for just one night and then she'd be free to go to the Eastern Mountains.

As she headed toward her chamber, she passed Phelan's door and stopped abruptly. Phelan. He was still here. He was well able to travel; he had been for many days now. Why hadn't he gone home? Was he waiting for her to recover?

Calantha drew in a deep breath. She must tell him. Somehow, she dreaded it. Reluctantly, she tapped on his door with the tips of her finger. Phelan's voice bade her enter.

She'd never been in his chamber before. It was similar to hers, but it felt clearer, less tangled—as tidy and certain as Phelan himself, even though the air sagged with weariness here, too, as everywhere.

Phelan sat on the window ledge. Calantha froze as she

saw the flute in his hands. His bandages were lighter than before, except for the one around the little finger of his right hand, but still....

Phelan quirked his crooked grin and clumsily put his flute down beside him.

Calantha sat down on a chair near the window. "I...I'm leaving tomorrow," she blurted. She couldn't quite meet his eyes. "I came to tell you."

Glancing at him, she saw the color rise in his face. He sat very still.

Shame pulsed through her. She should have thought of him before. "I...I just now asked Roarke for a horse and cart. You'll be going home, won't you? You could come with me."

He stared at the flute beside him, turned it over with his bandaged hand. Then he looked up. "Where are you going?"

Calantha flushed. She sensed something implacable in him, as though...as though she was doing something wrong.

"You know where," she said breathlessly. "But I'm going through the Plains first. To Grenlea. I'll leave some seeds with Gatherers along the way and the rest with Kasmira."

He kept turning his flute over and over.

"Phelan, I have to. I must...I must reach her." Her voice cracked.

He looked up and nodded slightly. Something about the way his ears stuck out made her throat swell. His hair was growing, a red sheen over his head, but it would be a while before it grew straggly enough to cover his ears again.

She leaned forward suddenly. "Phelan, come with me. There. To the Sower of Tales."

A brief light flickered in his eyes, then died. He shook his head. "No, I won't leave the Plains." His face was tired, so tired.

Calantha sat back, stung. "I have to go, Phelan." She pressed her bandaged hands together. "I thought you'd understand. I must find her and help her any way I can.... It's the only way to bring back the story pods. To save the tales."

Phelan hesitated, then said softly, "And who will help the Plainsfolk?"

His words slipped into her like a knife. Calantha stood up and left without saying another word.

They ate their evening meal together as usual, but mostly in silence. A polite silence.

She'd told Theora. Theora had worried and protested, as Calantha had expected, but then at last she had agreed. She'd given Calantha a good supply of salve and bandages for the journey.

After the meal, Calantha went to Roarke's chamber one last time, to spin her tales. She avoided Phelan's eyes. A crowd of people gathered around to hear her.

When she finished her second tale, Roarke sighed. He fidgeted, then said tentatively, "Calantha. Can't you stay here? At the castle. Be...be the Storyteller?" His pale green eyes looked pleadingly at her. "It'll be a new post. Created just for you."

The murmur of courtiers' voices subsided.

Calantha's heart thudded. *How could he ask?* He had every comfort imaginable already, and he knew she must leave—he knew she had more important work to do.

Her mouth tightened. "I can't," she said.

Roarke flushed and looked away.

The King's head jerked up, the scar on his temple contracting. He'd hardly spoken the past few nights, but now his voice was harsh. "She'll stay if you want her to."

Calantha stiffened. The silence around her grew rigid.

The King's eyes turned toward her, darting anger and blame. "I'll throw her in the dungeons, if need be."

Roarke shook his head. "Father, no. No. I—"

The King shouted, "I'm still King here. She'll do as she's commanded."

Roarke's face shrank with terror. "Father, no. I beg you."

The King looked at his son, and as quickly as it had started, the rage subsided. "Very well. As you please."

Calantha sat back in her chair, trying to still the shaking. The King would have thrown her in the dungeons! She should never have started with the tales; their wants never ended. More, they always wanted more.

Roarke turned to Calantha, his eyes wide, his voice high, "I'm sorry, sorry. I never meant..." His dark lashes blinked rapidly. "Calantha, all I meant was...I want you to stay, because...no one tells tales like you."

The words burst from her mouth, "Then you
must learn to tell them yourself."

Roarke's face was forlorn. "But I don't remember
them like you do."

Calantha sat very still. A seed of an idea began to
sprout and take hold. She turned to him. "Roarke,
maybe you can learn to tell tales." Something clear
and clean shot through her. "Yes, you can. You can
make them up. Or tell about something you did.
Like...how you met me."

She turned pleadingly to Phelan. Understanding
lit his face. "Roarke, remember how you came and
rescued Calantha and then me?"

Roarke frowned. A faraway look came into his
eyes.

One of the courtiers, a middle-aged man with a
sagging belly and pouchy eyes, rumbled, "Master
Roarke, I never did hear about that."

Other voices called out in encouragement.

Roarke looked about the room, slightly puzzled.

Calantha nodded at him.

Roarke licked his lips. "Let's see. It was because
I first saw Calantha in the chambers with Father that

I wanted to find her." He paused.

"Go on," urged Calantha. "What did you think?"

Roarke grinned. "I thought you were a witch, with your hair all snarled and your eyes all wild and excited."

A few guffaws broke out and Phelan flashed his crooked grin.

Roarke settled back. "But still, I wondered about the Sower of Tales. After what Calantha said about seeing her. And I wondered why..." Roarke's voice dropped, "...why Odhran wanted to stop her speaking so badly. And Phelan too."

There was a slight chill at the mention of Odhran's name. The King's back went rigid.

Calantha nodded at Roarke to continue.

"So I thought to myself, since...since Father wouldn't tell me any more..."

Calantha's eyes swiveled to the King. His head was bent but he blinked hard.

"I thought maybe I'd see if I could find the crazy girl for myself."

"How did you do that, Master Roarke?" asked a thin, balding man with watery eyes.

Roarke smirked and tapped his fingers against the chair. "The spare keys. I know where Father keeps them."

A few titters broke out, and then laughter. The King lifted his head.

"So..." Roarke leaned forward, and dropped his voice again, "early in the morning, I crept out of bed, and I made my way to Father's chambers, where the spare keys are kept. And..." Roarke paused, "I took them."

Calantha sat back. Roarke and his listeners were caught in the telling.

Cool drops of hope dewed and welled inside her, like the words of a story flowing perfectly into place. Of course! They must learn to tell their own tales. They must. It might take coaxing and suggesting, but they'd learn. Their tales would mesh with the Essences and help to heal them until the story pods came back. And afterward they'd still keep on, so that the Sower of Tales would be sustained even more.

Something released inside her. She needn't worry about the Plainsfolk, they'd be all right! Oh, the air felt lighter already. She could go to the Sower of Tales.

She smiled and turned to look at Phelan. His eyes were on her, steady, resigned. But under it something else; not disapproval, but that same stubborn expectation. Her smile faded.

At last, Roarke finished his tale with how he'd found and released Calantha and Phelan. Silence soothed the chamber—a cleansing, light silence.

"Well done, Roarke," said Calantha. She caught Theora's eyes and Theora smiled and bobbed her head quickly. Yes, Theora understood; she'd keep Roarke telling his tales.

Roarke was smiling, half proud, half disbelieving. Calantha leaned over and said, "You must keep telling tales. For everyone. And draw others to tell them, too." Her voice lowered. "It will help Theora, rest and uplift her so she can undo the knots faster."

A glint came into Roarke's eyes and he nodded. It was just what he needed. A purpose.

As Calantha sat back she noticed Justhorn lurking by the door. She hesitated, then said, "Justhorn."

He tensed. His eyes shifted, looking in different directions.

Calantha moistened her lips. "I never thanked you for your help, Justhorn. If it weren't for you, we'd never have reached the King." She turned to look at Roarke and the others, and her voice rose, as though telling a story. "If it hadn't been for you, Roarke would never have seen me, or come to rescue me. You defied Odhran. And you proved your loyalty to the King and to Roarke. Your courage is a beacon that will always be remembered. It will make a fine tale, Justhorn, and you must tell everyone of your part."

A dark red crept up Justhorn's neck, onto his face and up to the roots of his hair. Slowly, he lifted his head.

CHAPTER TWENTY-SIX

S ome of the tightness in Calantha's back eased as the cart carrying her and Phelan finally left Jaerlfin castle and rattled through the cobbled streets of JaerlzGate, to begin the long trek down the North Plains road to Grenlea. Phelan sat listlessly beside her, his head down. He'd go with her as far as Grenlea, he'd said, and rest there before returning to his own village in the southern Plains.

Others accompanied them—a few Plainsfolk who had come north and hadn't yet returned, some because of injuries, others because they'd stayed to help. There were a couple of other carts, three horses, and a few people walking, some still carrying the weapons they'd brought with them. Leading the horses of Calantha's cart were two of the King's soldiers, grizzled, wiry men. Roarke had insisted that they go with her—in case she encountered some of Odhran's men who may yet be at large.

Calantha's mind darted again to the highest peak of the Eastern Mountains. Would the armed swordsmen still be there? She turned to look but she couldn't see the mountains; the trees along the road hid them. Last night in her dream, she'd been the closest yet to reaching the Sower of Tales. She'd run after her, calling and calling, but just couldn't reach her, and the Sower of Tales had never turned around. She'd kept walking, and once again, she'd disappeared over the crest of the hill.

Calantha pressed her hands together. *Oh, Sower of Tales, wait for me, I'm coming, I'm coming.*

As the cart jogged on past the trees and emerged into hot sunshine, Calanatha sighed. How empty, how wrong, the roadsides looked with no red story-pod stalks springing among the weeds.

Spurts of blue caught her eye. Skydrops grew here and there, the blue of the flowers just like Xenyss' eyes. Theora had told her that when Xenyss' body had gone to Grenlea for burial, the Plainsfolk had strewn it with wildflowers. Calantha's throat tightened. Grenlea would never be the same. If she were staying, her heart would break missing him.

Blinking hard, Calantha sat back in the cart. She glanced at Phelan. He sat slackly, his back swaying with the jerk of the cart. Scabs covered the burns on his scalp. They hadn't spoken much since yesterday.

Something rough and hard turned inside her. What right did he have to expect more of her? Why did he always intrude and intrude? And without even saying anything? It was his certainty and insistence that made him so unyielding—just like the time he'd wanted to hear the story pod, so long ago in the sharo grove.

Her anger died.

His hands were curled stiffly in his lap. Oh, how his fingers had danced on his flute...like rowdy butterflies. She still had the tales, but he...? The heaviness of the air showed in his body—in all the travelers around her. They were somber and weary, weighed by the collapsing circle. Since she'd started to tell the tales, the humming had grown stronger in her, and she wasn't as crushed by the grayness as before. But the faces around her were so bleak.

Calantha shifted uncomfortably. Grenlea. Her mother, Kasmira, all her family—they too would be bowed by the twist in the air. She thrust the hair from her face with the back of her bandaged hands.

Out of the corner of her eye, she saw Phelan fidgeting, his bandaged hands fumbling at his pocket. The flute. It fell onto his lap. He tried to pick it up. Again and again it fell. Faint moisture broke out on his forehead.

Calantha averted her head, but she could still see him trying, trying. At last, he managed to bring the flute to his lips and blow. A long, plaintive note rang out before the flute fell from his fingers. But the note pierced the gloom, parting the heaviness momentarily. The Plainsfolk trudging beside them, some on foot, some on horses, turned to look.

Phelan tried to lift the flute again, impatience and frustration leaking out of him.

Calantha waited for her lips to steady. She drew in a deep breath. "Once," she began, "there was a young man who yearned to catch the moon."

Phelan sat still. As she continued, others drew nearer to listen, to breathe in the lightened air.

When she finished, she sat silent for a moment. Then she turned defiantly to Phelan. "Well. Don't you have anything to tell?"

He blinked, then nodded. "I went on a journey once, and I met a strange girl."

The Plainsfolk alongside came nearer again.

A gleam came into Phelan's eyes. "A strange and wild girl. Hair all matted. Snarling, snapping."

"Snarking bograts," muttered Calantha under her breath.

"Exactly," said Phelan. "Exactly what she said."

The sun dazzled slantways, lighting dust motes floundering in the hazy air as the cart jogged into Grenlea late that afternoon. In each of the three villages they'd passed, Calantha had handed out a few of the precious seeds from her pouch to the Gatherers. She'd told them to plant the seeds only when they heard from the Seers that the wind had been restored. The last few seeds were still in the pouch around her neck.

Calantha straightened up as the familiar woods along the North Plains road came into view. A pang tore through her. Somehow it hurt more to see no story pods growing here. There was the wide, red chernow tree with its low, sweeping branches. How often she'd hidden there! It felt like years since she'd thrown the clay at Freya, then run back along that road to the Green and bumped into Xenyss.

Xenyss. They'd need a new Seer now.

The whitewashed houses were coming into view. The sagging in the air was here, too. Everything felt sorry, tired.

It was Delmer, the Herdroffe, who saw them first. He stood still for a moment, brushing at his moustache. Then recognition dawned on his face and he boomed, "Calantha!" He waved his lanky arms, then turned and ran, swaying side to side, toward the Green.

A few folk came out of their houses and ran up to greet her and the others. Calantha's head spun.

They seemed glad to see her, as though they already knew what had happened in Jaerlfin. Some of the Plainsfolk who'd returned earlier must have told them.

As they reached the Green, a crowd of people came hurrying toward them. One figure led the way. Her mother.

"Calantha," Luvena cried.

Somehow, Calantha got out of the cart.

Luvena's chest heaved from running. She looked at the bandages, then at Calantha's face, and her own face twisted. She pulled Calantha into her arms and held her, weeping and weeping.

Calantha stroked Luvena's back. "Mother. I'm all right."

Her mother pulled away, wiping her face fiercely. She nodded. "Yes, yes. Of course you are."

Then her father was hugging her. He seemed thin, all angles, his eyes watery. Beagan clung to her, and Freya wrapped her arms around her, bawling and howling. Calantha caught her lip between her teeth. She didn't want to start crying; she wouldn't. But she had a horrible urge to shriek out laughing. If she were staying, she and Freya would be fighting again soon.

But not in the same way. Never in the same way.

Disengaging from Freya's wet embrace, she turned to the others. Argenta hugged her, stroking her back. Frensha, Benigna. They all looked older. Lined. They were feeling the loss here, too, feeling it badly.

Then Kasmira pushed through the crowd. She seemed to have shrunk. Her face was furrowed, but her brown eyes looked clearly at Calantha. Calantha stared at her, daring her to cry.

Kasmira's eyes moistened. Her smile was labored as she took Calantha into her arms. "I knew you'd come back!" she rasped. "With your hair as wild as ever."

Calantha caught sight of Phelan in the cart, watching, suddenly shy.

"Mother, Father, this is Phelan." She met his eyes above the heads of the others. "He's my friend. Without him we'd never have been able to stop—" Calantha broke off. She didn't want to foul the air with that name. It wasn't the time.

Calantha took the pouch from around her neck and handed it to Kasmira.

Kasmira held it between both hands. "Seeds?" she whispered.

Calantha nodded. She was free now. Free to go. She turned to look again at Phelan, half-defiantly, half-pleadingly.

He smiled slightly, but his eyes were as implacable as ever.

CHAPTER TWENTY-SEVEN

Somehow, she couldn't tell them she was going again. She just couldn't. Kasmira guessed it, and Calantha knew she understood. But the others seemed to think she was home for good.

Beagan chattered eagerly, clinging to her. Her mother plied her with her favorite blue plum cake, saved for special occasions, and her father couldn't take his eyes off her. She'd always thought of Anwyll as strong, and he was, but for the first time Calantha noticed the lines of weariness on his forehead and around his mouth.

Phelan was staying with them, too. Her mother had insisted he stay the night, sharing Beagan's chamber; she'd taken to Phelan as lorshcake takes to stew.

After supper, Calantha tidied her hair with
Freya's help and went outside to wait for Kasmira.
She'd asked Kasmira to come by—the walk to
Kasmira's was too difficult for her now.

Luvena looked after her anxiously, started to
speak, then pinched her lips together. She came
outside, too, pretending to tweak the sorry mess of
wilted flowers.

Phelan waited beside her, along with Beagan. It
was quiet along the road, with few people about for
this time of day. The air was thin, lacking. How
strange everything seemed. Empty.

Calantha drew in a crooked breath as Kasmira
came down the road alone, her Gatherer's cloak
swirling about her. How weary and bent she'd
become.

Leaning on her stick, Calantha joined her. With
Phelan and Beagan alongside, they headed for the
Green.

As they passed Berwin, sitting on the doorstep of
his small house, his mouth dropped open slightly.
"Greetings..." he began, before the words dried on
his lips. Blinking uncertainly, he got to his feet.

Near the Green, they met some Earthroffes talking to Saeward. Saeward's peaked eyebrows shot upward like flying crows when he saw them. He and the Earthroffes fell into an uneasy silence. Glancing back, Calantha saw her family, as well as Berwin and a few others, trailing after them.

There weren't many folk about the Green. Mostly children, wandering aimlessly.

Calantha hesitated. Kasmira said, "To the fireplace. That's where we used to meet."

Calantha nodded, and they crossed over to the fireplace near the north end of the Green. No fire burned, and the lorsha torches circling the sitting area were straggly and untrimmed. Everything felt strange—sagging, defeated. There was no sight of Argenta, or any of the Elders of Council.

Calantha sat down on one of the stone benches beside the cold fire, with Kasmira and Phelan on either side. Beagan huddled against her knee. The children wandering about the Green stared at them, then began to edge closer. Old Berwin came nearer too, his face astonished, hopeful. But her mother hovered at a distance, her arms crossed, mouth creased with worry, with Freya and Anwyll beside her.

Kasmira turned toward Calantha and smiled uncertainly, her brown eyes anxious.

Calantha's heart twisted. How strange that she should have to show Kasmira the way. She hesitated, then brought her hands together as though they held a story pod. Loudly, she said, "Thanks be to the Sower of Tales, she who scatters the seeds!"

As Kasmira and Phelan murmured the words after her, a few of the children came and sat down, also repeating the familiar words of thanks—some eagerly, some awkwardly, as though rusty. Calantha drew in a deep breath, then began to tell the tale of the man who tried to capture the dawn.

More children crept nearer, then Berwin, her mother and father, and a few others. Someone, Calantha couldn't see who, ran away and came back with more villagers. Benigna was there, then Delmer and another Herdroffe. Argenta's silver head gleamed among them as she wove through the villagers to come and sit down beside the cold fire in her usual place.

As soon as Calantha's tale ended, Kasmira began the tale of the lion who wanted to grow flowers in his mane. It was silly, but it made the children laugh.

When Kasmira finished, a collective sigh seemed to go through the gathering. They looked around at each other, shifting awkwardly; it was as though they wanted more, but felt foolish.

Calantha recognized a big, burly shape near the edge of the crowd. She leaned forward. She must do it now. She wouldn't be here tomorrow.

"Hardwin," she called out. She had to say his name twice before he heard her and came closer. "Hardwin, remember long ago when you climbed the Eastern Mountains?"

Hardwin's forehead twitched into a frown.

"Remember, when I was very small, and I asked you if you'd seen the Sower of Tales?"

Remembrance dawned on his face. He tugged at his ear. "Aye, I remember."

Calantha said, "Tell us about it. Tell the tale of how you climbed that mountain. What you saw."

Hardwin frowned. "Why, nothing. I told you then. Nothing but rock and rubble." .

A suspiciously strangled sound erupted from Phelan.

Calantha darted a sharp glance his way. "But what made you want to make that journey, Hardwin? What happened?"

"Ah, it was the time I went down to the Southern Plains, to trade the iron pots I'd made."

Flikketting lizards, it was like trying to lead Eythun's mule out of the bog. Hardwin was not going to shine at telling tales. But when at last, and with much prompting, Hardwin finished his account, his face was lighter. And some of the Plainsfolk around him were smiling—maybe more at Hardwin's difficulty in telling it than at the tale, but still, smiling.

Calantha glimpsed Julissa at the back of the crowd. She hesitated, then remembered what the Sower had said: *The tales are for all, even Odhran.* Before she could change her mind, she called out, "Julissa, can you maybe tell a tale?"

Julissa turned an unbecoming shade of purple.

Snarking bograts! Julissa thought she was mocking her.

Calantha said quickly, "Just start a tale. In any way."

Julissa blinked, then said uncertainly, "Once, there was a princess with fair golden hair." She stopped.

Folk were shifting impatiently.

Calantha called out, "Can anyone else continue? A tale can have many tellers. Eadric. Can you go on?"

Eadric grinned and said, "All right, let's see; er, and she was greatly loved and admired, but most especially by a young Herdroffe..."

Chuckles and laughter spattered the air and Eadric turned bright red, while Julissa tossed her hair, trying unsuccessfully to look displeased. At last, with several people chiming in, they managed to finish the tale. It wasn't the cleverest one, but the villagers laughed anyway.

Quickly, Calantha called to the little ones to describe their day. Beagan loved it, talking about the nest of snakes by the river and how he'd found them. As the crowd around the fireplace continued to grow, Calantha looked around at the familiar faces. Maybe half the villagers were there, more than there used to be at Talemeet sometimes. All were hungry for the gathering now.

As it grew darker Tabbert and Neola brought wood to the central fire and lit it. Others, Frensha and Laerissa, lit the lorsha torches. They hadn't been trimmed in a while and they smoked fiercely.

"Friends." Kasmira's crackled voice carried strongly. She seemed to have straightened during the evening. "We will meet nightly here for..." she glanced at Calantha and Argenta, then said firmly, "for Talemeet."

Argenta banged her stick and nodded. "Yes, we will gather each evening as before."

Kasmira said, "And now, one last tale. It's too long to finish in one telling, but I will begin it tonight."

Calantha looked curiously at her.

"Once," began Kasmira, "there was a young girl who longed to be a Gatherer of pods. She lived in a village in the Plains. But her mother had grander schemes for her. She wanted her to be..."

Some of the villagers had caught on. Calantha

flushed. She'd never seen them look at her like that, never. She bit the inside of her lip. They'd just tolerated her before, while others had ignored and even mocked her—she didn't want them idolizing her now.

In any case, she wasn't worth it. She was going tomorrow. She *must* go. The horse and cart and the two soldiers provided by Roarke were at Kerwin's. Maybe tomorrow, before her family was up, she'd go there, quietly wake them, and continue her journey. That way she could avoid the protests of her mother, the pain of her father. And Phelan, well, he'd learn to understand. He'd have to. She sensed his eyes on her, but she didn't look at him.

Kasmira was winding down the tale now. She stopped with Calantha's dream and the visit to Xenyss' hut. Xenyss. Calatha sat motionless. She sensed that the villagers, too, thought of him. He'd given everything to help her. To help all the Plainsfolk.

Slowly the villagers began to stir. The air was heavy but not as heavy as before. They lingered by the fire, talking, reluctant to go.

Neola called out, "You'll continue the tale tomorrow, Kasmira?"

"I will," said Kasmira simply.

Gripping her stick, Calantha stood abruptly and walked away to the dark of the Green, beyond the circle of the lorsha torches. Tomorrow she'd be gone. When Kasmira finished the tale she'd started, would she tell how Calantha had fled, silently, like a thief in the night?

Walking deeper into the dark, Calantha watched the folk around the fire as though from a great distance. Even if they didn't know it, they had started something important tonight; they'd started to come together. They'd started to mesh the Essences— enough to hold them until the Seers freed the Essence of the wind, yes, enough to hold them.

Calantha shivered; she was cold, so cold.

How long would it take to restore the wind? When she'd last asked Theora, she'd said, "Soon." But Theora had hesitated before answering, and there had been pain in her eyes.

The chill inside Calantha swirled and spread like a bleak and bitter wind. Oh, what if the story pods never returned?

You will always have the tales to sustain you, no matter what. The Sower of Tales had said that. Calantha wrapped her arms tightly around herself.

But the Plainsfolk? The Plainsfolk?

Calantha stood still as though turned to stone. No. They couldn't ask that of her. There were others who knew the tales, others who could tell them— Gatherers and such. In time, more would learn. They'd learn.

Something else the Sower had said rang in her ears. *I'd never abandon the people.*

Calantha caught her lip between her teeth. Sour blood welled on her tongue. She must go to the Sower of Tales. She must. She'd promised.

The Sower's face flashed in her mind, her fingers pressed against Calantha's mouth. *Don't make that promise, Calantha. There may be reasons why you cannot return.*

Mourning wracked her body. Calantha's stick dropped from her hands. She sank down onto the damp grass, her face crumpled with grief. The Sower of Tales had known it all along; oh, she'd known it. Her words echoed in Calantha's head.

Everything that has a beginning must also end.

Calantha bent over double with pain, her body shattered with weeping. Deep inside her, words whispered, then grew, reverberating through every part of her body.

If the Sower of Tales you seek to find
Unravel the knots that tangle your mind
Let the song of the story pods ring in your heart
Let go of all else, let the tales do their part.

"Let the tales do their part, let the tales do their part, let the tales do their part..." She rocked back and forth, holding herself, repeating the words over and over, like a dirge, a prayer.

At last she stopped. For a long while, she remained still, crouched on the grass. Then she sat up and fiercely wiped her face.

She must stay.

It was what the Sower of Tales had wanted her to do. Expected her to do all along.

She must stay and spread the tales. Here, on the Plains. Not just to lighten the air, to help the Essences mesh sooner. Not just to mend the circle.

And not just until the story pods returned.

For the story pods might never return.

The Plainsfolk must, they *must* learn to tell the tales. Tales from the story pods, yes, but more—they must also learn to tell their own tales. Mend their own hope, stoke their own strength. Oh, they must learn to tell their tales to fuel their own joy and delight.

And even when the story pods returned—if the story pods returned—they must still keep telling their tales. That was how the tales would be saved. It was the only way the tales would be saved.

Calantha stared upward at the eastern sky. If only she could see the mountains. They were shrouded in darkness. Was the Sower of Tales still...?

I'd never abandon the people.

At last, the cold made her move. Finding her stick, she pulled herself, slowly, painfully to her feet. The villagers were long gone. Some of the lorsha torches had been taken with them; the others were black. The central fire was cold.

Alone in the dark, she walked home.

Her mother was pacing about the main chamber,

a candle worrying feebly on the table. She looked at Calantha, and her lips trembled. Putting her hand against Calantha's cheek, she managed to say, "I...I'm so glad you're home."

Calantha nodded. She couldn't speak.

Silently, she went to her chamber. Freya was already in bed, but she turned around when she heard Calantha.

"Oh, thanks be..." she breathed. "Do you need help undressing?"

"No," whispered Calantha. But it took a long time to struggle into her nightdress, and by the time she crept into bed, Freya's breath sounded evenly beside her.

Exhausted, worn, Calantha lay staring at the curtain fluttering with the cool breeze. She knew what she'd dream that night. She'd never catch up to the Sower of Tales now.

She let herself drift into a tale, the one of the old woman who led her village to a river deep in the forest when the drought had dried their lands.

Calantha awoke with a gasp.

She sat up in bed, her heart racing, rubbing the sleep from her eyes. It was still dark, but she sensed that it was near dawn.

Silently, she got out of bed. Outside. She must go out to the clear morning air. She pushed her feet into her shoes and wrapped her shawl around herself. Leaning on her stick, she went outside.

A sleepy chitter of bird song greeted her. The sky was still dark, with only a promise of light yet to come.

Stiffly, almost without thinking, she started to walk down the road, then through the dew-spattered Green, and down the Mid Plains road—past the houses, the sharo grove, the empty lorsha fields.

She was nearly spent by the time she reached the Field of Gathering. She stopped to catch her breath. Then she made herself walk into the field.

The light was sufficient now. Grasses swayed in

the field, lonely without the darker stems of story pods singing through them. As Calantha walked deeper into the field, colors began to appear with the strengthening light—green tinting trees, shades of gold and bronze in the grass. But no misty shades of story pods danced across the top of the grasses.

She turned her eyes to the Eastern Mountains. Something clean and sweet flashed through her.

"You were leading me," she whispered. "All the time you were leading me. And I just didn't understand." Her heart filled with gratitude as she remembered the dream.

She'd struggled after the Sower of Tales as in all her dreams, calling out to her. Then, suddenly, the weight that had always held her back lifted, and she bounded toward the Sower, closing the gap between them. At the crest of the hill where she had always disappeared before, the Sower of Tales stopped. She turned around. Joy flooded Calantha as she ran up to her. The Sower of Tales smiled like a flash of sun and held out her arm. Her face was older, thinner, her hair streaked with more gray than before, but she was there, a vivid, real presence. She put her arm around Calantha, turned her about, and pointed downward. They were on top of the mountain, but below, unexpectedly clearly, Calantha saw the Plains. A flash of understanding washed through Calantha as the Sower of Tales nudged her forward.

Calantha turned before starting downhill. "Will the story pods return?" she asked.

The Sower of Tales smiled. "If the tales endure."

Calantha nodded. She asked then, her heart filled with longing, "Will I see you again?"

The Sower of Tales said nothing, but a burst of warmth filled Calantha, like an embrace, a blessing. Then the Sower of Tales was gone. Words drifted in the air—*I am the tales, the tales are me.*

Calantha blinked as the grasses in the Field of Gathering swayed with the morning breeze, tickling her arms. She smiled shakily. At last, at last, she had caught up to the Sower of Tales.

"I'll do your work here," she whispered, staring at the highest Eastern Mountain. "I promise. I'll spread the tales. But one day I will come back to you. And I'll be your apprentice."

Her eyes stung and stung. She would keep that

hope alive. She must. She stood gazing at the mountain, until the sun's rays rose above the summit. Softly, she said, "Thanks be to the Sower of Tales, she who scatters the seeds."

She turned and walked back along the road and through the Green. It didn't matter if anyone saw her.

In the distance, a sweet, plaintive note thrilled the air. Then another. It was Phelan's flute, calling her home.

Berwin, who was wandering the Green looking for mushrooms, nodded at Calantha as though it was quite normal for her to be out and about in her nightdress.

Eythun passed her and stared. "Calantha, are you all right?"

Calantha nodded. "Yes. Perfectly."

She clicked open the gate to her house, then walked around to the back to go in through the cooking chamber.

Phelan was sitting outside, on the back porch, his head bent low, staring at the flute in his bandaged hands.

Calantha paused. If only there were something she could do for him.

Then, suddenly, she knew just what to say. "Phelan," she called out.

He started and looked up.

"Phelan, the songs, they're inside you. Not in your fingers. Not in your flute. They're in *you*. No matter what." She stared at him, willing him to understand.

A startled look crossed his face.

Before he could speak, the back door burst open and Luvena rushed down the steps, her eyes alarmed. "Calantha. I was afraid you'd—"

Calantha managed a smile. "Not yet, Mother," she said. "But I will be going soon. To the other villages in the Plains." She glanced at Phelan and saw his face light up.

Luvena's mouth tightened forbiddingly, then slackened with bewilderment. "I suppose there's no telling you what to do anymore," she said. Her old snap was gone.

"No," said Calantha gently. She stared at her mother, at the pity, grief, and worry struggling across her eyes.

Then, surprisingly, through it all surfaced a gleam of hope.

"Well, I suppose there never was," said Luvena. She smoothed Calantha's hair and, with a fair imitation of her old vigor, added, "Mule!"

About the Author

RACHNA GILMORE is the author of many critically-acclaimed books for adults and children. Her children's novels are consistently popular, and her picture book *A Screaming Kind of Day*, also published by Fitzhenry and Whiteside, won the Governor General's Award for Text in 1999. *The Sower of Tales* is her first work of fantasy, but fans will recognize Ms Gilmore's sure hand in character and place here, as in all her novels. Her vividness and immediacy are the result of the way she works, which is to pay attention to the ideas that grab hold of her imagination and her heart, and don't let go.

Rachna Gilmore lives in Ottawa, Ontario. For more information, check out her Web site at http://www.makersgallery.com/gilmore/